T0269739

NOT THE KILLING KIND

NOT THE KILLING KIND

A NOVEL

MARIA KELSON

NEW YORK

Published in the United States by Crooked Lane Books, an imprint of The Quick Brown Fox & Company LLC.

Crooked Lane Books and its logo are trademarks of The Quick Brown Fox & Company LLC.

Library of Congress Catalog-in-Publication data available upon request.

ISBN (hardcover): 978-1-63910-967-8
ISBN (ebook): 978-1-63910-968-5

Cover design by Heather VenHuizen

Printed in the United States.

www.crookedlanebooks.com

Crooked Lane Books
34 West 27th St., 10th Floor
New York, NY 10001

First Edition: September 2024

10 9 8 7 6 5 4 3 2 1

For Lucha Corpi and
Stella Pope Duarte

BLOOD FLOATED ON top of the carpet as though hesitant to soak in, sorry for the mess. No war zone here. Here, a family room in northern California, 2009. A misty morning in redwood country, in a town where you could expect not to get killed if you minded your own business.

Someone tidied this little house neat as a church nave. Except for the knife gone from its block. Except for droplets of the boy's blood flung on the couch cover, scattered up the breakfast bar. Except for the blood pooling under his neck.

He was a big kid. Around five-foot-eleven, two-forty. He lay on his belly, arms pulled back and bound, the back of his head and the soles of his shoes pulled toward each other by the ends of the rope that tied his hands. One end looped around his forehead like a bandana, knotted in back. The other stretched to his sturdy ankles to lash them together.

The gash across his throat nearly threw me out of consciousness.

I knew him. I'd watched him and my son wrestle in my front yard when they were both in middle school.

He could've been my boy.

Something kept the shock of the scene from completely washing over me. A prickle in the back of my mind, a thorn-tip of recognition trying to break through.

His concave shape. A rope pulling the head back, the feet up. Had I seen this before?

And where was my son?

CHAPTER

1

seventeen hours earlier

THE COAST STRETCHED out under a low sky of thin milk and iron. I searched for a perfect sand dollar to give Jaral, my son. He was late again.

I walked around a flock of sandpipers playing tag with the rising waves. Beyond the skittering birds, the telltale white arc of a sand dollar shell, what scientists call the "test," poked up from the tide line. When I picked it up, it was only a broken piece, less than half a shell. I needed an intact test. Currency I could exchange for my teen's attention. Something to buy me a little goodwill.

He'd been acting tense, closed off, angry for no reason I could tell. And I wanted to talk about what he'd do after graduation, which was only a month away. I wanted to ask him about it. But I didn't want to come across as controlling and clueless. Make no mistake, I was controlling and clueless. But I didn't want to seem that way.

I guess I thought I'd lead with "Here's a cool shell" before diving into "What is going on with you, and what's your plan, anyway?"

We'd been tide pooling out here every month since I adopted him. Mucking around on the edge of the cold Pacific normally relaxed us both. But wondering where he was, and worrying about what I'd say, was anti-relaxing.

A few yards down from the broken test, I found another sand dollar, perfectly round. Barefoot, I walked into the surf to wash it off. When the ocean poured over my ankles, an icy pain detonated deep in my feet. The water played higher, licking the edges of the black suit pants I'd rolled up over my calves. Then it paused, swayed in place like a drunk, rushed to recede.

I rinsed my treasure in the tidal suction. Once clean, it showed the white of sun-struck concrete. Tiny holes stippled a perfect, five-petaled flower across the top.

Gorgeous. A small win.

I slid the sand dollar into a polyester pants pocket. The other pocket screamed once. Then twice. A barn owl call. Jaral's ringtone.

"Hey, son! Didn't you tell me no one under twenty-five makes phone calls?" Hiding my irritation that he was late, so I didn't alienate him right off. I walked my sand-crusted feet toward my shoes, higher up the beach.

"Mrs. Marez?"

"Excuse me?"

"Are you Mrs. Marez, mother of one Jaral Marez?"

Don't panic, a voice said deep inside me. Don't panic . . .

"I'm his mother, Ana Marez. What's going on?"

The parchment voice of an old man told me he could either call the police or I could come down to his store and "retrieve my errant offspring."

"What did he do?" I asked.

"Committed a crime that will cost you thirteen dollars and eighty-seven cents to rectify. The boy isn't carrying any means of payment, yet he feels entitled to depart my premises with merchandise. How soon can you be here?"

"What merchandise? Is he okay? Why do you have his phone?"

I'd gotten calls about Jaral before. As a single mom, his trouble came straight at me and no one else. "Mrs." Marez, your son is skipping school, shoplifting beef jerky, skipping school, riding his bike down the museum steps, skipping school, sneaking into movies, skipping school.

I adopted him when he was twelve, and we handled each call as it came. Me lecturing him or grounding him, sometimes banging kitchen cupboards, him suppressing a grin if he thought I was ridiculous, or tightening his arms against his sides if I stomped around too much.

But I thought those days were in the rearview. When he turned sixteen, it was like a switch flipped. Maybe he realized he needed material things from me to ease his social life, like a car, and he decided to play nicer with me to get them. Or maybe he got a zap of maturity. Whatever it was, it was great for us. We rowed along with attempts to push the other into a good mood when one of us needed something from the other. Not the healthiest dynamic, maybe, but it beat trying to enforce house arrest by grounding him three out of four weeks a month.

Now that he recently turned eighteen, I was expecting to exert good-mood pressure with a nice seashell and a big meal at his favorite restaurant, so I could ask him to start talking about options for his adult future. He'd turned around his academics enough to be on track to graduate, thank goodness, but then what?

I was not expecting to hear from a local business owner calling him "errant."

"Is he okay?" I said again. "Where is he?"

"He's right here at my establishment, Broadway Drug, 1824 Broadway on the north side of town. He wisely chose to dial your number so that I could speak to you after I told him the alternative. Using my own equipment to telephone the authorities."

"But he's okay?"

"Morally, no. Physically, the boy appears sound."

"What are you saying he did?"

"Ma'am, I cannot spend all day providing parental guidance. We can settle the details when you arrive. If I don't see you in ten minutes, I will notify the police."

"I'm on the north jetty. I'll be there as soon as I can. Hello?"

The screen on my phone at least had the decency to tell me the call ended.

I put the phone back in the dry pocket.

As I finished pulling on my shoes, my cell broke into the Thompson Twins, "Hold Me Now." Jaral programmed my general ringtone, for all non-Jaral callers, with an '80s music shuffle. He assumed I loved '80s pop because my age fit the profile. He personally couldn't get enough of '80s top-40 tunes and knew all the words to the biggest hits.

I picked up the call. A robot claiming to be the. Eureka. High School. Attendance Office. Told me Jaral missed hours 1, 2, 3, 4, 5, 6, and 7 today.

When I reached my car, I saw a brown juvenile pelican circling the parking lot.

"I hope you know what you're doing," I said to the bird.

I set the sand dollar on the shotgun seat, slammed the door, and peeled out across the bridge over Humboldt Bay. The mainland town of Eureka waited to catch me on the other side.

CHAPTER

2

JARAL, HEART-SHAPED FACE and whip-thin. Skin that glowed like a smooth tan-oak acorn, and a mind made for shaping the world around him. When he decided to give school a try at sixteen, he found a home in the high school's theater program, where it didn't matter that he was just tuning back in after years of apathy. Never a very verbal kid, except when singing to himself, set design became his passion. Spice canisters and napkins at home became mock-up materials. He loved to draw and redraw layouts, triple-checking his figures on height and square footage.

As eighteen-year-olds go, he seemed solid enough. More so considering how different the Jaral of today was from the boy who became my son six years ago. At twelve, he'd come out of two years in foster care suspicious of everyone, skilled at folding his smarts behind sidelong glances and a bouncing leg, a tapping hand. Now he'd sing to himself in front of me, laugh with friends, and show at least some of his teachers what he could do if he tried.

With his diploma four weeks away, why mess up now? What thirteen-dollar treasure had he tried to lift?

I crossed the bridge and merged onto Broadway, heading south. Just past Drive-Thru Donuts, I hit the first light. Beyond that sat Broadway Drug.

I parked my ancient Toyota beside Jaral's ancient Honda and went in.

Jaral leaned against the photo counter with one leg crossed over the other, next to a hunched little man with large ears and a comb-over about seven hairs strong. My five-feet-nine towered over the man. Instead of peering up at me, he addressed my salt-spangled pantlegs.

"I understand congratulations are in order."

"Excuse me?"

Jaral rattled a light-green bottle of pills. "He means these." He pushed off from the counter and handed me the bottle. A stork with a bouquet of pastel balloons in its beak perched on a corner of the label.

"Prenatal vitamins?" I turned the label around to face the owner. "There must be some mistake. This kid has no girlfriend. You think a brown boy by himself in a store must be shoplifting? Check your bias, sir."

"Moms! I had them on me. I took them."

I looked at my boy as though he'd stepped into a spotlight. He tilted his chin up higher than normal. Tensed his jaw. His gaze floated past the two adults in front of him. He flicked a glance at me, to measure something in my face.

"Why?" I said. "Why would you need these?"

A gnarled hand on my sleeve. "Aurmmm . . ." A wordless, gravelly hum warned me that Father Time would explain the facts of life to me, if he had to.

"Yeah, okay." I pulled my arm back. "I get it."

But I didn't get it. I wanted out, so I could berate my kid in the comfort of my own home.

"What do I owe you? Thirteen something?"

I caught a whiff of jasmine. A susurration of pastel linens materialized at my side.

"Well, Boots Marez! I wanted to catch you before the parent meeting tomorrow! Hmm-hm."

Lusanne Bewley, one of the parents at the school I ran, had the body of a volleyball champ and the voice of a fifth-grade girl. She also had a verbal tic that scattered little hums throughout her conversations. They underscored her usual self-satisfied and judgy tone quite nicely.

She saw the vitamins in my hand. "Oh my! Hm. What a surprise! Hm. I mean, aren't you a little . . ."

I cut her off before she could say "old" or "single."

"Here!" I handed the bottle back to Jaral. Then I turned to Lusanne.

"It's not what you think!" Heat rose through my neck and face. "Or hell. Maybe it is!"

She gawked at Jaral. Everyone at my school knew Jaral.

"This is . . ." I started, but found myself tonque-tied. "What is . . ." Having a jury of three weigh my cluelessness made my fingers curl into claws. I attempted a big, bold laugh. Jaral frowned at me and took a step back.

"Ta-da!" I shot my arms out to present the boy, like I made him appear from thin air. "This! Is the guy with all the answers."

I took out the last of my cash, a twenty, slapped it on the glass. Without glancing at the owner or Lusanne, I got out of there. Jaral knew enough to follow.

We walked to my car.

"Get in," I said. "I'll bring you back here to get your car later."

He opened the passenger door and saw the sand dollar.

"Aw, nice!" he said. "Thanks, Moms." Gone was the tension of the last few weeks. He seemed suspiciously calm.

I got in and slammed my door shut as hard as I could. Jaral flinched in his seat and turned away from me.

I tried counting back from ten to let my anger settle. It felt more like a countdown to launch. I slammed the door one more time. That felt a little better. Jaral's shoulders curled inward, just slightly, after that second slam. I wished it didn't give me some satisfaction to see that. But it did.

Those were the ingredients of an ugly brew that simmered in me. A lifelong rage that boiled over on those closest to me and a sick contentment when I saw it had an impact. I fought against these poisons, but sometimes my head and chest filled with such pressure I worried I'd burst like a putrid whale corpse washed ashore.

"So," I said, through gritted teeth. "Are you a teen dad? Are you going to be?" I wanted to shout this so loud the windows shook, but that was against my rules. Absolutely no shouting. I could bang and slam things to let off steam. But no shouting.

Jaral put the pills in a cupholder between us. I squeezed the steering wheel to keep my hands from shaking. Jaral put one of his hands over one of mine. I loved the paradox of those hands. He had a man's voice, but a youthful roundness softened his knuckles. Some childhood still remained in him.

"Nope." He squeezed my hand once, then crossed his arms. "Not a teen dad. A kid trying to help a friend."

"Well. But. Stealing, Jaral?"

He shrugged. Was thieving a native talent of his that I only now uncovered? A survival skill from years with his drug-addicted birth mom?

"I'm sorry I messed up mother-son time." He pulled the seat belt over him.

"Yeah."

"You were gonna take me to Lumberjack Cookhouse after we walked around on the beach."

"Yup."

"Because you know how much I love all-you-can-eat-oysters on that crackly wax paper."

"Because I wanted to ask you what's wrong. You've been so strange lately. So quiet." I let out breath I'd been holding since my phone rang. His deep brown eyes shone. "That's what the dinner would've been all about. What is really up with you?"

"Got big boy problems," he said. Then shrugged.

I started the car, backed out of the parking space, unsure where to drive.

"You're not going to freak out? I mean, like, legit massacre me?"

"For this?" I waved my hand over the green plastic bottle as though to make it disappear. "Or for cutting school? You're only four weeks from graduation. But you're not going to make it if you stop going to class."

"Moms. Missing one day of school ain't no thing. Graduation's all buttoned up. I got this."

I braked too hard at stop signs, revved too fast to get back up to speed.

"I know you're not using, or buying, or selling. I know you're not."

"You know I'm not."

"I know you don't even think about mind-altering substances. You hate what they did to your bio mom. But check this out. What if now is the time you've been waiting for? This moment you've got graduation All. Buttoned. Up. You think, 'Screw it,' and decide it's okay to just see what it's like. Get loaded. Is that what you did this morning instead of going to class?"

"I went to class!"

The effort not to yell made my teeth rattle. Yelling meant someone about to get hit, when I was a kid. I'd let anger ricochet around inside me before risking that.

"I got a call from the school. You ditched."

"These are just vitamins! Not even prescription drugs. Just let me take care of my own business. Stop the crazy. Shiiiii . . ."

I hadn't even started the crazy. But the sweetness of the half-cuss pierced me. Maybe he still cared what I thought.

"You know my mother would have smacked me if I ever cut school," I said to him.

"You want to smack me?"

I reminded him that after my mother disappeared, I went to live with my Uncle Max and Honey.

"I got this whole ramble memorized, Moms. You loved them, they loved you, but Max had his hands full taking care of Honey, who was dying of AIDS, in and out of the hospital all the time. So your uncle let you do whatever you wanted, you made bad choices, now you're trying to be the guiding force you didn't have when you were a teen. But I do not make it easy. Did I forget any parts?"

I would not let him get me more worked up than I already was. So what if I'd gone over this story before? At least now I knew he'd been listening.

"I know where we'll go," I said, turning toward the south end of town. "It's too late to go back to the beach, but Sequoia Park is close. Still up for a walk?"

When he didn't answer, I glanced over. Under a furrowed brow, Jaral's eyes snapped with a secret excitement. He leaned forward, back straight, staring into the distance.

Because he'd never been a big talker, I'd learned to examine Jaral's face, the angles in his back and neck, the small muscles in his hands, for giveaways, little signals of fear, unease, nervousness, or the expression that calmed my mother's heart most, relaxation. Right now, the kid cabled nothing but self-assurance, top to toe.

Part of me worried this confidence hid something risky, something that made him afraid. I wanted to scoop away Jaral's surface, pull out whatever he hid.

But just as intensely, I wanted not to become my own mother. She would bang things, yell, hit, to get real and made-up confessions out of me. Yes, I had left the back gate open so the dog got loose. But he came back, so what was the big deal? No, I hadn't stuck a fork in the blender or done something else to mess up the blades. It just stopped working because machines stop working sometimes. But whatever she thought was my fault, I had to own as my doing.

I carried my mother's violence like a blood-borne disease. Harmless when dormant, but when stirred awake, it had an energy, a trajectory, a will to live all its own, separate from me. I was afraid of its power in me.

Fear had roused it this time. Fear about whatever Jaral wasn't telling me, fear that I couldn't protect him if he cut me out of his life. I felt the heat of my fear-turned-violence all the way to my fingertips.

We had a jerky drive over to the park as my right foot punished each pedal. Brake. Gas. Brake. Gas. Brake.

* * *

The playground at Sequoia Park held a Monday evening peace. Two sweethearts perched on swings. A set of parents who spoke an easy-rolling stream of Spanish pushed three kids on a merry-go-round, a squeaky metal disk with bent pipes for handles. The kids shut their eyes and hung on, laughing. A solemn redwood forest rose behind the playground.

I loved walking out here. The soft give of woodsy earth under my feet felt like a gentle welcome. When my mother was in calmer moods, she'd take me and my little brother on walks in the state park near where we lived. We'd compare the smells of different leaves while she told us about the oils and odors plants use to defend themselves. We'd turn over rocks to hunt for lizards, laugh as we tried to bound like jackrabbits. Southern Colorado was an arid place to learn to love the earth, but the junipers and chamisa on the state park trails held plenty of life if you knew where to look.

Later, when I lived in California, Uncle Max took me to the redwoods after Honey died, saying the two of us needed some majesty and mystery to heal. He said the mystery of a forest is that a thousand forests exist beyond the one you can perceive. At the time, I didn't understand what he meant, but even so, the redwood forests were magical to me. From the spongy bark on the tall trees to the big banana slugs sliding over broad leaves in the undergrowth, the redwoods were a marvel. That set me on track for college up here. Then I'd just never left.

"We'll take one of the forest trails," I said.

Jaral settled into a state of excessive cheer. "Great! I love this place!"

We passed a stump higher than my head and big around as my kitchen, a remnant from those first lumber-boom years in Eureka. Younger trees sprouted all around the big stump.

What I said to him at the start of our hike? "You either tell me what's going on or I take your phone, your car keys, maybe your skin."

"Thing is, Moms . . ." It took him a while to finish the thought. The trail was too narrow for us to walk side by side. He shuffled ahead in a teenaged amble. I crowded him at one shoulder, trying to read his face. He kept his eyes on the trail and shrank away from me.

"Thing is, there's just one reason you want me to tell you what's up. It's so you can dig in with questions, scrape more details of my business out of me, then shove in a heavy pile of what you think I should do. That's how you always are. But I don't care what you think I should do. I don't need your help. No point even telling you anything. Don't you get that?"

"Don't I get that?" I echoed. Then I looked up at the treetops and yelled, "No!" Technically, I wasn't yelling directly at him. That still seemed to matter.

Then I got after it. Where had he really been, and who had he really been with? I asked. And who was the father of the pregnant friend's child, and did her parents know, and was this why he'd been so tense lately?

With too much momentum to wait for answers, I went on and schooled the back of his head as he kept down the path. Told him how he should know any friend who needed him to steal was no friend at all, and how he should get some adult help with this, there were medical clinics offering free prenatal care if that's what this friend needed, how he should show his best student-self these last weeks, finish strong instead of skipping class, he'd need good recommendations from teachers for whatever came next, and he should work on deciding what that was.

By the time I realized I'd just done what he said I always did—choked the space between us with questions and shoulds—it was too late. I'd shut Jaral down. He'd lost interest in his fake good mood, and just muttered "There it is," after I burned through my fear-fed fire of parental panic.

But in the end, I still let him have his phone, his car keys, and his skin that night.

Blame the pond at the bottom of the trail, lively with frogs. Blame the heavy-blossom fog of azalea perfume we walked through on the way back.

A redwood forest can decompose mistrust and fear, the hard metals of negativity, into just another decaying layer underfoot.

Plus, I felt guilty for going off. Maybe he was just trying to help someone.

By the time Jaral spoke again, I had no appetite for conflict.

"I actually need my car tonight. I'm handling something, Moms. Start grounding me tomorrow."

"When are you planning on telling me what this something is that you're handling?"

"Tomorrow, Moms. I swear."

"Okay. Here's the deal. I'm trying to trust you, here."

"That's good, that's real good."

"God, I don't know if I'm stupid or what, but you say you're handling something? Fine. Have your car tonight. But you will be back by eight PM. I'm sure you have homework. Or you can study for finals. Eight PM and then hit the books. Got it?"

"Sir, yes sir!"

I smiled. I couldn't help it. He was being goofy, and I was relieved I didn't want to kill him anymore.

He turned to head back up the trail.

"No, wait. I want you to turn around and hear the rest of this."

He spun back around on one foot and flashed jazz hands.

"I'm serious," I said, laughing.

He dropped his arms and said "Yeah, you are," pleased with himself.

"Starting tomorrow, the only thing you use your car for is to get to and from school." I forced my face back into an expression of earnest agitation. Which brought back up how I really was agitated. "And I'm going to follow you. I'm going to watch you walk inside that building. I have a parent meeting at Daybreak tomorrow afternoon. When I get home, I better see you there, too. Deal?"

"Eight PM tonight, nothin' but school and home tomorrow. You got it, boss."

We returned to where the forest opened onto the playground, now empty. Shadows crept out from the bushy salal where they'd hidden all day.

"Maybe nine, tops," Jaral said. "I won't be any later than nine. Promise." He pulled on each of his fingers, one at a time. The tiny cracks of each joint spoke the worries he tried to hide.

CHAPTER

3

WHEN JARAL WASN'T home at nine, I was annoyed. By ten, I was frantic. I knew people could disappear. I'd had it happen to me before.

When I was twelve, my mother vanished.

She taught science at the high school in the little town where I grew up in southern Colorado. She'd walk or take a bus to or from work when the weather was good. It was a brilliant October day when she disappeared.

She walked to work in the morning. Then never came home.

The police got closer and closer to me like The Blob on that black-and-white movie I liked to watch. That first night, there was just one at the door, talking to Dad. The second night, two of them made it inside and sat at the table. By the third night, I had one sitting on the edge of my bed while I sat on the other end, my back to the wall, squeezing a pillow to my chest like a shield.

"Your mother is considered a missing person," the officer said.

He asked me what she was like.

Angry a lot, I wanted to say. *For no reason at all.*

"She makes really good beans," I said. "And that's about it."

I was the one angry right then. I was angry about how overwhelmingly I wanted her back, when all I wanted when she was home was to get away from her.

It felt like the cops made her go. I was old enough to know that didn't make sense, but that's how it felt. My mother had been replaced by this slow creep of cops into my world. They terrified me.

In spite of that fear, I almost called 911 that night as I waited up for Jaral. Even in his first few years with me, during the old class-cutting era, he'd never gone far. I'd find him sneaking a cigarette in the ditch behind the school or hanging out at McDonald's. Nothing too scary. But now he was eighteen, old enough to get into real trouble. Out at night and not communicating.

Eleven PM came and went. Then twelve. At 12:15 AM, I called my gym teacher, Jodee.

"You have teenagers, don't you?" I asked.

"You called me in the middle of the night to ask if I have teenagers?"

"Jaral . . ." I couldn't bear to finish the sentence. "Jaral didn't come home tonight."

"Oh, Boots," she sighed and made a chuffling sound.

"What's funny?"

"Midnight is not 'didn't come home.' Midnight is just . . . he decided to be a jackass and do whatever he wanted. 'Didn't come home' doesn't start 'til like noon tomorrow."

"Ohhh-kay. Say he's just being a jackass. What am I doing wrong? I listen. I support him. I care about him. And he just brushes me off like I'm dirt. Do you think it's drugs? I mean, how would I know if it was?"

"I get it," Jodee said. "You're one of those people who thinks they can figure other people out. Do not try that with your own kid. You'll drive yourself crazy. Even if you guess right, you won't have all the pieces."

"Great pep talk, Jodes."

I hung up able to add "foolish" to the stinking pile of emotions I felt. I was shoveling worry on top of extra worry only because I didn't know what I was doing as a parent and couldn't tell a minor pain from a major problem.

Then he walked in.

"Why didn't you call me? Or text?"

"Because." He wouldn't meet my eyes, just headed for the stairs. "You'd stress and blow up my phone. With your thousand questions."

I ran to block the staircase. He stopped in front of me and glanced up. His eyes were clear, but he seemed tired. And distant. Like he was thinking something over that had nothing to do with me.

"Give me your keys," I said.

"Fine." He handed them over and pushed past me up the stairs.

When he reached the landing, I called up to him.

"Your friend. The one you're helping. Is she okay? Do you . . ." I climbed a few steps toward him and stopped. "Do you want to talk about anything?"

I wanted to sound caring, but it came out like just another demand.

He pressed his hands against the base of his neck and rolled his head around once, slowly. Then he glared at me with his eyebrows slightly raised, like I was the one who's behavior needed explaining.

"Honestly, Moms, it's fine."

After he'd been in his room long enough to fall asleep, I went out to check his car. His fender had some mud on it. Had that been there before? I opened the car and rummaged through the glovebox, trunk, door cubbies, under the seats. Nothing but dirt and Taco Bell wrappers. But when I breathed in the guy-funk of the car's interior, I caught threads of perfume, warm and woodsy, like an amber fragrance from a scented page in an Avon catalog from the 80s, with an extra hint of spice or resin. A nice smell. Jaral's "friend" had good taste in fragrance.

I quietly closed the car and went back inside. Before going to bed, I opened the window in my first-floor bedroom the one and a half inches permitted by the dowel I'd placed in the slide bay. I wanted to be able to hear if he tried to leave the house. Where he might go on foot, I had no idea, but I didn't want to be caught off guard again.

The night air came in cool, layered with saltwater and evergreen scents.

He's here now. That's what matters. He's here. He's here. I said this over and over in my head, until I fell asleep.

* * *

The next morning the wind started early, shredding the silken marine layer of fog before we left the house.

I gave Jaral his keys back when it was time to go to school, followed him in my car. Watched him walk in the building. Then drove off, microdosing optimism.

Jaral was right. Missing one day of classes ain't no thing. In any case, I planned to be back before the last bell. Parked in a corner of the lot, waiting to follow him wherever his "business" took him.

Until then, might as well throw my shoulder to the wheel of the day's work. I drove through the glaring sunshine to Daybreak Academy, my school on a coastal bluff.

I'd been one of the school's cofounders. One of the best decisions I made in that first year was to hire Mrs. Murray as head office admin, to provide both order and heart in the front office. She had a round face set in continuous concentration. She was the most caring unsmiling person I'd ever known.

She nodded when I grinned good morning to her as I headed to my office door, tucked behind her desk. I started unlocking the door. She got up to wait behind me.

She followed me in and closed the door behind her.

"Hey, that's a treat." I said. "Confidential business before coffee."

I settled in and offered her a chair. She stayed standing, put her hands on my desk, and leaned forward.

"That federal contracts woman. She's here."

"I already told her we couldn't do ESL classes by telecast. We're not set up for that. She's not taking no for an answer?"

"She said she wants to see the place for a possible on-site contract. I sent Elena to show her around. Now I get this text from Elena."

Mrs. Murray took out her phone, flipped it open, and showed me the screen.

She's asking 2 inspect air ducts. Weird. Smthg abt allergies?

"Yeah, that's weird. But whatever. Send her to the adult learning room when she's done nosing around. I can talk to her while my class does group work."

Mrs. Murray nodded and left, then returned holding something behind her back. She put it right in the middle of my desk like I might completely miss it otherwise. She'd printed it on hot-pink paper.

"The association secretary just sent this in," she told me.

Parent Association Meeting Agenda.

I. Call to order.

II. Vote on school charter.

"That's today? Noooo . . ." Even though I mentioned the meeting to Jaral yesterday, a late night waiting up for him and a rushed morning pushed it out of my mind.

"You worried about this?" She tapped item II.

"I'm so not worried, I forgot it was today. Of course the current charter stays. Our parents love us. What I'm worried about is Jaral. He's sneaking around. Acting shady. I wanted to get back to Eureka High at the last bell so I could make sure he goes straight home. Now I don't know what to do. Make him wait for me. Or make the parents wait."

There'd be a vote at today's parent association meeting about whether to recharter the school with another education company. Yes, if they went with another company, I'd be out on my rear. But the immigrant parents would never vote against me. I'd built our whole adult education program for them. They brought me presents on my birthday and Christmas every year. They knew how much I'd done for them. When they called me "maestra," the word had so much warmth in it I could've worn it as a shawl.

"Don't make the parents wait," Mrs. Murray said. "Think of them as your supervisors. At this job. Which allows you to provide for your little family of two."

I made a noncommittal noise.

Mrs. Murray moved on to a quick summary of the emails, letters, and phone calls I needed to get to that day, then went back out to her desk to greet a roly-poly fourth-grade boy waiting to read the Pledge over the P.A. system.

I lifted and straightened an already straight stack of papers on my desktop twice, just to hear the crack of a well-ordered tap against the desk. Although I'd only been away less than twenty-four hours, it was good to be back. Things might be rocky at home, but work was my anchor. I'd be a fretting mess of a mama if I didn't have this job to focus on.

I left my office for the school's foyer. In the last few minutes before the bell, I liked to stand right in the crossroads area where students streamed in from the patio and off down their halls. I tried to smile a smile that beamed beneficence on every one of them. The younger kids smiled back.

"Hi, Ms. Marez."

"Hi, Ruby. Hi, Jake. Hi, Pedro."

The morning bustle soothed my teen-jangled nerves. All these kids where I could see them, walking into places I knew they'd be safe. Left for the elementary wing, right for the middle school wing. Kids going where they should be going.

Mostly.

Instead of going to class, Jaylea Bewley was being forcibly steered toward me by her mother, Lusanne.

I pulled the tote hanging over my shoulder in front of me a bit, as though it were a talisman to ward off a second encounter with the overcritical woman. The bag was a luxurious leather "executive" model I couldn't afford but bought anyway. I was glad for the status symbol, even if my Penney's chic wardrobe didn't back it up.

When they reached me, Lusanne spoke to the top of the girl's head. "Why don't you tell Ms. Marez about the Pledge. What you told me. Hm-hmm."

"Nice to see you again, Lusanne," I said. Jaylea looked like she needed a Heimlich. Her face reddened. She appeared not to breathe.

"Tell her," Lusanne said, nostrils flaring. "Tell her what we talked about! Mm!"

She squeezed her daughter's shoulder with the force of someone juicing an orange.

Jaylea took a shaky breath, then said, in a rush: "I don't like saying the Pledge in Spanish because I speak English. I want to honor the American flag in American."

"In English," Lusanne corrected. "America's language."

Jaylea swallowed hard. "Yeah."

"Mmm, Ms. Marez." Lusanne tilted her head at me. "Forcing all kids to say the Pledge of Allegiance in Spanish is indefensible. It's reverse discrimination. I intend to bring it up at the parent meeting today. Hm-hmm."

I could've countered that reciting the Pledge twice each morning, once in English, once in Spanish, made us doubly patriotic. But hers being a stupid that would not quit, I ignored Lusanne.

"Jaylea," I said, "that was very brave of you to share your concerns with me."

The girl searched my face to see if the compliment hid any barbs of disapproval. When she saw I wasn't mad, her shoulders relaxed. Her head straightened.

"Go to class, munchkin," Lusanne said.

Jaylea turned toward the middle school hallway and left us without a goodbye.

"There's an even more grave matter on the agenda," Lusanne said to me, lowering her voice. "Hm-hmm. I tried to warn you yesterday in the drug store, but *you* had a lot going *on*."

For an instant, she bared a few of her expensive, unnaturally white teeth in a tight grin gone so quickly, it could've been another tic.

"I saw the agenda, Lusanne. If the parents vote to recharter as a parent-run co-op, I'm out of a job. I know. Not worried."

Chimes playing "De Colores" sounded over the P.A. This let students know all colors were valuable, and they had five minutes to get in their rooms or their asses would be grass.

With one finger under her chin, I snapped Lusanne's mouth shut. Her eyes got big.

"Thanks, though," I said. I did what I hoped was a sashay down the elementary hall to my adult education room.

CHAPTER

4

I HAD TWELVE STUDENTS in my room that morning, seated at four kidney-shaped tables. All of them mothers with kids who attended Daybreak. Most spoke Spanish as their first language, but a few from indigenous communities in southern Mexico and Central America were raised with Purépecha or Mixtec, Huichol or Quiché, and knew only a few words of Spanish. Two students came from Laos, one from Burma.

"Good morning!" the more outgoing students called as I came in. A few women chatted with each other. Some started copying words they saw on the whiteboard into their notebooks. I set my phone on my desk and tucked my bag in the big bottom drawer just as the bell rang.

"Good morning," I said. "Please stand for the Pledge."

We faced a flag that jutted out from the far wall. Hands over our hearts, we began, "I pledge allegiance . . ." The voice of the fourth grader leading us blasted out from the round silver speaker above the flag. It was hard to distinguish one word from the next. He took a sharp breath in after every other phrase.

"Take a step back from the mic, sweetheart," Mrs. Murray said in the background, sounding miles away.

"Ay, Jesusito," one of my students said, covering a giggle with the back of her hand. The boy on the loudspeaker was her son.

When the English Pledge was over, we began again. "Juro fidelidad . . ."

After we finished the Spanish Pledge, I moved to the whiteboard and selected a marker.

"These are word families with different 'e' sounds," I said, tapping the end of the marker at two lists of words I'd written the previous afternoon. "I'll read, you repeat."

I scanned the first list—words with a short /e/ sound.

death, breath, red, bed

"Eh, eh, eh, eh" I said, to get the class ready to use that sound.

"Excuse me."

A voice interrupted from the doorway.

I turned to see a brassy blond White woman with a short hair style that gave her head a bullet-like appearance. Elena, our janitor, looked out from behind the woman and shrugged.

"I'm here about the contract for English classes," the woman said.

I glanced at the words on the board behind me that I'd been about to read.

"You just go on and finish your lesson," she said, like I'd asked for her permission. "That'll give me time to observe. Then we can talk."

"Uh. Okay?" I mirrored my employee and shrugged back. "Thank you, Elena," I called to her, so she'd know she wouldn't have to waste any more of her day with this pushy person. Elena hustled back down the hall.

"If we spoke on the phone, I'm sorry I don't recall your name," I said to the stranger. I was pretty sure we'd never spoken. I didn't recall her voice either.

"This is Braulio Tenorio's school, correct?"

She had an accent from the north end of the Confederacy, vowels so round each one arrived on a satin pillow of sound.

At the sound of Tenorio's name, an eruption of murmurs rippled through the classroom.

The woman took a step inside and scanned the room, ramrod straight with a stare that demanded answers.

"He doesn't own it," I said, over the tops of my students' heads. "His education company holds the charter to run it."

I put down the marker I was holding and walked over to the woman. Hoping to kill the interruption with kindness.

"I'm Boots Marez, head of school." I extended a hand.

She gave a firm one-pump shake. "I left a message with your secretary. Originally, I asked if you'd be interested in a federal contract for English Language Learner classes off-site. But now I'm interested in your site here. I need to see if it meets the physical plant requirements for our programs."

She was fluent in that dialect of industrial-speak common to agency personnel, military, and feds.

"Go ahead and wait in the reading nook. I need to get this group going on vocab exercises."

She moved behind the partition I'd put up around the sofa and bookcase that made up our reading nook. I could see the top of her head as she walked around the small area, then came back out.

"Prefer to stand, if you don't mind."

I sighed, moved toward the board to resume my lesson. No use getting in a power struggle if there was a chance she'd give the school money.

Just then, my phone had a mini seizure on my desk. I checked the caller's name. Jaral.

Had he forgotten something for school?

I never picked up during my lesson. But yesterday in Sequoia Park, Jaral said he was handling something. What if he needed my help? I took the call.

"Moms, you have to come! There's so much blood! Oh God, I didn't know. I didn't know she was this dangerous!"

"Where are you?" I turned to my classroom window as though I'd find my son in the vista sweeping down to the shore. "What blood?"

"Poor Nando! Someone got him! He was just trying to help. You have to get over here! There's a bloody knife on the counter." Jaral's voice sounded thready, like he might pass out.

"Jaral. What about Nando?" I glanced at my student Rosalva, as I said her son Armando's nickname. I lowered my voice, put a hand over my mouth. "What do you mean, someone got him?"

Rosalva stood up. "Nando?"

Our boys were the same age, used to be best friends.

"Oh no, no, no, this is so messed up, no, no . . ." Jaral's voice came back to life.

"Where are you, Jaral?" I reached for the drawer with my bag, took it out, hung it on my shoulder. "You're at school?"

"No, don't be mad, I'm at Nando's, don't be mad, Moms, please come and help him."

"Son, listen to me. Did you call the police?"

"Police?" my students murmured. An English word they all knew.

"Son. Jaral?" He hung up.

I dropped my cell, fingers numb. Rosalva said something next to me, her voice imploring. I bent down to pick up the phone, struggled to put it in the phone-shaped pocket on the outside of my tote. Rosalva spoke louder. "Why you say Nando, police? He okay? What is problem, maestra?"

"Let's go find out. I'll drive you."

She reflected my panic on her face.

"I'm sorry, class," I said. "We'll continue our lesson tomorrow. Class is done. Ya termine."

One student bit her lip nervously, another raised her eyebrows at me, hoping for more information. The stranger standing to the side of the class looked grim.

"Who's Nando?" she called, as I walked out of the classroom.

"He my son you talking," Rosalva shrieked, hurrying out behind me.

The two of us trotted down the hall, one after the other.

As I passed the office, I pulled my phone back out, waved it at the admin. "Call if you need me. Class is canceled." Mrs. Murray frowned. Rosalva rushed alongside me with clasped hands pressed to her heart.

I thumbed the phone.

"Por favor, maestra, no la policia!" Rosalva grabbed my arm. I had already dialed 911.

CHAPTER

5

"WHAT'S YOUR EMERGENCY?" The female dispatcher sounded chipper.

I don't remember what I said to her. I kept repeating Armando's address.

Then Rosalva and I drove off in my car toward El Pavo, a poor neighborhood east of the fairgrounds where most of my ESL families lived.

To stop a scream I felt at the back of my mouth, I tried to focus on the harmless part of Jaral's call. "I'm at Nando's, don't be mad, Moms."

When did he go to Nando's? I knew he went to school first thing that morning. I knew because I followed him, like a crime boss tailing a rival.

Why did he go to Nando's? They hadn't hung out in years.

Blood. Knife. Dangerous.

I tried to push Jaral's more alarming words from my thoughts. If I let them sink in, I'd lose it.

I drove through downtown Eureka. A mistake. Bagel place, coffee shop, sushi place, light. Coffee shop, gallery, knickknack store, boutique, light. California Indian Services, shoe store, old hotel. Light.

Through all ten stoplighted blocks, my brakes groaned.

"The police will help." I said. We turned on Broadway. "An ambulance will come too. They'll take Armando to the hospital."

"Why he need help, maestra? Why hospital?"

She squeezed the top of her purse with both hands.

"I don't know. Do you want to call your husband?"

"I no have phone."

"Use mine."

I picked it up from the cupholder, glanced down to tap over to a dial screen. When I looked up, a cat was crouched in the road. I yanked the wheel right to avoid it. Left to keep from going up the sidewalk. Then handed Rosalva the phone.

"Jeez Louise!" Her favorite Americanism. I tried smiling.

"We're okay," I said. She already had the phone to her ear.

Blood. Knife. Dangerous. Don't think about that.

"He working. No answer." She dropped the phone back in its spot, then clutched her hands together. "Her!"

Heading our direction on the sidewalk was a short Latina teenager. She wore a large sweatshirt that fell over one shoulder, jean shorts, high-heeled sandals.

"Maestra! Alto, alto! Stop, teacher!"

Rosalva rolled down her window.

"¿Mija, dónde está Armando?" She leaned out toward the girl. "¿Y tú? Why you no in class?"

Then she turned back toward me. "Alto, maestra, please!"

I started angling the car to pull over. When the girl recognized Rosalva, she charged us like a bull.

I braked. Rosalva shrank back. When the girl reached the car, she slammed her palms on the hood and leaned in Rosalva's window.

"Your son is in deep shit. After how he was last night, he's in for some hurt."

"Go back to Mexico!" someone shouted at us, as they drove around me.

My turn to wedge my torso out the window. "Go back to Dumbassville!"

A car honked.

"Mija," said Rosalva, reaching out to touch the girl. The girl leaned back to dodge Rosalva's arm.

"Mija, something wrong. Come with us. Please. Right now."

"You say something's wrong? You got that right, Mrs. P. Why I'm walking the other way. There's cops outside your house. Ain't no one got time for that."

She turned and show-horse pranced away from us.

Cops at Armando's already? I shunted the car back into traffic, nearly cutting off a city bus and riding the bumper of a minivan ahead of us.

"Police bad, maestra. Because we don't have papers."

"It's okay, Rosalva." Something I couldn't know. "We have different types of police. Not all police are 'migra.' That's ICE. City police, or sheriff, can help sometimes."

"Help what, maestra? Why you calling for police?"

Not ready to repeat Jaral's terrifying call, I told her, "Jaral said someone was hurt."

She gasped as though she'd touched a hot stove. I changed the subject so her panic wouldn't spiral.

"Who was that girl? What did she mean, how Armando was last night?"

The road took us past Sequoia Park. Between a blur of fence posts, I could see the path Jaral and I walked yesterday, leading away from the parking lot.

"She good girl," Rosalva said, her voice quiet. "She girlfriend de Armando." Then she clapped her hands together. "You son no good!"

"What?" I said, glancing at her. "What are you talking about?"

"Maestra, these boys."

My phone rang, a number I didn't recognize.

"I think it's your husband." I handed Rosalva the phone.

She spoke in a continuous stream, voice hushed as though I weren't right next to her. Her husband, Eusebio, a calm man with impeccable posture, chauffeured Rosalva to English class every morning. He ran a busy roofing business, but always made time to transport his lady to Daybreak. He'd walk Rosalva and their third grader Lizzie right up to the door, then hold it open for them with a small bow. Day after day. His gallantry turned my heart over each time.

From Rosalva's words, I picked "policia." Then Jaral's name. She said "maestra" in an accusing tone.

I drove past the fairgrounds at the edge of the city. The neighborhood where Rosalva and most of my adult students lived was on the other side of the rodeo arena, next to the poultry building. Residents named it El Pavo, the turkey, after the enormous birds on display in summer.

We turned onto a street with every house painted a different color. Purple with turquoise trim, yellow with orange trim, light green, dark green. The structures were compact—none of them bigger than eight hundred square feet. I turned right again, onto another street of similarly tidy, colorful homes.

I was afraid I made a mistake calling 911 right after Jaral called me, without having much information.

After all, every mother in America with a brown son feels a distinct horror crawl through her thoughts at some point. *A brush with the law could end in death. If anyone sees this boy as even a whisper of threat, he could be dead.*

Yet I had just set up Jaral to become "young Latino male found at the scene." At the scene of . . . what?

Rosalva ended her call and handed the phone back to me. I gripped it in one hand as I drove, ready to document any brutality that might, even right that moment, be underway against my boy.

The sweet smell of hyacinths drifted in through the car vents. Short clubs covered in blooms edged every tiny El Pavo lawn.

In front of Rosalva's pale pink home, Jaral's car sat empty, with all four windows partly down. He left it like that sometimes, careless or forgetful. One sheriff's department cruiser waited behind it. I braced myself for the sight of Jaral in the back of the cruiser but only saw a lone officer with his face turned away, watching the front of the house.

Maybe he was waiting for backup before making a move. No ambulance had arrived yet either.

Instead of pulling up on the street, I drove around the corner and through an alley to park behind Rosalva's house. We pulled in beside a small green car.

Rosalva started to get out of the car. I told her to wait.

"I'll go in. If there are already police in there, let me talk to them first." As much as I'd tried to reassure her that local officers weren't the deporting kind, I didn't want to take any chances.

"But Nando, he is okay? Why his car back here? Why he no in school?"

I put the windows down a few inches so Rosalva could get some air. Took one deep breath, and said, "I'll find out. You wait here."

She dug through her purse.

"Is lock. Here."

I took her keys but didn't need them. When I turned the doorknob and pushed, the back door shucked open.

A dim hallway led to the living room at the front of the house. I stepped inside.

A pair of legs stuck out on the living room floor, with the feet tied together and pulled up over the backs of the knees.

"Jaral?" I called, flipping a switch on the wall to light the hall.

The legs, the feet, didn't move.

Whose shoes? Not Jaral's. White socks. Wrinkled. Against the cutting pressure of a yellow rope.

CHAPTER

6

I HADN'T SEEN ARMANDO in years, but I recognized his thicket of hair. His large hands, bound together. His eyes were closed, his head tipped back, pulled toward his hands by a yellow plastic rope around his forehead. After making a few loops around his hands, the rope ended in the knot that held his ankles together.

Where had I seen that before?

A gash opened his throat deep enough to allow his head another inch or two of give in its pull back toward his shoulder blades.

Armando.

He used to carry his little sister home from Head Start on his back.

Armando.

Had a hard time with math but was a genius at wrestling.

Armando, now dead.

I still had my phone in my hand. In a daze I took a photo of the boy in front of me.

Seeing the horrific image again on my screen snapped me back to the moment. I ran behind the breakfast bar.

"Jaral!"

No one there.

A bloody cleaver lay at a haphazard angle on the counter, as though thrown there. I backed away from it.

"Jaral, Jaral!"

I ran down a narrow side hall and scanned three bedrooms. A bathroom.

Every room empty. Was there a basement? An attic? I didn't think so.

I ran outside, past my car to the back alley.

"Jaral!"

Houses kept their backs to me and gave nothing away.

I ran alongside Armando's house, smack into a khaki-uniformed deputy. He grabbed my arms.

"Okay, ma'am, calm down. Who is Jaral, ma'am? You need to calm down. Tell me who you're trying to find."

As he spoke, he steered me with one hand on my right shoulder, the other on my right arm, to the center of the tiny front lawn. He was White, young, with a steel grip.

"Who were you yelling for?" he asked again.

"He's . . ." He's maybe not here because he's worried about being found at the scene of a murder.

"He's the brother. Of Armando. The boy in there. You need to see." I was so panicked about not being able to find Jaral, so unsure what to say to keep any suspicions from sticking to him, that I ended up tongue-tied and truth-impaired when speaking about him.

I thought it would be better to say I was yelling for someone else who lived there, like a brother, instead of a kid who was supposed to be in school and had no good reason for being there.

"What is your name, ma'am?"

That one, I could handle.

"Ana Marez. Boots, I mean. That's what everyone calls me. I said 'Boots' to the dispatcher." I glanced at my phone when I said that. The screen had gone dark.

"You're the 911 caller," the officer said. I nodded.

"And what is your relationship to the residents of this home?"

"Armando, I think he's eighteen now, he used to be my student. Now his mother, Rosalva, she's in my car back there, she's in my adult English class. That's where we were when Jaral called to say something happened to Armando."

"This Jaral made a call to Rosalva? His mother?"

I nodded, squirming inside from the discomfort of having to play out the sloppy lie I started, about Jaral being Armando's brother. I couldn't trust my voice and didn't know where to look. If I stared the guy down, I'd seem like I was daring him to challenge me. If I cut my eyes away, that said I'm lying so hard I literally can't look you in the eye. These calculations left me flicking glances up to his face, down to his shoes, back up to his face.

"Okay, ma'am? You're going to need to wait here for the detective to arrive. Can you do that for me?" We had stopped in the middle of the yard.

"Yes, yes, uh-huh."

"Good," he said. "You just wait right here." He left to go around back, where I'd said Rosalva was waiting. I wanted to follow him so I could tell her he wouldn't deport her, but I'd been ordered to stay put.

I tried calling Jaral. I heard applause and cheers coming from his car. The ringtone on his phone. Shit. I disconnected.

Had the officer in back of the house heard? He didn't seem to be coming back to check on the sound. That was good. The less attention on Jaral or his things the better.

Who else could I call to try and find out where Jaral was? I pushed the button to wake up the phone, then stared at the screen. My wallpaper photo showed a close-up of white needles on a rare white redwood that grew near my yurt in the north county. A hand tilted the needles up for a better angle. Jaral's hand.

Where are you? I shifted my weight from one foot to the other like a boxer before the bell. The grass felt oddly crisp under my feet. I bent to pat it. Fake.

Time jerked forward in jolts. Now the officer was back and pressing a hand against my collarbone. Or was I leaning into the hand? Yes, I was trying to get past him. I wanted to get out into the street where I could see. Where was Jaral? My boy. Where was he? Where? Where?

I was taller than the officer by a head. Up close, I could see how fine his buzzed, sandy brown hair was. I slouched a little, thinking, don't intimidate him. They don't like that. He had one hand pushing against me. The other covering his weapon.

"Relax, ma'am. I need you to stay here a few minutes. Like we talked about."

I backed away as I craned my head to look farther down the street.

In that snick of an instant, I saw Jaral. He stood up from behind a low fence a few doors down, on the other side of the street. He faced me for a moment, not moving. I couldn't see the expression on his face.

A dark stain marred his bright turquoise T-shirt around his belly. Dark splotches covered the front of his pantlegs.

He turned and leapt over a side fence, then disappeared behind a row of cedars.

I gasped. The White officer in front of me glanced over his shoulder to follow my gaze.

"You see something?"

I opened my mouth, but no sound came out. I tried to lunge past the officer toward where I'd seen my son. Was he hurt?

"Ma'am!" The officer stiff-arming me again. "I cannot let you leave this scene. We have to calm down, all right? Now what did you see over there?"

My breath came quick and shallow. If I pointed him toward a bloodied Jaral, things would not go well for my boy.

I stepped back once again, tried to take a deep breath.

"I saw . . . I thought I saw . . ." A cat that looked like one I used to have. A car with someone waving. A neighbor I recognized. Any of these would have been handy lies to get the focus off me and my surprise at seeing Jaral. But lies didn't yet come easily to me. I was rattled from finding Armando's body and already lying once about Jaral. Ideas for what I could have said wouldn't cross my mind until hours after this tense exchange.

The keening of approaching sirens made us both turn our heads the other direction and saved me from spilling the words "I saw Jaral" off the tip of my tongue.

A fire truck, an ambulance, another marked car, and Rosalva's husband all arrived within thirty seconds of each other. The melee of lights and sound superimposed themselves over the image of Jaral's dark-stained clothes that I couldn't stop seeing. And behind that image, a grisly presence. The mangled body of Armando. Blood pooling beneath his throat. I felt lightheaded.

The sight of a short Black woman in uniform exiting the new cop car with her weapon drawn on me sheared the present moment back into sharp focus.

"This one's okay; I've got her," said the cop in front of me. "Go on in."

Eusebio ran toward the front door calling, "Rosalva! Armando!"

"Detrás de la casa," I called out to him, glad I remembered the phrase for "behind the house."

Eusebio turned away from his front door, then ran between me and the weapon aimed at me on his way around back.

"Sir," the female cop called. "Is this your house? Wait, sir!"

She glanced at me, lowered her weapon, and followed him.

Another cop appeared. Where had he come from? This one was also White, but older and taller than the cop insisting I stay on the front lawn.

He followed the first woman along the side of the house.

"They don't speak English!" I called after the two of them.

"I speak English!" Eusebio yelled.

I heard him murmur something low, probably trying to coax Rosalva out of the car.

The female officer called out, "Thiel, the door is already open back here. Let's go in."

I heard the two cops move up the back steps, shut the door behind them. Then nothing.

CHAPTER

7

I USED TO WORK at the public library in Eureka as head of an adult English tutoring program. In summer 2003, the exhibit area on the second floor had something called the Heart Gallery. Enlarged photo portraits of kids covered the walls. Maybe thirty of them. Boys, girls, middle schoolers, high schoolers. Latino, Black, White. I kept coming back to this one image. A slight Latino boy with a heart-shaped face. Short, coarse hair. A half smile that might've been a question I could answer.

The placard next to the portrait said his name was Jaral. He enjoyed singing. He had a loving, loyal personality, was working hard on anger management. Extremely bright, would do best as an only child in a home with stable boundaries where he could be challenged to reach new heights.

Was I interested in learning more about adopting an older child? There was a number I could call.

If there had been a placard next to me back then, it would have said, "Because of trust issues, Boots Marez's emotional life is an empty begging bowl. She likes feeling needed, while avoiding real vulnerability. And watch out for that temper. She is single, thirty-three, likes being tall enough to stand eye to eye with most men but hates feeling like an absolute plow ox next to most women. Would love a reason to dump the search-for-a-life-partner drama down the drain."

I was seeing a guy at the time. He was a writer for the independent weekly and a major adrenaline junkie in his free time. We met when he did a story on the library's literacy programs. In our first six months together, we'd gone through bungee jumping, scuba, hang gliding, skydiving, and high-stakes poker, trying each thrill once before planning the next adventure. The heights stuff made me dizzy and sick to my stomach, but I never backed out, thinking I could train myself out of the nerves.

What I couldn't take was how hard I really fell for him.

I didn't like feeling electrified when things were going well, then buried in layers of mud when we argued. I was plate-smashing jealous a time or two, and his disdain for what he called my childish tantrums left me no oxygen. Not that I could breathe well when we were "on" either. It was just too intense.

Maybe taking care of someone as a parent, as a mom, would cleanse out the crazy.

The first place I took the boy after our ten-hour drive up from L.A., where I picked him up, was my little getaway in the north county. He had never seen a redwood tree. As we hiked up the trail to my yurt, the only thing he said was an awestruck, "Damn."

When we got to the clearing that held the thirty-foot diameter canvas structure I'd named "Mouse Manor," he'd started singing. "Big Trees. So much larger than life. I'm gonna watch 'em growin'!"

I didn't know what I had done to deserve the unexpected feeling of buoyancy that being near this kid gave me. But I was suddenly aware that as long as I knew he was okay, nothing could push me under.

"Hey!" Jaral turned to me. "We're gonna live in town but come up here to relax. That's cool. Who else is in the picture? You got a man? Someone you didn't want the social worker to know about? Maybe he's a thug type? Living underground?" Jaral dropped his voice. "He grow ganja? This is the Emerald Triangle, right?"

I laughed. "Nope. No thug. Don't need one."

Had I been wrong, trying to single-parent a teen boy? If he'd had a dad, could Jaral have avoided whatever tangled him up now?

I swore celibacy when I adopted him. Thought I needed a singular focus, like a nun's love for Christ. But Jaral was no Jesus. I was no nun.

Standing in the middle of a fake lawn in El Pavo, the strafe of sunlight strange on my skin, I felt my sense of knowing what was "best" burn away. How could I, how could any parent, ever know where our choices for our children led?

A sound like frogs or insects started up behind the house.

The lady cop came out the front door and walked to the fire truck. She spoke to the driver before the truck left.

Then she walked up to me. I hadn't realized how short she was. Stocky. Hips made for bearing a duty belt.

"Come talk to me around back" she said.

"What about the ambulance? Isn't anyone else going in there?"

I didn't like the thought of Armando all alone in his living room.

"Crime scene investigators are on their way."

I followed the short officer to the rear of the house. The sounds I'd heard came from Rosalva. She kept saying, "Oh, oh, oh." Shoulders hunched, two fists curled under her chin. Eusebio had his arms around her.

The officer pulled two plastic chairs away from the house and placed them alongside the driveway, facing each other. Then she found a third chair. She motioned for me to sit. Another uniform spoke to the grieving parents and walked them over to the front yard. I heard a car start.

The female officer sat down next to me. Her badge read "Sgt. Det. Alvarez." The long-legged officer joined her. His badge read "Thiel." One White, one Black did not mean fifty percent less bias.

A primal imperative rang through my head like the strike of a farrier's hammer. *Get out of here, quick, and find Jaral, find Jaral, find Jaral before they do.*

I needed to shield him from a justice system known to be a hungry machine that could eat up brown boys.

What was the quickest way out? Lying to try and protect Jaral had made me so jumpy, I was sure I'd trip up and make things worse. I'd try the short-form truth.

CHAPTER

8

"YES, JARAL IS my son. His last name is Marez. Yes, Rosalva Peregrino is the victim's mother. No, the victim doesn't have any brothers. Yes, Jaral called me saying the victim, Armando, was bleeding. No, I haven't spoken to Jaral since that call. Yes, he said he was here. Inside the house or outside the house? I don't know. No, I didn't tell him to leave before the cops came. Where is he now? I hope he's back at school. Yes, I will have him contact you as soon as I hear from him."

"So, Ms.? Mrs.? Marez . . ."

"It's Boots." I wanted control of at least one corner of our interaction.

The detective glanced at the basic flats on my feet. Wrote something down.

"Childhood nickname," I said.

"How did you know the victim?"

"Stop saying The Victim. Kid has a name." I felt like Armando might get sewn back up and come to life again. That made no sense, but it was how I felt. Protective.

Alvarez made a noncommittal grunt.

"You knew him well?"

"My boy and Armando were best friends in seventh and eighth grade at my school. But by tenth grade they stopped hanging out. They hadn't spoken in years. What's my school's name?

Daybreak Academy. K-8 plus adult education. No, I didn't know anyone who would want to harm Armando. No, I do not know what my son was doing at Armando's house this morning. No, he hasn't told me anything about problems Armando was having."

Alvarez asked for my license. She handed it to the young kid who'd kept me in place when we were in front of the house. He wrote something down on a clipboard, nodded, passed it back to Alvarez. He asked if he should call for a tow for the tan car. Jaral's. Alvarez told him to get it pulled into evidence right away. When he returned to the front of the house, I heard another vehicle drive away.

Alvarez turned back to me. "So you get this call from your son. Jaral. Then you call 911. Why did you tell dispatch that someone was hurt in an accident?"

She cocked her head like a small bird considering a very tall worm. I said nothing.

"Why lie to that nice young man, one of our sheriff's deputy officers, about who you and your son are? Didn't your mother teach you not to lie?"

"Do you have children, officer?"

"Detective. Sergeant Detective."

"Kids?"

"Three."

"Then you know how mothers worry. Encounters with the criminal justice system don't go well for our kind. I mean, the odds are not good."

"What kind is our kind?"

"Brown people. We get lumped together, even though we're different. Like me, my father's half Japanese, and my mother's Mexican American. My boy, I adopted him, his mother's Salvadoran and his father's Mexican. In any case, we're brown. I think you know why I want to speak to my son before the police do."

"I'd rather hear you tell me."

"I want to be sure he doesn't . . ." I stopped myself. "I want him to know his rights."

Alvarez wrote on the bottom of a form attached to a clipboard. Then she flipped the page over the clasp and continued writing on the next page in a goading silence.

"Whoever did this, whatever *this* is, it couldn't have been him!" I stood and loomed over the seated detective, trying to see what she was writing.

"Yeah," said Alvarez, with no more than a quick glance up from her clipboard. "And why's that?"

"Because he is not a monster! He's supposed to graduate next month. He just . . ."

Alvarez rocketed up, thrust her card at me. "I'm sure we'll be in touch again soon."

We heard more footsteps along the side of the house. Rosalva walked straight up to me.

"You son, he devil!" She poked me in the throat with one finger. Her eyes opened wide with rage. I didn't know what she was talking about.

Eusebio followed behind her. He pushed away her accusing hand gently.

"No, mami, no, ya, ya."

She wrenched her hand free and raised it again with an open palm, as though taking an oath.

"Jaral is a demon." Rosalva spoke to Alvarez in Spanish, eyes blazing. "The death of Armando proves it!"

The cop smoothed her pages. I hoped she hadn't understood Rosalva. But then she gave the grieving mother a Mexican expression of sympathy.

"Señora, te acompañaré en tus sentimientos."

Something inside me crumpled. Who would accompany *me* in my panic to find Jaral?

Alvarez addressed Eusebio. "We'll need to talk to you both again, later today. For now, is there a neighbor's house where you can go for a while? The crime scene van is on the way. Once they get what they need, the ambulance will take your son to the coroner's office. Then a cleanup crew will take care of your front room."

Eusebio stiffened. He ran his tongue over his lower lip.

"Okay," he said. "How much will cleanup cost? We can do it ourselves."

"No!" Alvarez and I said at the same time. The uniformed woman rushed to speak. "Sir? I advise you to ask your landlord. It's Braulio Tenorio, right? Surely he has the money to take care of it."

"But it's not a problem with the house," Eusebio said. "It's not for fixing anything. Anything to be cleaned, that's supposed to be us. We take care of the house."

"I'll talk to Mr. Tenorio," I said. "Don't worry. It's okay. Let me talk to him."

"Thank you, maestra," Eusebio said, bending his head toward me. "But no. I'll clean."

"Mother of dogs," Rosalva snarled at me in Spanish.

CHAPTER

9

I WENT HOME HOPING Jaral might be there. There was a cop stationed at my curb. The sandy-haired buzz-cut guy. Again. Pulling into the driveway of my little green home, I threw him a stink eye. Inside, I checked each room, closet, bathroom, basement, garage. No Jaral.

I opened my top dresser drawer, pushed aside underwear and socks. The emergency cash envelope I kept there was empty. I knew there'd been at least a hundred in the envelope. I remembered feeling like a loser last time I'd checked it, seeing how little I could actually save. If Jaral took the $100, did that mean he'd been back to the house earlier this morning? Or had he taken the money weeks ago? If he really needed it now, if it would help keep him safe, I wished I'd had more for him to run off with. If he'd taken it earlier, though, and used it for something not good, something not vitamins, then I wished I'd never left anything there.

I pulled down a first aid kit stored on a shelf in the garage. An undisturbed layer of dust covered the red tin box. If Jaral had been here, he hadn't used it. But maybe he was still on his way, walking, or running, over from El Pavo.

With his phone in the car the police were going to tow, he'd have no way to call a friend, or me, for a ride. I guessed it would normally take someone around forty-five minutes to walk over to my house from El Pavo, and I had to believe that blood I saw on Jaral's clothes was Armando's blood. I couldn't stand the idea that Jaral might be wounded too. He seemed strong when he jumped over the fence. Maybe he was running here right now, would be here any second.

But just in case . . . I dusted the first aid kit off and left it out on the kitchen counter.

I was desperate to find my kid, make sure he was okay. But the only other place I could think to try was the high school. And I had a feeling he wouldn't be there. He was running loose inside a nightmare where he'd found one of his closest friends tied up, cut open, and bled out like slaughtered livestock. Now cops were looking for him. I thought he'd try to get as far away from people as he could while he figured out what to do.

But I had to do something. Go somewhere he might be, even if the odds of finding him were slim. I didn't know where any of his current friends lived. A giant mom-fail.

Before leaving, I made sure front and back doors were unlocked, in case Jaral didn't have his house key and did want to come back. I scrawled a note that said, "Not a word to cops. Back soon. Love you so much, Moms" and stuck it on the fridge.

Was this my life?

On my way out the door, the cop who'd been in his car got out and approached me.

"I need to be sure you haven't removed anything from the home, ma'am."

I carried nothing in and brought nothing out. I turned my pockets inside out, to convince him.

"You be safe out there today," he said and got back into his car without turning it on. His courtesy may have been condescending, or even sinister, but at least he didn't try to stop me.

On the drive to the high school, my thoughts ping-ponged against a horrifying wall. Where was Jaral? What were Rosalva and Eusebio going to do with their crater of loss? And where was Jaral? What unimaginable shock must Rosalva have been in when she called him a devil? And where, where, where? On the other side of that wall was the unthinkable: that Jaral could be in danger from this same killer.

At the front office of the high school I spoke quickly, sounding manic or high. I introduced myself as Jaral's mother, asked the secretary to check if Jaral was in class.

She worked her keyboard, squinted at her screen. "His third-hour teacher hasn't put in his attendance yet. Want me to call down there?"

I nodded and asked her to send him out to talk to me, if he was in class.

He wasn't. The secretary took my number and said she'd ask the school resource officer to keep an eye out.

As I left the high school, thinking of all the uniforms looking for Jaral, I realized that when this kid turned up, he might need a lawyer.

I headed back to my own school, Daybreak, with the idea that someone at the parent meeting would hook me up with pro bono services. Someone with an attorney spouse, friend, neighbor—someone would know someone who would help. Even though I was at the top of my school's org chart, I was "house poor," with little cash left after paying my middle-class California mortgage and bills each month and bad at saving whatever I did have left over. Whenever I went shopping, there were always holiday decorations, or a few new basketballs, or a package of headphones on clearance I could get for the school.

Yes, the parent meeting was supposed to be about whether to end the school charter with the company I'd founded, whether to request proposals for a new company to run the place. But I thought only a few fringe members of the group supported that idea.

Like Tenorio, I counted on the loyalty of all the immigrant families I'd helped to be the ones voting to keep the school charter as-is. I'd stay on as head of school, of course.

Some of these immigrant families I'd known since my days at the library's adult ed program. More than one told me I was their hero. So the parents I'd helped would help me by voting my way. And maybe the more affluent parents would get a kick out of flexing their largesse by connecting me to counsel. I had until that afternoon to figure out how to put feelers out for an attorney without coming right out and saying, "My only child was at the scene of a murder this morning and police want to get hold of him." That reputational hit would not help either of us.

And just to find out what I was dealing with, I also planned to call a few defense attorneys' offices and get an idea of going rates.

To get back to my school, I came up the same driveway switchbacks, lined with the same second-growth stands of redwoods and cedars, that I had come down a couple hours before. The school building was the same as it had been then. Elementary wing on the south side, middle school wing on the north side, glass double doors opening to a foyer in the middle. Same student art on the walls, same office off to the right. But everything had changed.

Now, every shape seemed hyper-defined, as though edged with a fine line of white light. I felt like I was a visitor to a made-up universe where kids could care about who to be friends with, teachers could care about who learned what.

In the real universe, a boy had been murdered, and the unknowns about Jaral, where he was, his condition, became the black hole around which everything rotated.

Maybe the killer had other targets. Where was Jaral?

Behind the school, students from grades three, four, seven, and eight played tetherball or basketball or sat on picnic tables talking. I'd set up the school schedule to have mixed-grade recess, but most kids stayed with others in their grade.

Jodee, the gym teacher, and Mrs. Goody, second grade, stood talking near the door. They stopped when they saw me come out onto the playground.

What had they heard about this morning's horror show in El Pavo?

As I walked up to them, I realized I would have to tell the whole staff about Armando. He'd been a student here. His little sister attended our third grade.

"Boots," Jodee said, when I was close enough to hear. I'd asked my staff to call me Ms. Marez in front of kids.

Both Jodee and Mrs. Goody had the same stiffness in their necks that they got when I walked into their classrooms for staff observation.

"Look over by the sycamore," Jodee said. She twitched her head toward the back of the play yard.

In the shade of a crooked tree on the far end of the yard stood a man who resembled a Mexican Sean Penn. Chiseled jaw, narrow mouth, a wave of hair cresting at his forehead, rolling back from his face.

Braulio Tenorio, who normally stood like a field boss with his arms crossed, legs apart, today had one hand over his eyes, craning his neck, squinting. Trying to find someone? On the playground?

Anytime we got a visit from the CEO of the business that ran this place, a current of bitterness laced with anxiety ran through the staff. He paid our salaries but could yank any one of us off the payroll in a heartbeat. He sucked in state dollars through his company's charter to keep the school going but then siphoned off a more than healthy chunk of funds for his own bloated salary.

"How long has he been here?" I asked Jodee.

"Just a few minutes. He's acting weird. Not talking to anyone." Jodee stepped closer to me. "Are you okay? We heard you had to go out to El Pavo. Is there . . . something wrong?"

"Later," I said. I didn't know exactly what to say about what I'd seen.

Mrs. Goody grunted. "Well, you know. We heard. Something."

Tenorio saw me and walked toward where I stood.

The bell rang. Mrs. Goody turned to follow Jodee inside. Kids assembled themselves into knots and whorls, packs and loners moving toward the door.

I waited to meet Tenorio, the usual bitterness and anxiety overwritten by the day's bright terror—*where was my son?*

CHAPTER

10

TENORIO MET ME at the edge of the blacktop, just past the white lines of the foursquare court. His cologne tingled my sinuses.

"Mr. Peregrino called me," he said. "What a terrible, terrible tragedy. Still, the main thing Peregrino wanted to tell me was that Nando wouldn't be at work tomorrow! That's the Mexican peasant," Tenorio said, a few words sharpened by his slight Spanish accent. "So reliable, even up to the point of death. That's why America needs more Mexicans of that class."

I winced. I didn't want to talk about Nando. Or about Tenorio's theories of social engineering. At least he'd said "peasant" instead of "peón," the word he used to favor when describing rural immigrants. No matter the terms, he still sounded like what he was: a worst-of-both-worlds cross between a Latin American dictator and a North American capitalist robber baron.

Tenorio was raised as a second-tier society boy in Mexico City. He came to the United States for college, stayed when he realized he could make his fortune in the people business. Yes, he was our major investor. But he'd made himself CEO of his own education corporation, through which Daybreak's public funding was channeled. In this way, he also became the person paid the most to do the least for Daybreak.

"You don't have anything to say about this horrible murder?" Tenorio asked, his voice tight. "Tell me. Why do you think your son was there?"

"Was where?"

"Why do you think Jaral was at the Peregrinos' house? They told me you got a call from Jaral. That Jaral was the one who supposedly found Nando. What was Jaral doing there, in El Pavo?"

"He did call me, but he was traumatized. I didn't get a lot of info."

Tenorio narrowed his eyes at me like he knew I was keeping something back. But I didn't know anything! Could he be thinking Jaral had done this? What could I say to stick suspicion on someone else?

"There was a girl!" The rest of Jaral's brief call had come back to me. "He said, 'I didn't know she was this dangerous.'"

I expected Tenorio to smirk at this—even as I said it, it sounded like something I was making up on the spot.

But instead, he pulled back as though I'd horrified him.

"A she? What she? Who she? Has he seen her?" Then he lowered his voice to a rasping whisper. "Does he have her?"

"I don't . . . I don't know what you're talking about. I don't know where Jaral is, but I think he's probably alone somewhere. He's scared, right? But there was this girl who ran up to the car when Rosalva and I were driving over to her house."

"Was she very dark skinned?" He ran a hand over the skin on his arm. "Negra?"

"You're asking was she Black? No. She was Latina and lighter skinned. Furious at Nando for something. Getting away from his house fast as she could."

"And you don't know her name and don't know where she is, I'm sure."

"Wait, I was trying to get to my kid who said there's all this blood, and I didn't know what was happening, so no, I didn't take fantastic notes on this suspect number one. I didn't even know Nando had been murdered when I saw her. But I'm not making this up. Talk to Rosalva about her."

Tenorio waved a hand dismissively, his attention on the last group of students to leave the schoolyard. A set of eighth-grade girls ignored us as they walked by.

"Who is that?" he said. "In the blue?"

He followed them in.

"Which one?" I said, from behind him. "Blue short sleeves? Blue jacket?"

He moved into the foyer, craning his neck as the girls continued down the middle school hallway.

"Let's do a walk-through of the middle school," he said, not taking his eyes off a girl in jeans and a navy-blue hijab. When she turned, we could see her light eyes, freckled nose. Then she entered her classroom.

Tenorio leaned against the wall and slumped forward with his hands on his knees.

"No," he said, sounding short of breath.

"What, you've never seen a Muslim convert? Don't tell me you're an Islamaphobe."

"No," he said again, still doubled over. From that position he gave a few shuddering coughs.

"You okay?"

"I thought I recognized her," he said.

"That's McKenna Lake. Her dad works at the greenhouse on Sea Breeze Drive. Her mom's the secretary of the parent association."

He squeezed his knees, distressed. But I wasn't sure why.

"No walk-through, then?"

I wanted to hustle him off the school grounds and process not only what had just happened, but also what was ahead for Jaral, for the Peregrinos, for me.

A few tardy middle schoolers' shoes chirped on the linoleum as they hurried to get into their rooms. Tenorio unbent to watch them, swiveling his head so he wouldn't miss anyone.

The late bell piped through the intercom. We were alone in the hall.

"What do you want, Tenorio? Why are you here?"

No answer.

He walked down the middle school hall, stopped in doorways, scanned one room after another.

"You looking for someone?"

No answer.

"I give up, sir. I'll be in my classroom if you need anything." I wasn't ready to face the bustle of the main office yet. I turned and started walking away.

Fast as lightning he was behind me.

I heard his voice in my ear at the same time I felt his hand at the base of my neck. I froze. He dug his fingers into my flesh like he was about to start either a massage or a takedown.

"You know I don't like losing what's mine," he said. His breath smelled like a clove apple. "Make sure that boy of yours knows it too."

Before I could respond, he was striding out the door at the end of the hall.

I rubbed the back of my neck as though to erase the hold he'd had there.

Losing what's his. Did he mean Daybreak? What did he think Jaral had to do with anything that was his?

I saw the glass door lunge back into its frame behind him.

I went outside to watch Tenorio drive away. His black Escalade revved out of the parking lot and squealed down a curve in our driveway. The forest at the edge of the parking lot blocked my view, but I heard the harsh, guttural notes of his engine all the way down to the main road.

My lower jaw ground side to side with anger and embarrassment. He'd never grabbed at me like that before. I could've tried knocking his hand off me. Could've chewed him out for being so bizarrely inappropriate. But I'd done nothing. One more little lamb he had no reason to fear. All right, then let him think that. I had a feeling he wouldn't be able to overestimate his own power forever. One day, a little lamb might take him by surprise with fierceness of her own.

* * *

Back in my empty classroom, I sent the school staff a confidential message about Armando's death. I kept it simple: he died at home, police were investigating. Refer students or staff who needed emotional assistance to the office. Don't discuss anything with students until I confirmed Armando's little sister, Lizzie, had been told.

I hoped no one would take me up on the referral for support. I needed support myself. And I sure as hell couldn't afford to pay a grief counselor for anyone.

To add to my despair, I dialed a few law office numbers. Criminal defense attorneys' retainer quotes ranged from $25,000 to $100,000. Impossible numbers for me. Even if I got a loan against my house, how would I repay it? And I hadn't even brought myself to utter the word "murder." When the office staff who answered the phone asked what charges I was inquiring about, specifically, I'd said lamely, "Just checking out options."

Coming back here was a mistake. What was the point? I knew my adult students all went home after Rosalva and I left. Now I had Braulio Tenorio in my mental space. I needed to clear him out. I took tai chi classes on the weekend and had learned a few visualizations for letting go. *I am nothing more than a piece of wakame. A rubbery leaf of seaweed. Bending in the tide.*

Except I wasn't. All the chaos of the day, all my helplessness, condensed into a clear bead of rage inside me. I had to act. I would go back to Eureka High, accost one kid after another until I found someone who could tell me where Jaral was.

"What did the Big Boss want?" Mrs. Murray called out as I passed the office on my way back out.

"Breathing down my neck." She must not have seen my email about Armando yet, because she gave only the smallest lift of her eyebrows in reply.

I put a hand on the office door frame and leaned in. "He almost had a seizure when he saw McKenna's hijab. I don't know if he has pathological intolerance or what."

She sighed and straightened a stack of papers on her desk. She was the last California woman to leave her hair in big rollers overnight. Like my whole staff, I loved her with equal parts awe and affection.

"Wherever you're going in such a hurry," she said, "remember the parent association meeting at 3:30 PM."

"I won't forget." I went in to grab something out of my desk drawer, then hustled out to my car.

CHAPTER

11

ON THE DRIVE back to the high school, I put together what I'd say to talk my way past the school's office staff. Earlier I'd been just a mom. Now I had a gold plastic name badge verifying I was Boots Marez, Head of School, Daybreak Academy. And I wasn't afraid to use it.

Eureka High was made up of three long, narrow classroom buildings, with one round building in front for the cafeteria and offices, a second round building off to the side for the theater.

I signed my name on a visitor log in the main office. Reason for visit? I wrote: "Classroom observation."

"Can I help . . .? Oh, ma'am, I'm sorry. No one's seen him." The same office admin I'd spoken to earlier gave me a quizzical look. She had chin-length, straw colored hair trimmed so level you could hang a picture frame with it. She wore a white polo with EHS Loggers embroidered in red.

"He'll turn up, I'm sure," I said. "I'm here for something else. I have an appointment to observe Mr. Noble's math class. At Daybreak Academy, we're trying to improve our eighth graders' high school math readiness." I'd repeated these last sentences over and over in the car before walking into the office. Dissembling like this made my skin crawl, but I delivered the lines without hesitation.

She handed me a white visitor badge on a red lanyard that had "Loggers" printed all over it.

"He's in the middle wing, right?"

"No, all the math is in the north wing. Fourth door on the right."

I walked out into the breezeway, straightened my spine.

I'd always thought of myself as charmingly blunt and prided myself on being an honest, open book. That's a persona a nearly six-foot woman with a nice face and good hair can pull off. But it was also a luxury. Forthright, authentic—all those traits that won you bonus points at self-improvement workshops—I saw now they were just a decorative crust for those with no need to eel upstream against the law.

Now that I was trying to aid a fugitive, I had to do what the kids called "frontin'." I'd flailed when I thought I needed to lie to a cop, but I could fool an overworked administrative assistant. That wasn't a win. That just made me a jackass. I felt necessity's carving knife shave a curl off the sturdy wood block of my self-perception. At least now, I was a jackass with access.

I hoped kids in Jaral's fifth hour would know what he'd been up to when he'd missed class yesterday. Maybe someone would have an idea of where he'd gone today.

I looked through the window in the door. About twenty-five kids sat at two-person tables, heads bent over their books. There appeared to be a Filipino boy, an Asian girl, maybe Vietnamese, a couple of Latino kids. The rest were White. Jaral would still be a minority in this room, but at least he wasn't an "only."

Mr. Noble, a man in a pale pink polo shirt with colorless, receding hair, noticed me peering in. I raised my eyebrows in a way I hoped was pleasant. He opened the door.

I introduced myself and told him my rehearsed lie about needing to observe his class to prepare Daybreak Academy eighth graders for high school math.

"Then you probably need to come back later," he said. "These are juniors and seniors. We have two sophomores. No freshmen. You want to see ninth grade math, you're welcome to come back seventh hour." He started closing the door.

I snuck part of one foot in the doorway and snapped my fingers. "Wait. Algebra II? Fifth hour? I think you are actually my son's teacher. Jaral Marez?"

"That's nice," he said. He sounded annoyed. "Where's he been? Right before finals is the wrong time to miss class."

"Don't I know it," I said, rolling my eyes and pointing to my badge. "I've got some eighth graders who would just skateboard their lives away, if they could! Why don't I get Jaral's make-up work, while I'm here?" I pushed past him as I said this. "I'll just ask one of his classmates. Where does he sit?"

"By me," said a White girl with a single purple braid down her back and gold-rimmed Lennon specs. She was at a table with one empty chair beside her. I walked over and dropped into the chair. A sustained beep came from a speaker in the wall.

The students started scraping chairs back, talking all at once. The girl beside me stayed put.

Mr. Noble tried speaking over the noise. "Review Chapter 24."

A few of the kids looked up and nodded. The rest were out the door.

"Do you want to see Chapter 24?"

"What?" Jaral's table mate had spoken to me in a small voice that sounded like she was about to tell me a secret. "Um, sure?"

"Thank you, Lee," Mr. Noble called to the student next to me. "And nice to meet you," he said to me with an icy tone, frontin' politeness. "I have my prep period now. I'm headed to the office, back in a few minutes. Pull the door closed when you leave."

He disappeared into the shuffles, shouts, and giggles of teen traffic out in the hall.

Inside the room, my fingers started a chaotic tap on the table as though I was sending a garbled telegraph.

"Here's the homework," the girl called Lee said. She opened her book to a section with problems in larger type, and answers at the bottom in smaller type. That's exactly what I needed for this monstrous day. An answer key.

"I'm worried about him," she said, nearly whispering now.

Was that girlfriend-level worry? What did she know about his life that brought on this worry?

"So you two . . . talked?"

She lifted her chin, and her voice came out stronger. "Two pans, you know. We have a bond."

"Pans?"

"Pansexual. It means . . . oh, wait, did he not tell you?" She pushed a loose strand of hair behind her ear. "Dang, I hope I didn't out him. To his mom, even. That is not cool. That's like . . . a form of violence."

It was my first time hearing this term, I still wasn't entirely sure what it meant, and no, he hadn't told me.

"Ahh," was all I managed.

"So you're not here for his homework?" she said. "You didn't write anything down."

I froze. She went on before I could answer. "He looked stressed yesterday, miss. Where'd he go?"

"You saw him yesterday?"

The warning bell sounded, and she started putting her book away, getting ready to leave.

"I guess," she said, without looking at me.

"You guess you saw him? Then wouldn't you be the one to know where he went?"

"I wish!" She stood and spoke to me in profile. "If that boy has a little honey somewhere he hasn't told me about, I'll kick his butt." She moved her shoulder bag over her head so the strap fell across her chest like a bandolier.

"Me too," I said to a silver snake ornament twining up the outer edge of her ear. "But why do you say that? About Jaral having a little honey."

I thought about the bottle of prenatal vitamins. I didn't know how to ask if they were for her without scaring her off. If she had asked Jaral to get them for her, that probably meant she didn't want any adults to know she was pregnant, not the drugstore owner, not her parents, and not some twitchy, clueless lady she'd just met.

When she reached the doorway, I leapt out of my seat and crossed the room toward her. She stepped away from me, into the torrent of teens, getting jostled a little as the human stream eddied around her.

"Is there anything else?" I said, when I stood in front of her. "Anything at all?"

"I don't know," she said. I waited. "I guess since he might already hate me for saying he's pan, I could just tell you this other thing too. Someone should know."

"Okay."

"Yesterday he made me hold up a blanket in the parking lot so this girl could get in his car. Like, he was hiding her from the security cameras in the parking lot."

Jaral had mentioned a dangerous "she" in his call, Tenorio had been uptight and tight-lipped about looking for someone, maybe a girl, and now here's a girl Jaral hid from security cameras. I felt like I was hearing echoes in a fog bank.

"What time was this? I got a robo-call from the attendance office that said he missed every class."

"He didn't go to any classes. He just texted me while I was heading to second hour."

She took out her phone, punched a few buttons. Turned it around to show me his text.

Jaral's name across the top of her screen startled me, like some evanescent outline of him appeared, just out of reach.

"Need help. Now. Pkg lot. Plz plz."

"You went out there?" I asked her. "To the parking lot?"

"Not right that second!" She snicked her teeth. "He knows I'm trying to rock perfect attendance. I can't have a tardy just because he can't decide which side to part his hair on today. So that's what I texted him, and I went to class. But when I checked my phone right before the bell rang, he said something really weird."

She pushed the down arrow to show the next text.

"I hv pregnant grl. She's scared. "

Lee's eyebrows lifted.

"Super weird, right?"

I nodded. "I have this pregnant girl . . . that's what he says, but you don't have any idea who she is?"

Lee shook her head, slid the phone in her back pocket as the tardy bell rang. She started walking, gesturing for me to follow.

"Are you going to need a note or something?" I asked her. "I can excuse you for being late to your next class." I waved at the plastic rectangle stuck on the side of my shirt.

"Nah," she said, as we moved outside into the courtyard. "Ruined my perfect attendance streak yesterday. No big deal if I'm late to one of my classes today. So yeah. I did go out to the parking lot. And there's this girl laying in the bottom of a car."

"And you'd never seen her before?" We kept walking.

"Never," Lee said. "A Black girl. With one of those head coverings? We don't live in a big city, miss. I'd remember if I saw a girl like that."

"And she's in the bottom of a car?"

"She was half sitting, half lying. Her butt was on the floor of the car and her head and neck were kind of propped up against a door. Her legs flopped over the hump in the middle. I didn't even notice she was pregnant right away, because her eyes. They were so dark and kind of shimmering, like she was scared and excited at the same time. And there was something unique about her face. A little birthmark. Right here." She pointed to the corner of one eye. "Shaped like a four-leaf clover."

We passed the narrow classroom buildings and were aiming toward the round theater. That could be how this Lee and Jaral had become friends.

She saw me looking at the theater and said, "I do need to go. Theater's my next class. I'll just tell you the rest, fast. Basically, I hold up this blanket Jaral gives me. He tells me 'lift it up between the cars so security cameras won't see.' This girl gets out of the one car and into Jaral's."

"What did the other car look like?"

"I don't know. Random? Small, greenish? When Jaral closes his back door, I shove the blanket at him and get a peek inside. The girl's laying exactly like she was in the other car. On the floor. Like, hiding. I say, 'What the hell,' but Jaral just gives me this quick hug and says, 'Thank you.' Says he has to leave, he'll explain everything later. Then he opens the back door, throws the blanket over the girl, and takes off."

"He didn't say where he was going?"

Lee shook her head. She had her shoulder against the door into the theater.

"Oh, but there was one other thing." She made a fist between us. "The girl was clenching this dull table knife. Like it was going to save her from something."

"That's it?"

"What do you mean, that's it? I just said way more to you than I've said to any adult like maybe ever."

"Thank you. I just meant . . ."

"You want to know how any of it is supposed to make any sense? Me too, miss. Me too."

She turned and went inside the theater building, leaving me outside with more problems to work, hunting for the tiny print with all the answers.

CHAPTER

12

I SAT IN MY car in the high school's visitor parking lot and tried to make sense of what I'd just heard.

"Pan" sounded like the hipster version of "bi," to me, but whatever. I could accept that my own vocabulary had some duds in it, when considered next to the firecracker box of youth. I could accept that Jaral might be attracted to humans of various and sundry types, as the prefix "pan" suggested. What I couldn't accept was that if this was an identity that required coming out, he hadn't come out to me. What I couldn't accept, although the last few days' evidence was piling up, was that there was an entire swath of my son's life about which I knew nothing.

I had become an outsider in a family of two.

Then there was this mysterious girl. *I didn't know she was this dangerous.* Was the girl he'd driven off with connected to Armando's death? Did he drive her over to Armando's on Monday, and then . . . and then what? On Tuesday, she murdered him? I couldn't picture a girl doing all that had been done to Armando. Hog-tying, in such a bizarre way. And slicing his throat open.

I dropped my head on the steering wheel and tried to slow my breathing. None of what I'd gotten from Lee helped me figure out where Jaral was. And that was the whole reason I'd come to Eureka High.

But if someone close to him, like Lee, had no idea where Jaral was, then I didn't know who would.

But as it turned out, someone did.

My phone rang with a lament from Prince: *How can you just leave me standing, lonely in a world that's so cold? Maybe I'm just too . . .*

I answered without recognizing the number in case it was Jaral on someone else's phone.

"Ms. Marez? This is Sergeant Detective Alvarez. We picked up your son."

"You found him? Is he okay? Did you bring him home?"

I had the keys in the ignition and was starting the car.

"He appears uninjured. And no, Ms. Marez, we did not bring him home. We booked Jaral into the county justice center."

"That's wrong," I said. I turned the car off and got out. "You do not mean 'booked,' like jail. You are not saying my son is in jail."

I slammed the door and started pacing around my vehicle.

"Yes, jail."

"For what? It's against the law to help a friend? It's criminal to call your mother? To leave a bloody scene when you're afraid of cops?"

"Let's talk at Sequoia Park. No interrogation room. Just us." That halted my pacing.

"Why would I agree to that?" I asked. "I need an attorney or something. The last thing I want is to meet your badge-carrying ass alone in a park. You think I'm stupid, officer?"

A tweaker with a scraggly beard passed by on the sidewalk. He pumped his fist in the air, saluting my side of the conversation. "Tell it, sister! Fucking pigs! Tell 'em to eat shit!"

That's exactly what I wanted to do.

"I am suggesting Sequoia Park out of courtesy to you, Boots." Alvarez spoke with the smooth voice of someone in power about to screw you. "You're a prominent community member. Your status depends on people trusting you. A marked car outside your house? Or being seen entering the basement of the county justice center? That's bad publicity. So I asked myself: where's a place we could talk close to Boots's house that wouldn't create a PR problem for her? Sequoia Park. It's only three blocks from your place. Pretty, too."

I opened my car and got back in. "There's no way I'm talking to you before I see Jaral. I need to get to the justice center."

"Oh, that's sweet. Never had a loved one in jail? He's got to go through intake and processing, get his togs, cell assignment, all that before his name even comes up in the system where they check visitors in. And then they have to regulate visits by last name. There's not enough staff to open the floodgates every day. Let's see, Marez, M. Your first chance to see him won't be until tomorrow, but that's only if he's processed by then."

I wanted to race to the jail and jump up and down outside holding signs or waving flags, anything so that Jaral might see me and see he wasn't alone. But while the sergeant detective had practiced her condescensions, I'd gotten an idea for a next move that might actually help Jaral.

"I'll see you at the park," I said to Alvarez. "Fifteen minutes."

Back at the city's redwood park for the second time in two days, I felt bad about disrupting the peoples' refuge with an officer on the scene. At least Alvarez didn't roll up in a marked vehicle. But when she got out of a spotless blue sedan, she had on her zookeeper beige uniform with its shiny sheriff's department badge.

"Let's hit the rim trail," I said, "so we're not hanging around stressing people out." We'd be out of earshot but still in the open. I didn't want to be tucked in the woods with her and her gun.

The short trail made for a fifteen-minute loop around the edge of the park basin. I thought that was all the time I'd need to get things moving my way.

As we walked from the parking lot to the trail, a dark-haired teen on the swing set greeted us with a series of oinks when he saw Alvarez's uniform. A set of lovers side by side on a picnic bench corked their effervescent murmurs when we got close. Toddlers on the creaky old merry-go-round squealed, "Again, Apá, otra vez!" while their father, who had been pushing them, moved to put himself between Alvarez and the little ones.

"Let's go over the basics," Alvarez started in. We left the playground behind and walked down a dirt path. "Your son is being held on a murder charge. Specifically, murder one."

"I know you had to bring someone in," I said, not missing a step. "Jaral Marez is the only name you have right now. But that just shows what you've really got. Nothing."

"I'm sure it's nothing that we picked up Jaral at the Greyhound station," Alvarez countered. "Holding a one-way ticket to Los Angeles."

I stumbled a little on the trail but kept moving. Jaral's birth mother lived in L.A. Did he think she could help him? And what, I couldn't?

"He paid cash," Alvarez added.

"No crime to have cash." Boosted from my skivvy drawer.

"Very true, Boots. But I'm wondering: what's in L.A.? You must have heard from the young man already. You know they get that one phone call, just like on TV. So what do you think was on his mind, trying to flee all the way to the other end of the state?"

I didn't answer. We passed a culvert where a little stream plucked its sputtering tune. None of the place's natural wonders did anything for my nerves this time. And I wasn't about to tell her I hadn't heard word one from my son.

"Change of subject," Alvarez said. She fell in behind me where the trail narrowed. A breeze played through the ferns and raised goose bumps on my arms.

"You said the boys hadn't spoken in years," Alvarez said. "But yesterday a call to your son was placed from the vic's phone. During what would normally be considered school hours. Plus they exchanged a few texts last night. What can you tell me about your son's day yesterday? Anything happen out of the ordinary?"

Yup. Jaral skipped hours one through seven yesterday. But what did I know about how he spent that time?

I stopped and turned to face the cop.

"I got one for you, detective. What do you know about the victim's girlfriend walking away from the scene this morning? Armando's mother and I saw her. When she saw us, she ran right at us. She was furious, said Armando was in for some hurt."

"That's fine detective work, Boots."

"I'm not saying I'm a detective. I'm saying I can help you. Armando's parents won't tell you anything. They're scared to death of anyone in uniform."

"Maybe so," Alvarez said. "Maybe the victim's mother didn't tell me specifically how Jaral Marez came over every day in middle school until something made her realize he was evil. Who's to say I didn't just make that all up right now?"

She turned and started back the way we came. There'd be no finishing the trail's loop. I didn't have much time to make my case.

"No one from El Pavo's going to talk to you. You need someone trusted by that community to help you find this killer."

I tried to sound confident, but my mind tangled in thoughts of Jaral locked up for a night. Two nights. More.

"That trusted someone is you, Boots? What makes you say that?" Alvarez sounded truly curious, which should have put me on my guard, but I kept at it. This was the only play I had.

"Just let him go," I said to her, "and I promise I'll do everything I can to help you. I know you want to find who did this. So do I. I'll talk to every single family at my school who lives near Armando. Anyone who knows anything, they'll have no problem telling me. Like I said, they trust me. But for you, they won't even open the door. I guarantee that. If you hold him for even one night, I swear I will not grease any wheels in that community to help you, and you'll have nothing but dead ends in your investigation."

"Whoooo, isn't this my lucky day!" She did a little jig on the trail, flapping her arms like a two-year-old hearing disco for the first time. Unbecoming on a professional woman with a duty belt. "Teacher-lady is here to show me how to do my homework! Thank the Lord!"

She rounded on me so quickly I had to back up to keep from running into her. "Is that the response you anticipated, Ms. Marez?"

My mouth fell open. She squared her shoulders, hitched up her belt, and turned to continue walking at a brisk clip.

When we came back in view of the picnic area, the people lounging at the tables must have heard her racket, because all eyes fell on us.

Alvarez followed me to my car and put a hand on my shoulder. "You can be sure the department will contact you, should we ever feel your services are needed." A smile teased the corners of her mouth. She withdrew her hand.

"In the meantime, your son will be arraigned at eleven AM on Thursday."

"Arraigned? What is that, anyway? A hearing?"

"You should probably ask your lawyer."

I spun a kick at my back tire.

"Oh, Boots, no. Say it ain't so," the detective said. "You don't have a lawyer?" She rolled her eyes. "Okay, an arraignment happens like this. The accused goes before a judge. The prosecutor, with the help of law enforcement, presents the evidence they have so far."

"Which must be zero," I said. "Innocent until proven guilty. You can't hold him for no reason."

"You didn't let me finish," Alvarez said. "The burden of proof is much lower for an arraignment than it would be for a conviction. All we have to do is show enough evidence for suspicion that Jaral might have committed this crime."

"What evidence do you have?"

"No comment. But I can tell you that if Jaral is found to stand for the charges, he will have a preliminary hearing two weeks later, when the court sets a trial date."

I wanted to slam a fist on the hood of the car but kept the urge in check.

I had forty-eight hours to stop Jaral from getting thrown into the teeth of the justice system. I couldn't risk the investigator thinking Jaral came from volatile people.

"I'm going home." I couldn't stop a tremor moving through me. I felt like someone had rammed a rod of ice straight down my spine.

"See you there," said Alvarez. "I'm going to your place too."

CHAPTER

13

IF NO ONE found Armando's real killer by Thursday at eleven, Jaral would be in jail for another fourteen long days. At least.

Alvarez drove her sleek car behind my rust bucket. In my rearview, I saw the blur of the detective's halo of hair above the dash. Why did she need to come to my house?

When I reached my driveway, just ahead of Alvarez, I found that she spared me the indignity of having one marked car in front of my house by sending two. She parked behind them as I pulled into the driveway.

Inside, I found my home occupied by three uniforms intent on the task of tossing my place all to hell. Only one of them glanced up as I came through the door.

"This is your homeowner," Alvarez called to them, over my shoulder.

Reality finally caught up to me then. Alvarez hadn't jailed Jaral on a chance she could work out a way to go forward with charges. Alvarez put Jaral in jail because he was *the focus* for an entire sheriff's department bent on smearing guilt all over the kid. In Sequoia Park, I'd thought there was still a tiny chance Alvarez might want help finding the actual murderer. But she only wanted me away from the house where she thought the actual murderer lived. My house.

Without a word, I stepped into the living room. All the furniture had been pulled away from the wall. My sofa cushions lay in a heap on the floor.

Bookshelves had been emptied, with stacks of novels and parenting books covering the end tables. I picked up a paperback copy of *How to Talk So Your Teen Will Listen*, tore off the cover and flung it to the ground.

Last year on Mother's Day, I was laid up with a stomach flu and didn't want to leave my room. Jaral coaxed me downstairs with "something to show me." Here in the living room, he'd created a beach set complete with wave sounds, sand sprinkled over flattened cardboard, and a blanket with plates of cheese and crackers for a picnic. "I got you lemon-lime soda too," he said. "In case that's all you want to have."

I remembered feeling impressed with his thoughtfulness and relieved I hadn't squashed it with inexperienced or inept parenting.

But now my living room was the set for a "home of the suspect" scene, and my parenting was judged on one fact alone: I had a son in jail. She's not a mother, their actions said. She's just dirt covering something up.

I didn't recognize any of the three busy strangers in my home. One of them, a White man in khakis with slim, dexterous hands opened a stack of my mail.

"She's behind on her mortgage," he said, glancing up at Alvarez.

"She sure is," I said, standing over him, "which happens to be none of your goddamned never mind."

"Slow that roll," Alvarez said. "I need to show you something."

"Where's the cam?" she asked a man with black hair pawing through my kitchen drawers. He left each one hanging open when he finished. It looked indecent.

The man nodded over to a plant stand in the corner where I kept a feathery Norfolk pine. A 35mm camera was propped next to the small tree.

Alvarez moved toward it, waving me over.

I heard a scraping sound upstairs.

"Wait, I can show you what you need up there! Wait!" I ran upstairs.

In Jaral's room, socks, shirts, pants, papers, pillowcases, tossed everywhere. Blue dust on his doorknob, blue dust on his dresser, cards for lifting his prints.

"The kid has a Hall & Oates poster, for Christ's sake!" I bellowed. "This is not a killer's lair!"

The officer in his room glanced up and went back to rummaging through the boy's closet.

The next hour cartwheeled forward, a whirl of wonder and alarm.

Upstairs cop calling down to Alvarez. "Hey, Triple A, I'm about done here."

She asks him, "What'd you find?"

Find Jaral, I didn't find Jaral, they found him first.

Upstairs cop now downstairs. "Kid had a nice seashell collection."

She sells parental failure by the seashore.

I'm pressed against a wall downstairs in my living room. There's no sense to be made of anything. But I try.

"Why AAA?" I ask Alvarez. "Your nickname is a roadside service?"

Alvarez ignores me, pulls up an image on the camera screen to show me.

"This is Jaral's phone." The picture is of a text message.

"Whatev u do, do not tell yr mom. That would jack up the whole thing." Jaral to Armando.

"It isn't roadside assistance. It's Affirmative Action Alvarez, Triple A," comes a voice like an acid bath.

Alvarez lets it wash past, then asks me, "Know anything about this?"

She shows me another pic she took of a text on Jaral's phone, this one Armando to Jaral: "I'm going to tell my mom."

I say, "I have no fucking idea what that's about."

"We call her Action, for short." Same voice as before. The man socks Alvarez in the shoulder.

Which, for some reason, cinches a straitjacket around my wild emotions just in time for Lionel Richie to start singing "Hello," from my pocket, "is it me you're l—"

"What?" I said into the flipped-open device.

"Boots, you're missing the parent meeting." The voice of Mrs. Murray had that part-near part-far speakerphone sound.

"I'll be right with you," I said.

Then I covered my phone's receiver with one hand and told Alvarez & Co. to get out of my house. But I was the only one who went out the door.

Standing on my lawn, I learned from Mrs. Murray that she'd called me from the flying-saucer-shaped speaker in the middle of the conference room table. And the assembled parents had a letter to read that couldn't have taken me by greater surprise if it had been written by Martians.

"We received this last week, hmm-hmm." The disembodied voice of Lusanne Bewley sounded even judgier than normal. She began to read.

Dear Parent Board,

I know this might not be cool to do, but I'm writing to ask if you can give my mom a break. Get her that tide-pool touch-tank she's been wanting to put in the science room and try to keep Tenorio off her back. She's really stressed. She probably doesn't tell anybody this, but some nights she hardly sleeps. There's some new medicine in our bathroom. I looked it up. It's for ulcers.

As some of you know, my mom is all I have in this world. All we have is each other.

I need to know she's okay. She'll take care of your school, no matter what. Will you take care of her?

More money would be good too. I'm sure it's not cheap to run a school, but we count every penny just to get by. When Tenorio gave her that one bonus when she first started the school, she used it to pay for part of our house, but it sure didn't pay for the whole thing. She says we're house-poor, but we might just be poor-poor, I don't know. We both drive piss-poor cars. She's kind of embarrassed to be the boss and still have those wheels but anyway. Please give her a raise. She works really hard.

Sincerely,

Jaral Marez
Former Daybreak Academy student and son of Ana Marez

"We want to know why your son wants money," said the voice of one of my advanced ESL students. "You ask him to write this?"

"And where's Mr. Tenorio?" That sounded like McKenna Lake's mother. When I said I thought he would've been there with them, since he was the CEO, another mom said, "We thought you would be here too."

"Family emergency," I said. "And that letter is news to me. It's touching, but I had no idea about it until now. Can we get this vote done? I have another matter to discuss."

I needed that pro bono attorney referral ASAP. A police van had pulled into the driveway, and officers had begun carrying things from the house and into the van like a line of ants dutifully rushing crumbs into their hole. In went the desktop computer Jaral and I shared, a few notebooks of mine, and armfuls of Jaral's clothing.

Mrs. Murray's voice came back on to say she would mute their sound for the vote. She came back after a few seconds. "The parent board thanks you for your leadership, Boots. Your contract will be terminated at the end of this school year."

"What? That's a mistake. Because of a letter? Because I miss one meeting in ten years of service? The parents are who I made this school for. You think any other school will bend over backward for undocumented families?"

"The parents have decided to recharter the school under their own organization."

"Lusanne! It was you, wasn't it? Somehow you strong-armed everyone into thinking that twenty seconds of Spanish in the morning is a threat to patriotism? Y ustedes . . ." I switched to Spanish and tried pleading in my third-grade vocabulary. I told Patricia, Maria Elena, Lupe, the Spanish-speaking parents most likely to attend these meetings, that it was okay to use their own voices and stand up to Lusanne.

Patricia replied in English. "We use our voices, teacher. It's that some of us don't like Rainbow class. We vote for new charter."

Lupe said, "I think is okay, but lot of people, no."

"The vote was nine to three," Mrs. Murray said.

"The Rainbow Curriculum?" I said. "This is California in the twenty-first century. You're throwing me out because kids can read books like *Heather Has Two Mommies*? That book's been out almost twenty years!"

"Is danger," said Maria Elena. "Teach like this for children very danger."

I didn't know I was this dangerous.

"Obviously I was a 'no' vote. Of course I support the Rainbow Curriculum. But now that these other parents are going to squash it, we'll be pulling Darren out of Daybreak," said another mom whose voice I recognized as Sarah, a woman who happened to be one of Darren's two mommies.

I tried speaking to her. One last wave from the drowning, one last chance to be thrown a life preserver for Jaral.

"Sarah, do you know a good lawyer? Who defends people accused of . . . accused of a crime? Someone available today? Like now?"

"No, Boots, I don't," she said flatly.

"Hmm hmm, no one's accusing you of a crime, Ms. Marez, mmm." Lusanne sounded almost gleeful.

"Hmm hmm, thank you for that, Mrs. Bewley," I said, and hung up. My filters were getting severely stress-tested.

I needed to clear my head, needed to think.

Jaral's unexpected letter, alone, would have been plenty to digest for one phone call. Although it seemed we were growing farther apart, the letter reminded me he cared, in his own way. True, it mentioned money. Maybe the letter wasn't as selfless an act as a homemade beach set. But it wasn't icy disregard, either. I wished I had the time to think more about where we stood, emotionally, as parent and child.

But then I also found out I'd been antagonizing some of the parents for whom I started my school, without even realizing it. Now they were upset enough to turn against me. With my immigrant parents, I'd thought being called "maestra" meant I was on a pedestal from which I could never fall.

"How many parents still support me?" I texted Mrs. Murray. Lupe and Sarah said they were on my side. Maybe others were.

"A fourth of the parents here, maybe half, school-wide." Mrs. Murray's reply was immediate, which I took as her own show of support.

The betrayal of the parents who voted to recharter was a kick in the teeth. But Mrs. Murray's words were enough to give me hope that I could still turn things around at the school. As soon as I got Jaral free, I'd rally the parents who backed me and call for a new vote.

To keep from curling up like a pill bug, I had to believe I could still get everything back the way it was. Lying to myself in this way became one more acid river inside me, working away at that ulcer.

I went to my car and dug out some chalky antacid tablets from a container in the glovebox. I took one for the parent meeting drama. And three more for the fact that Jaral might have to start things off with a public defender. Based on immigration cases I'd tracked, public defenders were an underpaid bunch with way too many cases.

Without money of my own for a criminal defense, I'd just have to make it my job to show the law that my kid could not have taken another person's life.

CHAPTER

14

WHILE THE POLICE finished searching my only partially paid for financial albatross of a home, I drove back to where the Peregrinos lived. Even though I wanted to let them alone to process the unfathomable fact of their son's murder, I had to barrel into their mourning with more questions. I only had two days to shred the case against Jaral before he appeared in front of a judge for the first time. I had to find some other explanation for Armando's grisly death.

Even if Armando's mother was out of her mind with shock and grief, I thought his father might sympathize with me, help me out with more information about who in Armando's life might have been the wrist-binding, throat-slitting kind.

And there were those texts. Jaral didn't want Armando to tell his mom something. Poor Rosalva. What was your dead son not telling you?

I also thought there was a chance I'd find Tenorio at the Peregrinos' house. At some point, I'd need to tell him about the parent meeting.

But there was no sign of his Escalade when I pulled in front of Rosalva and Eusebio's home. Jaral's car was gone too. It had already been towed. When I turned my car off, my phone gave a mechanical shudder. I flipped it open before it could start up with another song, thinking it might be Tenorio.

"This is the. Eureka. High School. Attendance Office. Calling to tell you that your son, Jaral Marez, missed hours one, two, three, four, five, six, seven in school today."

And that was the least of his problems.

I hesitated at the Peregrinos' door. When I'd left this morning, Rosalva called my son the devil. She'd been wild with shock and grief. If she truly thought I was the mother of her son's murderer, would I push her over the last edge of sanity by showing up here again?

But much had changed since this morning. While the sun repositioned from one side of the sky to the other, I'd gone from being Humboldt County's hero of the undocumented to being the desperate mother of a kid in lockup.

I squared my shoulders and knocked three times, hard.

Eusebio opened the door. His brow tightened as though he were squinting against a painful light. A chemical bouquet of Tide detergent and frying oil billowed around us.

"Oh, excuse me, maestra. We don't want to talk right now."

He waited for me to leave so he could close the door.

Something roared on the TV behind him.

"Te acompañaré en tus sentimientos." I tried the standard expression of sympathy to buy myself time. I didn't know what to say to convince them to talk to me.

"Gracias, maestra." The pained look on his face did not change.

"The police came to my house and . . . and I'm worried about you. I want to see if you're okay, or . . . if you're scared."

"Yes, scared, of course, maestra. And police? Yeah, it's okay, we already telling the lady, Alvarez, everything. About Armando. This family. This neighborhood. Everything. Thank you, maestra," he said again. "I will keep this house safe." He started to push the door closed quickly.

"Wait!" I slapped my hand against the door. "Are you okay with . . . with immigration?"

For a fast, ugly moment I thought about lying my way into their house by saying immigration was asking me about them, since a crime happened in their home. I needed more information from Armando's parents, needed to get them talking, and every second of delay lengthened the time Jaral spent behind bars.

"Migra?" Eusebio asked. "Of course it's okay. Señor Tenorio takes care of that for us. He have this house. He keep everything okay."

Earlier that day, Rosalva had admitted they didn't have papers. But I didn't press the point now.

Dark blue shadows deepened the clouds shifting in the low sky behind their house. The north wind pushed against me.

"Please," I said, my throat tightening. "It's my son under suspicion. Please. Can I just talk to you and Rosalva for a few minutes?"

* * *

Unless you're the devil on his worst day, if you're invited into the home of a Mexican immigrant family, you're going to be given a cup of hot Nescafé. I held mine carefully as I sat on a sofa cover that had been tucked Marine Corps tight around the cushions. I felt bad for interrupting its smoothness.

A heavy rectangular mirror with an elaborate, gold-painted frame hung behind me. I had an unaccountable vision of it falling on my head.

Eusebio pushed the button on the TV to shut it off just as an alligator bellow roared on-screen. I begged all my students to practice their English as much as they could. Listen to the car radio. Keep the TV on at home. How *Swamp People* became a go-to in this house, I'd never know.

Rosalva sat on the other end of the small couch, seeming to pretend I wasn't there. Eusebio took up his position in a recliner. He placed both hands on his knees.

"Sooo . . ." I brushed my fingers over a blue flower on the sofa cover, bracing for another wave of devil-talk from Rosalva.

From somewhere down her dark hallway, a washing machine churned and thumped.

"I'm going to find out who killed Armando," I said.

Eusebio scowled. Rosalva shook her head side to side, not focusing on anything, expelling breath between her teeth in a hiss. Then she went still again, as tightly tucked as the sofa.

"Did he have any enemies in school, or at work? Any trouble in his social life?"

With a shudder, Rosalva came to life. She got up and moved around the room, picking up framed pictures of her son, setting them down. She handled each one gently, as though it were a delicate artifact.

She brought me a portrait in a silver frame. "His first communion. He have seven years."

In the picture, the boy's hair was slicked down. He wore a gray suit, pressed a black Bible between his hands. The gold-embossed word "Holy" showed above his fingertips. A blue plastic rosary lassoed his pinkies together.

"First communion," I said. "That's Catholic. I thought you were evangelical. Don't you go to the big church over on Clements?"

Rosalva eased the photo back to its propped-up position.

Eusebio cleared his throat twice. "We were saved. All of us. When we came to the United States and discovered River of Hope Church. Yes. The very big building on Clements."

I nodded, distracted by watching Rosalva. She handled every prayer plaque, every picture frame, except one. In the image she wouldn't touch, Armando stood next to a girl, holding her hand. She had on a formal, knee-length dress with a turquoise skirt. He wore a tux.

I pointed to the photo. "Rosalva, that's the girl we saw this morning, isn't it? The one who ran up to my car, yelling?"

Rosalva stood behind Eusebio's chair. Her husband tilted his head up at her with his eyebrows raised.

"Not important," she said, finally looking directly at me.

"The girl? Are you saying that girl is not important?" I thought about the prenatal vitamins Jaral had stolen. Had they been meant for the girl in his car—or maybe for Armando's girl?

Rosalva stared at me, blinking rapidly, her mouth a border sealed with an angry line.

"Okay," I said, trying to soften my voice. "How about Nando's work? Can you tell me what kind of work he did?"

Eusebio shifted in his chair. "He worked for Mr. Tenorio."

"Braulio Tenorio," I said. "He's the boss for everyone in El Pavo who wants a job. Right?"

"That's right." Eusebio carried the conversation for both of them.

"So what did he do for Mr. Tenorio?"

"Landscaping."

"Did he work with a crew?"

"Maybe two others," he said. "Every morning. Six days a week."

"Didn't he have school in the mornings?"

"They work very early, miss. Six-thirty in the morning until eight-thirty only. Armando had a free class for his first hour. Usually he comes home to shower, then goes to his second-hour class. On time. Every time."

Eusebio tightened his jaw. I couldn't imagine his pain. I didn't want to stoke it. But I had to pry more.

"Who were the people in Armando's work group?"

"We don't know."

"They didn't live in El Pavo?"

"We don't know, maestra."

"Okay. Landscaping. For Mr. Tenorio. Where?"

"Various places."

I stood up. "Imagine this. What if someone investigating decides Nando got killed because he worked in the illegal drug business? I don't think that. But lots of people in Humboldt think that's the only reason immigrants would be here. I don't want anyone thinking that about Nando. That's why I need to know more about what he actually did for work. I know it's not drugs, or anything to do with drugs, but maybe getting details about his work and about who he worked with will help me learn if anyone wanted to hurt him."

Yet what if Nando really had been involved in drugs? Even though I was only using the idea as a wedge to crack open this conversation, maybe it was something I should consider.

Eusebio spoke up. "When Mr. Tenorio brought us here, he told us he will give us 'Decent work for decent people. No drugs, no violence.' That's what he tells everyone. That's his law."

"That's important," I said, "but look where he brought you. We are part of an area called the Emerald Triangle, a three-county zone that grows so much illegal marijuana, law enforcement can only stop a sliver of what's out there. If—and I'm just saying *if*—Armando was a dealer, he would be one of many young men in the Humboldt drug trade."

"A dealer! Of the drugs!" Rosalva aimed a stream of Spanish obscenities at me, accused me of performing unspeakable acts with animals, and assured me it was only my status as brainless foreigner that could lead me to think her son had the tiniest rodent-bit to do with such wickedness.

She demonstrated utter fluency in the pages of anger that fill the book of grief.

"Cálmate, ya," Eusebio said, reaching to stroke her arm. "Maestra is only confused. Uncertain. She wants only the truth."

Rosalva bent over him and spoke in Spanish, her eyes resting on me. "Maestra is the enemy of truth. She's trying to make the police think Armando was a drug dealer, so they won't discover her own son is a killer."

The washer in the hallway emitted a four-note warble to tell us the cycle was done. We all ignored it.

I set my coffee down on an end table and stood my full five-foot nine-inch height. "No, Rosalva, no. Jaral is a good . . ."

"He's satanic!" Rosalva straightened to address me in Spanish with a preacher's thunder. "His evil is a disease!"

CHAPTER

15

MY FEET TOOK on the task, unordained by me, of moving me so close to Rosalva I could see the hard line on each of her teeth where silver met enamel. I thundered back, "Jaral loved Armando like a brother."

Her chin tipped up defiantly. The next thing that came out of her mouth could not have surprised me more if it were a winged serpent dropping through the roof.

"Sodomita." She dropped the word into the room softly as a pencil scrapes a page.

I took a step back.

"What?"

In Spanish, she said, "Your son Jaral did not love my son like a brother. Your son Jaral is a homosexual."

A million pinpoints rose to prick my skin from the inside.

"Impossible," I said in English. "If my son were gay? He would have told me. He trusts me." But even as I said the words, I heard Lee-the-pan's voice in my head: *Did I just out him to his mom?*

Rosalva switched back to English. "The devil have your son and my son for a little while. Then we give our son back to Jesus. Jesus forgive everything." Her eyes said nothing about forgiving.

"¿Es cierto?" I said.

She pulled her brows together.

"Very certain. Grade ten. We find them. Here, really." She motioned to their living room floor. A throw rug had been placed where the pool of Nando's blood stained the carpet.

"Here . . ." I echoed, following her gaze.

"I think is because you teach him," Rosalva said.

"You think . . . what?"

"You teach that this sin is no sin. Yes?"

"We teach acceptance at Daybreak Academy. We call it being open and affirming. That means . . ."

"He kill his soul, no problem, you say."

Rosalva started pulling dead leaves off a peace lily next to the sofa. She snipped each one off with her thumbnail, then crushed it in her hand over the potted soil.

"Eusebio?" I turned to Armando's father. He sighed, gave a sad shrug.

So that was why the boys hadn't spoken in years. Armando's parents must have forbidden them to see each other. But why hadn't Jaral even hinted at any of this?

I needed some air. I moved to leave, opened the front door.

"Impossible," I said to the wind that met my face with a slap.

"Maestra," Eusebio called, rising from his seat. He followed me to the door. "Maestra, wait."

I hustled down his steps. In the middle of his concrete walkway, I turned to look up at him. "I just can't figure out how this person I knew, this person I thought I knew, who I lived with, had a life so completely . . ."

Eusebio, standing in his doorway, interrupted. "We came over in washing machines." He closed the door behind him and walked down the front steps to join me.

"Came over?" I said.

"From Mexico. The border. We crossed in a truck full of washing machines. We each got inside one, like this."

He crouched low to the ground, curled around himself.

"At that time, Armando was two years old," Eusebio said over his shoulder, still crouching down. "I told him it was a game. A hiding game. He was so quiet, his eyes big." He cupped his hands around his face. "Like an owl."

Eusebio stood. His voice trembled. "A little owl with huge eyes." His own eyes flicked side to side, frantic.

I touched his elbow. "It's not your fault," I said softly.

He pulled away from my hand. "In my mind, I was bringing him to safety. There was so much death in our city. My neighbor was shot outside a supermarket."

"Oh." I drank in the cold wind. It felt like quicksilver pouring down my throat.

"And my brother! The only thing they found of him was his head. My strong, honest brother."

"Eusebio."

"So I think if we come to the United States, we will be safe. But I don't know. When I bring him, I don't know there is a knife here, waiting for my boy's neck."

That very morning, this man's son bled to death like slaughtered farm stock. I wanted only to try and comfort him. To accompany him in his pain. But I had to drive the conversation on, to try and save Jaral.

"There is evil in what happened here," I said to Eusebio. "But you didn't bring it on. And neither did Jaral. Jaral is not satanic. He is not a disease. He's . . ." My throat felt suddenly tight. "He's in jail."

"That's very bad, maestra," said Eusebio, his eyes focusing on me again. "He's too young. Too skinny."

I wrapped my arms around my belly, driving out the implications of what he'd said. "It's bad, yes, but he won't be there long. Somebody else will be locked up instead. The real killer."

Then I sprang close to him and grabbed his arms. "Help me find whoever did this. Protect your daughter. Protect your wife. Tell me. Who do you think hurt Armando?"

He set his jaw and stared me down. I let go of his arms and took a step back.

"I remember your boy, maestra. Very quiet, but sometimes singing. Polite. I don't think it's him." He took a shuddering breath and went on. "My wife, she can't think good right now. Sorry, maestra. But that girl. I don't know. She always angry at Armando."

"The girl from the picture? We saw her this morning. Rosalva and I. When we drove here."

"Ay, that girl." He clenched his fists, then quickly put his hands behind his back.

"What is her name?" I asked.

"Marta. Marta Rizo."

"Why is she always angry?"

He shook his head and shrugged.

"Have you noticed anything special about her lately? I mean, is she . . ." I didn't want to blurt out questions about pregnancy. Shaking up this family once more, over nothing but a guess, might make it harder to keep them focused on finding the killer. "Has this Marta changed at all recently?"

"Changed?" he echoed. "She always think every day he should be with her twenty-six hours. Very jealous. No change."

"You said she was angry with him?"

"Always angry."

"Did they know each other from school?"

"Yes, school."

"That's good," I said. I'd talked my way into Eureka High before and felt I could do it again.

"No good!" he said. "She is no good for him."

"No, of course, you're right. Someone always angry like that is no good. Anybody else giving you, or Armando, or your family, any trouble?"

"No trouble, maestra. We live here fifteen years, very peaceful. Absolutely no trouble."

The wind withdrew for a moment. Overhead, two crows exchanged caws before another gust blew them sideways.

Eusebio took something out of his pocket and passed it to me. It was a simple business card that read "Tenorio Roofing

Company, Eusebio Peregrino, General Manager," with his cell phone number. Underneath was a tiny cross with the words, "The Lord is my Shepherd, I shall not want."

"You call me if you really think I can help you, maestra," he said. "But you know many people in this city. I think you will find this bad person, or the police will."

This man who had just lost his only son was now pitying me. The shame of it was unbearable. I had a headache so powerful it had a litter of seedling headaches sprouting from its trunk.

But instead of being ashamed, I should have just been grateful. It turned out Eusebio was alone in wanting to help me.

After I spoke to the Peregrinos, I went door to door in El Pavo, hoping to gather information, speculation, ideas, gossip, anything to start weaving an answer to the question: who killed Nando? But my trust with the people I had spent the last six years trying to help appeared to be gone.

All the Peregrinos' Spanish-speaking neighbors wove into a mesh I couldn't pierce, made of long-established trade networks: eggs, flour, milk, warnings. Do not speak to this woman, I imagined them saying to each other. Do not answer your door. She is the mother of a killer. Rosalva's monstrous misconception of Jaral as murderous devil must've caught on. Or maybe no one wanted to face me after the vote to leave me jobless in a month. Maybe both.

In any case, I knocked. I rang. I got no response from anyone.

So I drove behind the one household I hoped Rosalva hadn't warned, the home of someone I figured couldn't care less about a Daybreak Academy parent meeting, and knocked on the back door. A guy I'd once heard Rosalva describe as "That Scary Man" opened the door.

CHAPTER 16

"Yo," SAID A White man with a yellow smiley-face marble in one of his eye sockets. "I don't need any churchin' but leave me your pamphlet or whatever, if you have to. And try using the front door next time." He smiled down at me to show this was just a friendly pointer.

"No churching," I said. "I'm actually a . . . private investigator." This lie shot out easier than my previous ones, maybe because the target was a total stranger. Maybe because my new identity as mother of a jailed son had finally laid my smug, self-satisfied, proudly above-board persona to rest.

"I'm trying to help one of the Mexican families that live in this neighborhood. The family that lives right across the street from you, actually."

"I love Messicans," he said. "My wife's half. Come on in then."

He stepped aside and waved me toward a small Formica table that sat against one wall of his kitchen, all of it right inside the back door.

"I love Messicans," he said again. "What are you?"

I'm prejudiced against people who say they love Mexicans. I've known some pretty thorny ones. Mexicans, I mean. My mother not least among these.

"Human," I said.

I sat down across from the man known as Happy Face Holland. Each forearm sported a tattoo I could not have distinguished from the mark of Voldemort. He wore a black t-shirt with a toothy cartoon cat on it, stretching up to peek into the cage of a chubby-cheeked yellow canary.

"Two humans! Right on!" He raised a meaty hand for me to slap. I gave a thumbs-up instead. He chuckled.

"So you're a P.I.? You're cuter'n Magnum, I'll give you that." The reference to the old TV show placed him squarely in my parents' generation.

"To be honest, I don't have much experience in the P.I. field. Actually," I sunk my shoulders into a pathetic sag, "this is my first case. I'm not doing so well."

I don't know where I got the zeal to ham things up, but I let it ride. If it got Happy Face to want to help me, it'd be worth the queasy silliness I felt.

"You say folks across the street hired you? What's that family's name again?"

"Peregrino. Rosalva and Eusebio." I straightened up again. "They brought me on to find out where their son was going every morning. He said 'working,' but never gave them any details. They worried, like parents do. Now I come out this morning and there's the boy, in his living room, dead!"

"That's terrible!" he said. "I wondered what was going on over there. I noticed the cop cars and whatnot. Come to think of it, I saw someone out there looked a lot like you, getting stiff-armed by a cop. That you? What'd you say to make him lay a hand on you like that?"

"Aw, that was nothing." I tossed my hair. "Occupational hazard."

Part of me felt foolish for this playacting, and another part felt I earned a second high five for trying to sell it.

"Well, it's a terrible waste, that boy dying. I saw the stretcher come out of the house with something covered up on it. Nice kid, he was. Always said hello. Patient with his little sister, respectful to his parents." Holland rubbed one of his inky arms from elbow to wrist. Then he slapped both hands on the table suddenly.

"Damn it!" he said. I jumped a little in my seat.

"Where the hell are my manners?" He got up and opened a cupboard. At least fifty different boxes of tea were stuffed inside.

"What can I get you?" he said, gesturing at the shelves. He slid a box off the top row. "This vanilla rooibos from the co-op is killer. Have you tried it?" He turned the box around to read the back. "Organic South African honeybush tea infused with fair trade vanilla."

"Sounds good," I said.

"You know, people give those Mexicans a bad rap," he said, loading a red tea kettle with tap water. "They say they're here to take our jobs, they bring drugs, they want to kill us." He put the kettle on the stove and turned a knob. A pale blue flame leapt up. "Shit, I'd take a Mexican for a neighbor any day. Those are hardworking people. Easy to get along with too. Can't afford not to be." He sat back down in front of me. "Always on their toes, waiting for de-por-tation."

I tried to watch the cartoon cat on his shirt while he spoke. But the glass eyeball teased at my periphery.

"Go ahead!" he said. "Get an eye-full! Ha! It's the reason I got the grand-slam of a nickname I got. I was born a Bertrand. Can you believe that? You bet I'd trade an eye to be rid of that one!" He guffawed with such force it became a percussive cough.

When calm returned, he cleared his throat. "Okay, little lady. Let's get down to business. You go ahead, privately investigate me." He winked the good eye.

I felt tired, heavy with the weight of a years-long day. I forced my head to the side in what was meant to be a flirty tilt, but with the headache throbbing, it felt more like cranking a rusty gear down one notch.

"Do you stare out your front window much?"

"No."

"But you saw the ambulance, stretcher, me and the cops, the whole show, this morning?"

"Yes."

"Do you know the name of the boy who died?"

"No, ma'am."

"It's Armando. Armando Peregrino."

"Yes, ma'am."

"Have you ever seen his car?"

"Not sure."

"He didn't usually park it out front?"

"Nope. 'Spose he used the alley. Just like you did, coming to my place from the back."

I left that remark alone. I didn't want Rosalva to see me go in Holland's house, but I didn't want to get off track explaining that to him.

"So you don't know if Armando Peregrino kept any . . . weird hours, or anything?"

"I didn't say that."

"You didn't say he kept weird hours? Or you didn't say he didn't?"

"Holy crackers and wine, lady. You stink at this job. I mean spectacularly. You know that?"

"Is that so?"

"See, right there! You did it again! You broke the first rule of interviewing! Which is?" He tipped back in his chair. "Which is?" The front legs of his chair thwapped back down. "Avoid yes or no questions!"

"Let me . . ."

"I'll give you an example." He barreled ahead. "Don't ask if I look out my window. That's a yes or no."

The tea kettle started wheezing. He rose to comfort it.

"Instead, tell me to describe what I saw this morning."

He dropped vanilla rooibos bags into two mugs and carried them to the table.

"Honey, milk, or sugar?" he said.

"Aspirin?" I said.

“Ah, so it’s that kind of day. Just a sec.”

When he returned, I downed two little white pills with a gulp of scalding tea and got open-ended.

“What did you see this morning? Starting from the first time you looked out the window.”

He told me a black Escalade with tinted windows parked in front of Armando’s house at 7:45 AM. He thought the driver was probably male, because “that type of an SUV is a very macho vehicle.” But he didn’t see plates or the driver. At about 8:15 the car made a U-turn, sped off.

Braulio Tenorio drove a black Escalade with tinted windows.

“I’ll tell you another thing.” Holland took a gulp from his mug. “You’d better be careful whose web you tangle in this county.”

“Why’s that?” I said.

He squinted both the eyeball and the marble at me.

“Feds,” he said. “Goddamned feds are everywhere.”

Paranoia was Humboldt County’s unofficial religion.

“Which feds?” I asked. “The government’s not just one thing.” The tea smelled good, but I couldn’t enjoy it. I’d burnt my tongue pounding the aspirin.

“FBI, CIA, DEA, even the National fucking Guard. They’re all so hard for Humboldt right now, with our taxpayer dollars buying their military-grade gear to fight the war on drugs. We got weed, yeah, but meth too. Only they can’t fight it. Not very well. ’Cause they don’t know the lay of the land like local folks.”

“You think that guy parked across the street was a fed?”

“They’re everywhere. That’s all I’m sayin’.”

“What do you do for a living, Mr. Holland?”

He grinned, turning the crags in his face to rounded swales.

“That’s classified.” God, I hated smug people and their smug secrets.

“One more thing,” I said, as I stood to leave. “I know a man named Braulio Tenorio owns most of the houses on this street, most of the houses in this development.”

"We know him," he said. "We were here when he started buying things up."

"We. That's you and your wife?"

"The very same. My old lady's shopping at the co-op right now."

I nodded. "You ever talk to Tenorio? You've seen him around here, right?"

"Not lately," he said. Either he truly hadn't been able to identify the driver of the Escalade as Tenorio or he didn't want to. "But Tenorio was in the paper today."

Holland retrieved the *Eureka Sentinel* from another room and handed me the page with the headline "18 Deported in Nursing Home Sting." I read the two short columns quickly. Responding to an anonymous tip, the sheriff's office investigated a Horizons Care Home location and found that all eighteen of the entry-level staff were unlicensed, undocumented. ICE detained the workers, all women. The agency would begin deportation procedures once each woman's identity and country of origin had been determined. Braten Staffing Solutions, responsible for the hiring and placement of the workers in question, did not respond to requests for comment.

I read the last sentence out loud. "Braten is owned by local philanthropist Braulio Tenorio."

"Well," I said, "he must be quite a guy." I set the paper back down on the table. "Are you one of those types who tells a little now, waits for a couple of Humboldt twenties to grease your palm, then tells a little more?"

"Huh-uh, honey, my days of trading favors are over." Holland moved toward the back door with me. "When it comes to trading favors, you hardly ever get what you pay for these days. And when you do, you get a bonus helping of loco to go with it. Just remember what I told you."

He clucked his tongue. Cocked a finger at my chest.

"Feds are everywhere," I said.

"Atta girl."

The day's light was almost gone. I drove home exhausted from working both sides of the truth-fiction line. Knowing I'd need some rest to digest this wild day, I hoped at minimum I'd find my abode cop-free.

CHAPTER

17

THE HOUSE WAS empty. I sat on my back step with a blanket around my shoulders.

The indigo air seemed to fold up the last of the restless wind into itself, leaving behind a chilly stillness.

It would have been a great time to call a friend. I would've liked someone to help me take stock of this mad day. But I'd let all my friendships crumble like abandoned sandcastles when I became a mom. Jaral and my school became my entire world. And now fate threatened to rip that world away.

My house was turned inside out. People I'd thought I was in lockstep with at school were against me. My son was in jail, waiting to see a judge in two days.

And Armando. The gentle giant who lifted his baby sister onto his back day after day. Armando was gone.

Had he died for love? Jealousy? Drugs? Something else?

All I'd really learned about the morning he died was that his girlfriend was coming from the direction of his house in a rage. And the man who lived across the street claimed a car was parked in front of Armando's house, an SUV that might have been Tenorio's.

Braulio Tenorio, Mr. Decent Work. Mr. No Drugs, No Violence. What was hiding underneath Tenorio's polished image, his spiky cologne armor? Jaral liked to say, "Everyone's frontin', Moms. Every. One."

And all I'd learned about Jaral today was that every guardrail and guidepost I'd put up to keep him on a good path couldn't keep him from lockup. Couldn't make him want to trust me enough to come out as gay, or pan, as his friend had told me he was. Jaral was going to sleep in a cell less than two miles from me, but I'd never felt farther away from him. Apparently he didn't even trust me enough to be his one call.

I heard a noise in the alley. This was the time of day Jaral had told me he'd be home after taking care of his "stuff." It made no sense, but I hoped I would see him coming around my neighbor's hedge, bounding up to me with a song.

Instead, an old man with a shopping cart came down the alley. Nothing but squeaks and shudders held the cart together. Same with the man.

They rattled over the potholes as they passed my house.

"Ernie!" I rose from my step, swung the blanket off my shoulders. "It's getting cold at night! Here, take this."

I walked up to him and draped the fleece blanket over his shoulders. He stopped pushing forward, ran a hand over the fleece.

"This is nice," he said. He studied the pattern of owls printed on the blanket. They appeared upside down on one arm, right side up on the other. "I'll take this to my daughter. She can use it for the baby." He clasped two corners of the blanket together in a fist at his neck.

"How many kids do you have, Ernie?"

"Four kids. Five grandkids." He grinned.

"How do we know we've raised good people? What's the secret?"

"Psssh," he said. "Wish I knew, miss. That boy of yours seems all right though. Where's he at, tonight?"

"Jail."

"Ooh, that's bad," he said.

"I'm going to see him tomorrow," I said. "Sometime before two, I guess. The last check-in for visitors is at one-forty-five."

"Hey, you can't miss that check-in time. They don't play. You're not there by the time they say, you're out of luck. I have a little bit of advice about that boy too. Now that I know where he's at."

"Ernie, I need all the help I can get. His arraignment's in two days. I'm trying to find evidence to prove they've got the wrong person. I have no idea what I'm doing."

"My advice is simple," Ernie said. "Those guys on the inside, they don't get internet. They don't have phones. What they live for is to hear news about life on the outside. So just bring him some good news, mija."

I patted his blanketed back. "Okay, Ernie the Wise. I'll see you around."

"Sweet dreams," he said. "Make sure the news you bring that kid is good."

"I'm trying, Ernie," I said. "Believe me, I'm trying."

Back inside, I pieced together the skeleton of a plan for the next day.

Before visiting Jaral, I'd find this Marta. Get her to talk to me. Somehow.

Then I'd catch up with Braulio Tenorio. Somehow.

I'd left him messages today. His phone went right to voicemail, like it was shut off. Tomorrow I'd talk to the temp in his front office. She'd tell me how to reach him.

I opened a cupboard, clanking aside cooking oils on the top shelf until I found what I wanted. I pulled a glass from the drying rack next to my sink and poured.

The best news I could bring my kid would be that he was free. But the only way he'd be free was if I showed a stubborn sergeant detective that she had the wrong guy. I felt ready and not ready, weak and tough at the same time.

I tried substituting rum for sleep that night and met the dawn with a hungry snarl.

CHAPTER

18

TURNS OUT HUMBOLDT County is a great place to lie. The geography of the place supports it, a land full of trickery. California tourism brochures call it the North Coast, but there's still one county further north before the California-Oregon border.

You drive five hours up from San Fran through dusty hills expecting redwood trees, but the first ten miles past the county line, all you see are more dry hills.

When you finally pass what seem like thick redwood groves, you are again deceived. Those stands of big trees along the road are often just "fringe timber," woods a few yards deep left up for looks by logging corporations that clear-cut hundreds of acres behind them.

By the time you get to Eureka, you might think you're smelling the Pacific, but it could just be the verdant decay of Humboldt Bay. And even the ocean misleads. A calm sea might con you into beachcombing, then roll your last breath into a sneaker wave.

I had lived in Humboldt since I was eighteen, when I came to attend the state college, but maybe it wasn't until that May, lying my way through one conversation after another that, at thirty-nine, I finally started to fit in.

Not because I was particularly good at deception. But because my family now depended on cover stories. This put me in league with the undocumented, the growers, trimmers, and runners, with the stands of fringe timber trees.

And I found out the more lies you tell, the easier they come.

Wednesday morning, I called Mrs. Murray and told her I would be out for a couple of days because I had family visiting unexpectedly. I didn't want it getting around the school that Jaral was a jailed murder suspect, since I still planned on convincing the parent board that I should be the one to run my school once all this was behind us.

Then I put on my darkest, most I-mean-business pantsuit, clipped on my little Daybreak badge, and drove back to the high school to find Marta Rizo. It was against privacy laws to tell any Jane off the street which student could be found in which classes, so I shored up my adrenaline for a new round of untruths to get to Marta.

The high school's office admin was gone, so I loosed a flock of falsehoods at a vice principal, who was watching the front desk. The name on his magnetic badge said Cordell. I fingered a corner of my own badge as I spoke.

"We had some vandalism at our school. Nothing serious, didn't need to call the cops. A three-foot tagging I could easily paint over. One of the Daybreak eighth graders recognized Marta Rizo on the security footage. I just want to talk to her, make sure she knows there are good channels for her creativity in Eureka. I could invite her to tutor eighth-grade art club kids, help them with a mural."

I'd sketched out this tale while I'd gotten ready that morning, and it seemed to hold up.

"Good luck convincing that young lady that you know best," said the VP. He told me most seniors were off campus for Beach Day. He looked up the kids' itinerary.

"They'll have a coastal ecology lesson at Moonstone Beach this morning," he said.

I groaned. Moonstone was half an hour north of town. I'd wanted to finish talking to Marta before Tenorio's office opened. Then I'd have to sift through whatever Marta told me and whatever Tenorio's temp told me for a key to Jaral's freedom.

All before today's visiting hours at the temporary detention facility. I had to be checked in, whatever that meant, by 1:45.

But now, instead of rushing down a breezeway to find Marta in a classroom, I'd have to race up the 101 and track her down on the beach.

"Want me to just call you when she's back?" the man offered.

"No, no," I said, distracted.

I leaned against the door to let myself out, then remembered to throw in a fake dash of context. "We're hoping she can start repainting after school today. I'd like to talk to her right away. Thanks."

As I started to push open the door, the VP said, "Thought you already painted over it." "Needs a second coat," I said. I rushed out before he backed me any tighter into a corner I couldn't escape. I had to race up to Moonstone and grab hold of the lumpy coal of Marta's bitterness. Then press it, somehow, into a diamond of good news for Jaral.

CHAPTER 19

Moonstone Beach was one of my favorite places in Humboldt County. An array of black rocks rose in the middle of the sand, some big as bungalows, others small enough to climb over, giving the eye a place to rest before rushing to the vastness of the sea.

Skirting the rock array, flowing right through the sand, ran a pert waterway called the Little River.

Groups of teens were clustered at various points along the river, with other groups making their way up a green bluff south of us. I walked along the river to the first group but didn't see Marta with them. One of them held a flow probe shaped like an elongated lollipop in the water, with a round digital face on top. I remembered those gadgets from tagging along on field trips with my mom's high school ecology classes.

The kids spoke to each other in little flurries of giggles or jibes, then waited to hear their classmate read out the numbers for the device's flow speed measurement.

I walked to the next group. They stood at the outer bank of a curve in the bed where chunks of sand hanging over the eroding bank dropped into the water every few seconds. The kids timed the intervals between splashes. Besides a gentle slurp when a clump fell in, this waterway was strangely quiet. Inland streams knock rocks in their beds as they flow. In contrast, the Little River's glassy brown waves roll toward the sea with no sound other than the press of water on water, water on sand. The unexpected quiet of the river's surge always gave me a shiver.

As I passed the group of teens at the cut bank, I scanned every face. No Marta.

The final group along the river sat in a semicircle with sketchbooks about fifty yards from the tideline. I recognized Marta in profile. Her glossy hair seemed to settle into spear-like points down her back, which the sea breeze lifted in playful hanks. She wore a puffy red 49ers jacket three sizes too big.

Is that what a killer would wear? Is that how a killer would iron her hair? What would a teen femme fatale sketch the day after killing her mate?

A female teacher stood to the side, gesturing to the water. When I got close enough to hear her, I realized she was explaining a standing wave the students were supposed to draw.

"This is the point where the rising tide is pushing back into the river flow. So the water here is going to be what's called brackish, part salt, part fresh."

I stood a few yards behind the kids.

She tilted her head up at me, squinting. "Can I help you?"

I pushed my badged shoulder forward.

"Sorry to interrupt." I walked toward her. "I need to speak with one of your students." I stepped into her personal bubble, my back to the teens. In a low voice, I delivered the same load I'd given the VP about Marta tagging my school. I added that Mr. Cordell, in the office, told me where to find her.

"Okay," the teacher said, "that's not weird. You drive all the way up here, march out to the beach in black dress shoes to interrupt my lesson. Because you decided this just could not wait until the one field trip these kids get all year is over."

I started to apologize, but she waved a hand angrily. "No, no! Please! I'm used to it! The last thing on administrators' minds is giving us uninterrupted time for open-ended exploration. If I stand here listening to you, that's two more minutes off our lesson. We only have ten minutes left until we have to get back on the bus, anyway. Make it short." She leaned toward me with her brow furrowed, mouth tight. "You might want to try a little compassion for this kid. She lost her sweetheart yesterday. That kid who got murdered."

The teacher straightened. "Marta! This woman needs to speak with you. Why she came all the way out here to do it, I don't know. Please go with Ms. . . ." She read my badge, without looking at my face. "Marez."

"Dang, miss, I already talked to the cops!" Marta sat up a little straighter to make the most of her spotlight. The kids around her glanced up from their notebooks, their invisible antennae rising.

"That's racial profiling, miss!" said a White girl sitting next to Marta, her hair pinned in two enormous auburn rings. "Picking on my girl cuz she's Mexican!"

"Okay, you can go talk to this nice lady too," said the teacher.

"Huh-uh," said the sidekick, suddenly intent on her notebook. The group of six kids tittered and fussed, glancing between Marta and me.

Marta blew some air out of her lips. "Ooh, poor me, I don't get to finish this stupid-ass drawing." Instead of tossing the sketchbook on the sand, she thrust it at the sidekick, who carefully tucked it under her own open sketchbook, resting them both on her crisscrossed legs.

I walked toward the tall rocks, hoping for a few seconds to compose my thoughts before starting in on Marta. The teacher had heard about what had happened to Armando. Had it been on the news last night?

The image of Armando's painfully tied limbs and the cut across his throat rose up, burning into the gray Pacific chill. The shock and trauma of the sight came back too. My stomach lurched. Again, I had that prickle of unnamed recognition. I felt I had witnessed a similar scene before. But where?

Some TV show? Had I read a description somewhere, detailing something like what I saw?

"Slow down, lady. I can't keep up with your big giraffe legs." Barefoot Marta strolled at the pace of glue behind me.

I didn't stop until I was out of earshot of the teacher, partially concealed from her. Marta made no sign of recognizing me. I'd had my hair in a workday up-do with sunglasses on when she charged my car yesterday. Her focus had been on Rosalva. I unclipped my name badge while I waited for Marta to catch up to where I stood.

When she reached me, she kept her eyes on the sand. Her tiny hands clenched. She recited a phrase so rote in Humboldt it was almost liturgical: "I don't talk to cops."

"You already did," I said.

"Not like talk-talk. They don't know everything I know about Nando." She turned away from me, swiped at her eyes.

I wanted to put my arm around her shoulders. This kid had a violent current to swim against. I had to remind myself she could have been the perpetrator of that violence.

Instead of hugging her, I cleared my throat. My voice came out scratchy and uncertain.

"I know about the pregnancy?"

"What?" She jerked her face away as though she'd been slapped. "He what?"

She tipped her head up, jabbed a finger at the sky. "I knew under all that baby fat and Bible shit, the boy was a player!"

"Wait, no," I said to her, now off my game. "I mean, somebody's pregnant, but it's not you? Do I have that right? If it is you, though, I can help you. I can keep you and the baby safe. But you have to tell me everything."

"Uck, get away from me!" She shoved the air between us and started walking away. "I'm not pregnant and I've got the tampons to prove it."

Lying to adults to get what I wanted was one thing. Maybe I seasoned my justification for lying to my fellow grown-ups with some cynicism: adult lives are full of self-deceptions and duplicities already, what's one more misdirection?

But I had no motivation to BS Marta. She was generous with her feelings and impressions, offering them quick and raw, as Lee had, as perhaps only teenagers could.

I wanted to honor her apparent sincerity with my honesty in return.

"Hey. Just be careful of showing attitude to Mr. Peregrino."

That stopped her. She didn't turn around, but angled her head slightly so I knew she was listening.

"Mr. Peregrino says you're the jealous kind. The angry jealous kind. He gets that idea too often, he'll talk to police about you. That could go bad for you."

She made a growling sound, shook her head. She turned back to speak to me.

"Nando doesn't text me back all Sunday night, then Monday his car's full of some other girl's perfume? And not like any regular perfume, no. This stuff was crazy strong, like incense at Christmas Eve Mass, but female too, you know? Hells yeah, I was pissed!"

"What other girl?"

"If I only knew!"

"Was this part of the story you gave the cops?"

"Ain't no story. Maybe try listening to me instead of trying to play me. I did not tell the police about some *smell.* Do I look like someone the police will believe? Whatever comes out my mouth, they think the opposite. I blame some other girl, they think I'm guilty."

"Then why are you telling me?"

She sighed and her shoulders slumped. Her stormy mood, or her grief, had worn her out. "You were in the car with Mrs. P. yesterday."

"I'm trying to help her. Trying to find out who killed her son."

"Okay, so that's why I'm telling you about this other girl. I'm helping too. I'm telling you so you can tell the cops when they come asking you about Armando. You got those boss lady shoes, that nice crease in your pants. They'll listen to you. You tell them it's this other girl they should be looking for. Some knocked-up ho, the way you're talking. Maybe that girl's the jealous one. If she even—" her voice cracked, and she paused to collect herself. "If that bitch even knew about me."

A bus rumbled into the parking lot. Marta glanced over at it.

"Tell them about the car," she said. "That smell in it. Then we're all sniffing around for the same person."

The sleeves of her Niners jacket swished as she trotted back to her group.

Another girl no one else knew about? Jaral's friend Lee said he drove off with a girl she'd never seen before. She'd described her as having an unusual birthmark. All Marta had to go on was a perfume smell.

Why did I keep running into stories with a mystery girl in them?

Out past the shore, the gray Pacific stretched to meet a gray horizon.

Instead of coming clearer, Armando's death kept getting harder to read.

Soon after I drove away from Moonstone Beach, I had a more immediate concern. As I wound along the sheer cliff drops and hairpin turns of the southbound 101, I thought I was being followed.

CHAPTER

20

THE MAROON EXPLORER stayed far enough behind me that I couldn't see who the driver was. It could have been one of the many tinted SUVs rolling around Humboldt at the time. But when I slowed down for about a mile on Highway 101, it slowed down too, always staying around fifty yards behind me. It had no front plate. The windshield had a big spiderweb crack across it on the passenger's side.

I remembered reading Carlos Castaneda as a kid, before I read that he was a fraud. There's a scene where he's driving on a deserted Mexican road with his mythical shaman teacher riding shotgun. His teacher, Don Juan, says, "Do you see those headlights behind us?" Castaneda notices a car following far behind them, never completely out of sight.

"That's death," Don Juan tells him.

I've thought of the fictional shaman's words just about every time I drive someplace rural, with another car anywhere behind me.

Don Juan is my copilot.

The southbound 101 between Moonstone Beach and Eureka is not exactly a deserted road. It's two lanes in each direction. But traffic was light enough that the maroon Explorer's consistent distance behind me was noticeable.

Should I call somebody? A 911 call would go to the sheriff's dispatch. For all I knew, it was one of Alvarez's investigators tailing me in an unmarked car.

Watching over my shoulder for the law—now that was really rocking it Humboldt County.

Highway 101 made a long oxbow inland. I rounded old dunes seeded with saltbush, descended into a cove out of view of the Explorer. Accelerating as much as I could, the centripetal force pulled one side of the car down, giving the other side that dizzy, roll-threat lightness.

The road flattened out about a foot above sea level. Waves hurled into the cove, slamming into the base of a low wall. On the other side of the road, a few birds paddled around a marsh with still, coffee-colored water.

The Explorer appeared at the top of the rise behind me.

It's illegal to make a call from your phone while you're driving in California, but I thought I could plead self-defense. As my car climbed up out of the sea-level bend, I glanced down to thumb through my contacts and selected a number.

My old flame picked up on the second ring.

"You okay? What's wrong?"

"Why does there have to be something wrong for me to want to talk to my favorite indie weekly editor?"

In the years since we were together, Yori Shimada had moved up at the *North Coast Journal* and also ran a popular blog called North Coast Cop Watch. I thought he must have pissed off enough people on the way that he'd have some know-how when it came to shaking off a tail.

"There's always something wrong when you call. It's the only reason I hear from you. You get worried about state charter rules changing and want me to do a story. You hear some anti-immigrant rant with made-up stats on the radio, you want me to do a story. What is it this time?"

"Well, if you must know. I'm being followed by a maroon Explorer. And I'm trying to find out who committed a crime in the home of one of my Daybreak families."

"I saw something on the news about a murder in El Pavo. Tell me you don't mean you're trying to solve a murder."

"I'd love to hear your thoughts on why that's a bad idea. But first, how do you lose someone following you?"

The scab-colored SUV kept its polite, fifty-yard distance.

"Jesus, Boots. Make a few quick turns, I guess. How would I know? Where are you calling from?"

"Okay, quick turns. Another thing. How would you find out what happened in someone's home? During a crime. Besides talking to the other people who live there."

"Oh, my God, you are digging into that murder, aren't you? What are you doing? There are some scary people underground here, Boots. You think you're going to make your undocumented flock love you more if you solve their crimes? Is that the ultimate social capital? You find out who took someone's life, then the family that's left behind owes you their lives for figuring it out?"

"Just answer me."

"I'm engaged. Did you know that? I've had things going on in my life. You could at least pretend to care about how I am."

"Yeah, I could. So. What would you do?"

"I don't know, talk to the fucking neighbors, I guess." He hung up.

We'd bungee jumped off a twelve-story bridge together. We'd tandem skydived, each of us strapped onto a pro like a human backpack. Even though I'd called it quits with him six years ago, the sound of his voice was still as thrilling as the moment before you tip into a fall. The exhilaration of one last second to think you're calling the shots. Knowing you're about to be breathless, out of body, airborne.

I squeezed the steering wheel, shimmied in the driver's seat.

Minus the paranoia, with decent weather a drive south down 101 to Eureka is damned serene. I wasn't going to make any quick turns. My brakes would squeak like a legion of rats fleeing a drowning ship. My pursuer would follow the sound. All I could do was keep going.

After I passed Arcata, the last town along the Pacific before the road curved around the north bay, I ticked off the familiar sights as our motorcade of two got closer to Eureka. PALCO lumberyard. Humboldt Bay holding a flock of sandpipers in the crook of its arm. Pete's Drive-Through Donuts.

When I turned into the justice center lot, I had exactly three minutes to find a spot, get through the metal detector, and sign in for visiting hours at the jail.

I shut off the car. Counted Mississippis like a kid waiting for a thunderclap. At "four Mississippi," the Explorer rolled down the street next to the lot. The guy at the wheel leaned forward as he drove. Young White man, copper hair in a bowl cut. No one I recognized.

The car pulled into an alley across the street, turned behind a brick building, continued out of sight. Braulio Tenorio kept his office on the second floor of that brick building. His office happened to be next on my to-visit list.

I'd have to think about that later. I locked my car, rushed across the street. A small green sign past the security check pointed to the right for the detention facility. I high-stepped a dress-shoe jog to the far end of the building, where a set of descending concrete stairs led me to a door sunk below street level.

I clacked down a hall that made a ninety-degree turn right, then left. About every four steps, a set of three blue tiles broke the floor's off-white linoleum consistency. There was no one else in the hallways.

After one more turn to the left, the hall opened on to a waiting area with orange plastic chairs bolted in rows onto metal frames. Across the room, three people stood in a line in front of a customer service window. My phone said 1:44.

CHAPTER

21

I TOOK MY PLACE in line behind the three others, disturbing the universe of office etiquette with sparks of impatience crackling in the air around me. An involuntary groan escaped my mouth. I rubbed my hands on my pantlegs.

The neck of the man in front of me, visible just above the collar of his jean jacket, seemed to contract ever so slightly.

I poked at one of his shoulder blades. “Do they count us as being here on time if we’re in line by our check-in time?”

I got the side-eye plus a set of shoulders that raised for a shrug but never dropped.

The woman ahead of him said, “Depends on who you get. She’s a good one though,” speaking of the corrections officer behind the counter. “Anyway, they’re nicer to attorneys.” She flicked me a quick once-over.

“I only wish I was an attorney,” I said. I was about to cross-examine my only child, and the answers I didn’t have fueled an anger inside me I did not want. It was starting to sting behind my eyes. Why hadn’t the kid just told me what was going on Monday night? Why did he skip school a second time Tuesday morning and go to Armando’s, the wrong place at the most dead-wrong time?

Along with the anger, I had the familiar maternal eagerness to lay eyes on my cub. That stung too, deep in my chest.

After a few minutes, I stood at a glass window facing a guard. She had tight, efficient curls in her chin-length brown hair. A resolute crease in each uniform sleeve.

My spine went slightly concave, the beginnings of an involuntary cower. I told her why I was there.

The officer slid a brown clipboard into a narrow metal basin under the window.

"I need ID," she said.

She took my license, typed something into a computer. I filled out the visitor log:

5/19/09 1:45 PM Ana Marez

The last column asked for a "Reason for Visit."

A sneaker wave.

A live wire.

A man-kid I thought I knew.

Jaral Marez.

The guard slid my ID into a beveled storage rack next to the computer. Then she broke into the universal chorus of bureaucracy.

"Have a seat. We'll call you." Made it.

I sat in a chair next to a soda machine. A toddler in a Superman shirt banged one of the buttons. Nothing came out.

"Marez?" A White officer with skin bronzed darker than the Mexican president's led me into a room with three round tables. Inmates sat at two of the tables, already talking with their visitors. One of them was a White guy with flaming red hair who looked to be in his late twenties, slouching over hands folded in front of him. The other was a Hmong guy with perfect posture. His round face held a deep crease between the brows. He seemed closer to my age, late thirties. They both glanced over when I sat at the empty table.

I knew that when I saw Jaral, I'd be scanning for signs of injury, wounding, violence. On his body. Or in his eyes. I'd be watching his posture, his arms, his hands, to gauge his emotions.

Just a day ago, he'd seen the murdered, mutilated body of someone he'd loved in probably more ways than one. What would that do to a young person's mind?

I expected to see a weakened, grieving son. Someone slouching in with a bowed head.

I wasn't prepared to see Jaral walk in straight-backed, purposeful. His eyes swept the visiting room as though his gaze could clear it of threat. He acknowledged me with a chin lift.

The jailer who accompanied him walked a few feet away to stand against the wall. Jaral pulled a chair around the table and sat down next to me, leaving one empty chair across from us. We might've been about to begin a parent-teacher conference.

My son's easy proximity to me made the guard's back stiffen, but he didn't move toward us. I had signed a form saying I wouldn't touch the boy, give him anything, or accept anything from him. I angled one foot up on my chair.

Aside from the regulation stripes, which lay loose on him like bands he could easily slip, Jaral looked like the young man I'd been trying to mold him to be. Slight shoulders squared. Heart-shaped face lifted, steady. Just barely eighteen. I'd never seen him so composed.

The grown-man act scared me.

"I . . . I . . ." Questions jammed my circuits all at once. Why'd you skip school Monday? Where were you Monday night? Why were you at Armando's on Tuesday? Who do you think killed him? Who is the "she" you didn't know was dangerous? And why couldn't you come out to me as pan?

"Moms, I'm okay," he said, before I could spit any of that out. "It can't be too much longer that I'm here. Right?"

That depended on whether I could find the killer. The cops were gunning for Jaral as the number one suspect. I sighed.

"You. Didn't. Call. Me." I tapped the table with each word. "Don't you get one phone call?"

He shrugged. "Someone's always listening." Then he started whistling the chorus to "Somebody's Watching Me."

My hands flew up in surrender. "I would've been happy just to hear your voice."

"No, you wouldn't. You'd have all these questions, same as you have now."

"Oh, did it show on my face? All right, let's start with this. I talked to your friend at the school. Lee."

"Moms. Don't even start in on that, okay. Don't even start."

The words were defiant, but his face was scared. He glanced over his shoulder, then back at me.

He leaned forward and made an exaggerated wince. "Please."

His voice was so low I barely heard him. He didn't seem like someone who was okay. I thought maybe he was on something.

His eyes slid down to his lap, where he kept pulling on the hem of his shirt, bunching and unbunching it in irregular, jerky movements.

In the few minutes we'd been sitting there, he'd gone from confident to pleading to spasmodic.

I leaned toward him. "I just want you to know that I know. I know there's lots you don't want to talk about. Don't want to tell me. There's even some things about kitchen stuff. Pots and *pans*. That's your business, but, you know, doesn't change anything with me."

It was my clumsy attempt at talking in code. I wanted to tell him I knew about the whole pansexual thing without outing him in the county jail.

And of course, I wanted to see if he'd volunteer anything about the girl he drove off with.

"You high, Moms? Talking about pots and pans, kitchen stuff. Huh. You want to talk kitchens, let me tell you about the mystery meat we get in here for dinner. And that's if we're lucky!" Carefree jokester, the next card he shuffled into his identity deck.

But his hands hadn't stopped their twitching. He looked down at them, then back up at me, down and up again.

"I believe the children are our future." Was he really singing Whitney Houston right now? "Watch them well, and let them lead the way."

Cute, Jaral. Eighties songs instead of real information.

"It's 'teach them well,' and we only have a few minutes. I want to hear how you're doing!" I lowered my voice and leaned toward him. "You're going to need my help to get out of here."

"Hold up. You want to help me?" He stopped his hands mid-twitch. "You think you know what's best for everyone, you think everyone needs to do what you say and their lives will be great, but I'm not the one who needs saving. You want to help?"

He looked down. His hands started pulling at his shirt hem again. He spoke without raising his head. "Are you even trying?"

I grabbed one of his arms and yanked him toward me. I yelled right into that beloved face.

"Do not make me your enemy! I am your only lifeline now!"

The guard moved behind me and freed Jaral from my grasp with one downward chop against my forearms, then he bear-hugged my shoulders and lifted me out and away from my chair.

He kept hold of me as I tried to get my footing, angling his body between me and Jaral.

"Ma'am, when I release you, you are going to leave. Immediately. Understand?" He tightened his arms with the question.

"Okay. I'll leave."

The officer released me. I turned my head toward Jaral. He stood behind the table, eyes wide. His voice came out in a rasp. "I wish I'd never gone to the white redwood."

The words stopped my breath. Was that really the knife he was going to stick in me now?

"The visit's over, son," the guard said to him, without taking his eyes off me. "Ma'am, leave now or I will detain you."

I took a few steps backward, watching as Jaral turned to go. The whole room was quiet. Everyone heard Jaral as he called back over his shoulder, "All my trouble starts there."

CHAPTER

22

A RARE WHITE REDWOOD grew at the edge of the clearing by my yurt in the north county. I took Jaral up there right away, the day I adopted him, because I wanted to show him our two lives were connected. Like the white redwood with its parent tree. Connected by the roots.

I told him how the three-hundred-foot parent tree sent nutrients through their shared roots to the thin white redwood, which, due to the rare genetic mutation that gives it pure white needles instead of green, was unable to photosynthesize on its own.

"Isn't it beautiful?" I said, tilting a sprig of white needles toward him.

"It's stuck needing a parent its whole life," he'd said. "Yuck."

I'd laughed. His play at tween bravado was endearing. He was just a scrawny twelve-year-old then.

But now Jaral was grown, accusing me of not helping him while at the same time trying to rip us apart from each other at the roots. At least that's what I thought he was doing. Saying all his trouble started there at the white redwood. Saying, I thought, that he wished I'd never adopted him.

I left the visiting area, retrieved my ID from the desk attendant, and headed back through the justice center's linoleum hallways. This time, I noticed how the sets of blue tiles interrupting the institutional off-white floor made patterns suggesting ocean waves.

I tried stepping over every group of blue tiles as I moved ahead, my mind desperate for distraction from the words I'd just heard.

At least Jaral hadn't seemed broken. I tried to comfort myself by picturing the way he'd come into the room walking tall. But when I reached for the door to exit the justice center, my hands shook. Outside, sunlight hit me with offensive brightness. What was it doing shining? Nothing had any business being light when my kid was caged in concrete.

I felt weak and realized I hadn't eaten yet that day. I wanted to go to Tenorio's office and swim toward the next wave coming at me, but I'd need food first.

In Los Bagels, around the corner from the justice center, they had my favorite brew on drip, Signature Costa Rican. When I sat down with a toasted Guac 'n' Lox on salt and that velvety cup of heaven, I felt some fortitude return.

I used this renewed energy to stuff my feelings.

My shame at losing control, at probably being the first one to lay a hand on Jaral in jail, was crammed in a carton labeled "I'll make it up to him."

My chagrin at hearing him wish out loud that I hadn't adopted him got shoved in a "kids will be kids" box. Doesn't every teenager wish they had different parents?

By the time I finished eating, I felt calm, cool, and collected. Aside from a spasm that seized my left lower eyelid at random moments.

I sentenced the waxed paper liner from the deli basket to a crumpled life in the trash, then left to go see Tenorio.

CHAPTER

23

ONCE OUTSIDE Los Bagels, I went back around the corner toward the justice center, then crossed the street and started walking through the parking lot toward Tenorio's office. I felt the high walls and narrow windows of the jail behind me. I hoped Jaral could see me out here trying, trying to be the mother he needed.

I thought Tenorio would have to tell me what he was doing outside Armando's house the morning of the murder. He would have to tell me why he hadn't answered any of my calls or texts. He would have to assure me that, as Armando's boss, he hadn't knowingly put Armando in any situation that could have cost him his life.

Or else I would assume he was in league with killers. Maybe a killer himself. Tenorio was the last person to be seen at the Peregrinos' house before Jaral found Armando's body.

Past a dumpster in an alley, I saw the car that had followed me. I memorized the plate, then walked to a worn wooden door between a boutique sock shop and a chocolatier. I pulled the door open and started up a stairway covered in musty carpet. The stairs gave out familiar creaks as I climbed.

The second-floor offices all had wooden doors inset with frosted windows. The lettering on top of Tenorio's door said "Braten Staffing Solutions." He told me once that he was especially proud of this American-sounding name for his business. "It's just the first syllables of Braulio and Tenorio put together," he said. The name must've served him well, because he'd grown a reputation for being able to provide work crews quickly, wherever needed, and it was his booming business that made him able to invest in my school.

Since I wasn't a homicide investigator, I really didn't know how I would go about questioning the major funder of my life's work. "Kill anybody lately?" That yes-or-no was definitely a nonstarter.

Even the concrete things I needed to find out, I wasn't sure I would get an honest answer for. Why was he at Nando's house early yesterday morning, the morning of the murder? If Nando worked for Tenorio every morning, where had he worked that morning, just before returning home to get ready for school?

And why had Tenorio gotten so threatening with me later in the day?

I had been in Tenorio's office a few times before. He kept a rotating cast of temp receptionists at his front desk.

This one was a copper-haired young woman in her twenties with a bowl cut, who looked like she would have run right through the wall to escape me, if she could. She opened her mouth partway. No sound came out.

"Can I see Mr. Tenorio, please?"

The young lady fiddled with a sticky note pasted to the countertop, rocking very slightly side to side on a yoga ball.

"He's usually in by now. I don't know where he is." She turned toward her computer and I recognized her boyish profile.

"Ah!" I made an involuntary noise of realization and tried to cover for it by rummaging in my purse for something I couldn't find. But instead of a tissue or a lip balm, I dug out another tall tale.

"Well, if he's not here, that will save me some parking money. I haven't fed my meter yet, and I just saw the parking cops out there. In fact, they were putting a boot on a car already. A maroon Explorer, I believe."

Thinking how Jaral could be either on something or hiding something from me, hostile to the idea of my help, made lying for his sake feel sickening again.

"Shit!" she said. "Can you wait outside? I need to lock up and run down there. I'll be right back."

I hadn't let my attack of conscience stop me, but I didn't want to lie any more. I leaned forward.

"Did you hear about the recent labor busts?" I lowered my voice. "All those ladies your agency placed in nursing homes who were deported. What's going on with that? If there's trouble for Tenorio's company, that could be trouble for me too. He funds my school. Daybreak? Out on the bluffs? Just let me access Tenorio's employee records to verify a few things."

"Those are confidential," she said. Her jaw tightened, eyes big as quarters. She stood to leave.

"You're okay," I said, trying to soothe her and at the same time project authority. "I'm not here to get you in trouble. I know you were following me. You want to tell me why?"

"I need this job," she said.

"Okay . . ."

"It's hard to get even a stupid office job in Humboldt if you don't know anybody."

"Right . . ."

"The temp service told me his tagline."

"Decent work for decent people."

"I mean, that doesn't sound too bad, right?"

Help Jaral, help Jaral, went the drumbeat in my head.

The photocopier indicated it was settling into sleep with a guttural whir, followed by a soft screech.

In the momentary shift of her attention to the Xerox, I moved around the desk to stand in front of the young woman. Without thinking, I put my hands down around the base of her neck. Not tightly. But firmly. As though taking a measurement.

"Why—" was the word I got out before she pushed her hands up between my wrists, then stood and flung her arms wide to break my grip. She snaked a foot behind my legs, pushed me down. I bounced off her yoga ball, pulled her to the floor with me. She kicked and spat, sprang to her feet, and raised the desk phone receiver above her head like she was going to brain me with it.

I scooted back against the wall with a manic grin. "Someone took a self-defense class. I did too, when I was your age. Repeated it three times, actually. A girl can't be too careful."

"Get out or I'll call 911," she said.

"You get out," I said. "Go move your car. I just need a few minutes here."

She pushed Talk on the phone.

"Or else I'll tell Tenorio he needs to hire another temp who is more careful not to be seen while she's tailing someone."

I heard the dial tone coming through the phone's speaker.

"You already won!" I said to her. "You haven't told me why he asked you to follow me. And I can tell you're not going to. I get it. You're doing your job. Just let me do mine. I need to check a few facts in those employee records."

The dial tone had gone from one long dash to a series of aggravated dots.

"I think it's up to $200 now, to get the city to unlock your tire." I nodded at the door, tasting bile. "Just go."

She lifted the phone receiver, then set it back down to disconnect the beeping line. She pulled the top sticky note off a pad on her desk, slapped it on a drawer in a dark green filing cabinet behind her. Then she sidestepped past me, flattening herself against the desk to stay as far from me as she could. She kicked the door shut behind her as she left. The frosted glass inset rattled in its frame.

"I wasn't going to hurt you," I called after her. Then I reached for the file drawer she'd labeled with the blank note.

CHAPTER

24

I GRABBED THE DRAWER handle, squeezed the release button with my thumb, and tugged it open. Multicolored files labeled by number filled the drawer. Three red files were labeled "1," followed by three orange files labeled "2," then three yellow files labeled "3," three greens labeled "4," on up to 37. I opened the first of three files labeled "1."

A name I didn't recognize was written in thick black marker on the inside cover. A clasp on the right-hand side held a stack of paper. The first pages listed work sites. Underneath lay a basic employment application.

Rifling through the other "1" files, I found the same materials. By the third "1" I realized all the 1s shared the same work sites. Same with the 2s, 3s, 4s. Each number must represent a work crew of three men.

I pulled out the drawer further and flipped quickly through each file, searching for Armando's name. I couldn't rule out the possibility that Tenorio's temp pasted a sticky note on a drawer full of nothing. Maybe she was just keeping me busy while she hustled out to grab a tire iron. Or call the cops.

I finally found "Peregrino, Armando" in the 34s.

His work site log showed that on Mondays he and his crew worked the grounds of a church and the school attached to it. On Tuesday, two sports complexes. I checked to be sure the other two files numbered "34" had work sites identical to Armando's. They did.

Armando's father had told me Armando worked in landscaping from 6:30 AM to 8:30 AM six days a week. It was possible the guys in his work crew were the last people to see him alive before he went home to face a killer.

I used my phone to take pictures of the site list and the employment application in Armando's file and the files of his two crewmates. After I tucked Armando's file under my arm, I returned the two other files and noticed a black ledger wedged in the back of the drawer with the spine facing up. The word "Accounts" was embossed on the spine in gold letters. I told myself I'd just have a quick look, worried the temp would be back any second, or worse, that Tenorio himself would bust in.

I pulled out the ledger. The pages fell open to a pencil drawing of a lovely young female face with a hijab covering her hair. The image was that of a teenager or young adult. Someone had drawn her face in three-quarter view, so that a birthmark at the corner of one of her eyes, four small, misshapen circles suggesting a four-leaf clover, became the focal point of the drawing.

Her skin had been shaded to evoke rich dark tones. Her narrow face and full lips reminded me of two Somali women I'd met at a literacy conference in San Jose back when I worked at the library. This was years before Somalis gained a higher profile in public positions, such as police officers in larger metro areas or federal lawmakers. Those would be the children of these earlier waves of immigrants.

The next few pages had drawings of the same face. In profile, facing front, glancing back over a shoulder. Always with the hijab. In each one, the eyes shone with dark intensity. In one of the portraits, she smiled, a dimple in her right cheek.

I flipped through the rest of the ledger. It was empty except for the words "Braulio Tenorio" printed on the inside of the front cover. I paged back to the first image I'd seen, snapped another picture with my phone and returned this chronicle of an obsession to its hiding place at the back of the personnel files.

I closed the file drawer and turned to leave. The sticky note the temp had been fiddling with on her computer monitor caught my eye. I leaned closer to see what it said. It had a description of my car and the words "Boots Marez, very tall, long hair, might be dangerous."

I grabbed a red marker out of a pen holder and scrawled "WAS HERE" under my name. Then I left the office more eager to find a church than I'd ever been.

CHAPTER 25

THE ADDRESS BOX on the employment application I'd just seen in Armando's file listed his parents' house in El Pavo. But on the applications of each of his crewmates, the address box just said "Holy Family."

I walked away from the brick building that held Tenorio's office and crossed the street to my car. Before I got in, I glanced back to see the temp watching me from the alley where her car sat untowed. I waved goodbye and got in.

As I drove off, I awarded myself another maternal demerit for not having paid extra to be able to search the Internet on my phone. Seven blocks away from the Braten office, away from the justice center, right at the edge of downtown, I pulled into the parking lot for the public library and circled around back to park.

I didn't think Tenorio was anywhere near his downtown office, based on the temp's spectacular underperformance. She hadn't even had her computer monitor turned on. She'd willingly left their files open to a complete stranger.

But in case he had anyone else following me, I wanted to wait a few minutes. When I didn't see any other cars pulling into the lot after five minutes, I ran into the library to grab a spot at the Express Internet Computers, 15 Minutes Maximum. Luckily, there was one station open.

Two search hits came up for Eureka Holy Family. I used a very sharp half pencil and wrote down the phone numbers for both listings on a small square of paper.

Back in my car, I started calling the numbers I'd written down. I needed to figure out where I'd be heading.

The first Holy Family turned out to be a Catholic parish. "The priest is the only one who lives here, hon," said the obliging woman on the line. I'd asked her if they had any type of worker housing or refuge housing for immigrants. She said Holy Family Episcopal on Eleventh and Sellars had been converted to apartments.

"You know who bought it?" she said. "That guy who owns the Spanish newspaper. Handsome guy. Real gentleman. What's his name?"

"Tenorio."

"Right. We always advertise with his paper. Gotta keep up with the Moonies, trying to pick off our parishioners! I think the building's empty now though. Looks abandoned."

I thanked her and ended the call.

Eleventh and Sellars. That was on the southeast end. I drove away feeling like I was just twisting around in a sticky web Tenorio had laid over this town.

I didn't think the place would be empty, and I needed something to sweeten up Armando's crew mates, listed as Francisco Gomez and José Lara in Tenorio's files. I stopped at a Mexican bakery to get a paper sack full of empanadas.

Then I drove home for a fast change into jeans and a Daybreak hoodie. I didn't want the implied authority of my sharpest, meanest suit to distance me from those I hoped to meet in worker housing. More comfortably outfitted, I sped off.

When I pulled up to the church-turned-residence, lights I had seen behind the front windows went dark. The faint blue exterior had wood-framed windows that rose vertically on either side of the door, with a swirled opaque bottle glass in them that no one had changed, despite the passing of three decades' worth of fashion.

I brought Armando's employment file and the bag of pastries to the door and knocked. No one answered. I heard a scurrying inside that sounded like it came from a second story. But the building wasn't tall enough to have a second story.

I looked around for a doorbell. Nada. I thumped the soft end of a fist on the door.

"Señor Gomez!" I called. "Señor Lara!" That's when I realized these were probably fake names. They were the Mexican equivalent of Smith and Jones.

I was mid-thump when the door swung wide. My fist nearly fell on a young man about my height, skin a few shades darker than mine, pale brown eyes flecked with green. I almost lost my balance.

"Hello!" he said.

Then he stepped out, yanked the door shut behind him.

"You from a church. A church group? Canned foods? Please, miss. No more green beans. No more evaporated milk."

"It's okay," I said, pointing to my paper bakery bag. "No green beans. No evaporated milk."

"You no from a church?"

I shook my head.

"Okay miss, you have good day." He flattened himself against the door, reached his right hand behind his back to grasp the knob, started to turn it. He rubbed his other hand on his shirt, over his heart.

"Bye, miss."

I took a step back, not wanting to scare him into the darkened building.

"Please wait," I said. It came out too high. "I'm a teacher." I sounded like a creepy old lady calling "Here, kitty-kitty" at dusk.

I put my hands out as though imploring him to read my palms.

"I need to find two guys. Francisco Gomez and José Lara. I teach here. Daybreak Academy." I pointed to the school logo, a stylized sun rising behind a redwood tree, on my hoodie.

"Frankie and José don't have no teacher."

"They worked with a man. A teenager. Armando Peregrino. He was one of my students. I'm trying to help Armando."

"What kind help? Why Armando need help?"

"He was such a good boy," I said.

"No good," the man said. "No good for working. Good for the girls. Bad for working."

"Why do you say that?"

"I'm his crew leader. Frankie Gomez, the guy you looking for. Nando come to work very tired, working slowly. He almost cut my arm with pruning shears, my God. We work early, but all night he's with girls, so he don't work good."

"When? Yesterday?"

"Yes, yesterday. That was Tuesday. But also Monday."

Hard to believe Tuesday had just been yesterday. Just yesterday, Armando started his day getting chewed out by his crew leader. Then he'd gone home to get ready for school. Then he'd been killed.

"Do you know anything about what happened to Armando?" I asked.

"He's deported." The man calling himself Frankie stamped his foot with satisfaction as he said the words.

"Deported?" I asked. I tried to cover my surprise with a quick comeback. "Then I think you should be worried. You and whoever else lives here. I support immigrant families. I can help."

"Braulio Tenorio helps us. We have all our papers."

"Because of Señor Tenorio?"

"Because of Tenorio, yes."

"Is he taking care of your papers? Or controlling them? What if someone makes him mad?"

"No one does, miss. No one makes him mad. Valoramos nuestras vidas."

We value our lives.

Either the man in front of me knew Armando had been killed but didn't want to tell me, or Tenorio lied to Armando's work crew about why he hadn't shown up for work. Whichever way it went, someone wanted the murder hidden.

I nudged Frankie's hip to move him aside so I could go in. He shrank from my hand as though it burned him. I pushed the door open, calling, "José Lara, estás aquí? I have to talk to you."

I crossed the tiny entryway in two steps. An unlit space that had once been the sanctuary stood bare except for a kitchenette in one corner. Nothing moved but dust motes. Apparently, no one considered the hollering of a gringa as a summoning bell.

"Empanadas!" I called. "Calabaza, piña, y . . ." I couldn't remember the word for "cherry."

A light scuffle came from the ceiling above my head.

"Oh, my God, lady. Now I really know you're not migra." Frankie chuckled behind me. "Nobody from la migra coming in like that, with empanadas like with cheese for a mousetrap. I don't know who you are. Don't know what you want. But okay. We listen to you. For fun only."

I forced a smile in return.

"Okay, por abajo!" the young man yelled at the ceiling. "Abajo, abajo!"

A panel in the ceiling swung open. A ladder slid down to the wood floor of the former church.

One man came down the ladder, then another. After the first two, men kept climbing down, one by one. By the time the last one stepped down, I'd counted twenty-two of them. They walked over to Frankie and me, not saying a word.

CHAPTER

26

THEY WERE BOYS, really, around fourteen to twentysomething years old. The tallest stood at my nose height, but most didn't reach my shoulder.

In old T-shirts and flannel, they swirled around me like a soft creek eddying around a fallen branch. Frankie stood off to the side.

We'd left the sewer smell outside. A fragrance of grass cuttings, cologne, motor oil, and stress sweat haloed the young men.

They emitted an articulate silence rich with questions. Finally, a few muttered to each other but kept glancing at me. I caught the Spanish words for "foreigner" and "charity," then other words that might have been Purépecha or Quiché.

The empty sanctuary had wood floors, no pews. Two long windows sat in each side wall. The stained-glass dappled the men's skin green, bronze, blue. I felt disoriented, like I'd woken in a strange fairy tale. Light Brown and the Twenty-Two Campesinos.

There I was with nothing but bakery items for currency, hoping the act of having taken a life, or knowledge of a life taken, would leave a ripple in the air around someone. A scent-trail I could hound. But beyond the cologne and body heat, the only thing I could sense was the crack of my own exhausted nerves short-circuiting.

I needed focus. I closed my eyes to imagine the window slits on the sides of the jail, running up the building in narrow gashes. Jaral's face appeared in one of them. I opened my eyes determined to get what I could out of this group. Jaral's future depended on it.

The men were very shy about taking the empanadas. Each one offered me half of his, so that I had a pile of half empanadas left in the bag, little open mouths of dough with jelly tongues.

I selected one of the cherry filled.

This set off a few quips in Spanish that broke the tension.

"Oh, she took mine!"

"No, that was mine, you blind ass!"

"Poor guys, you're all a little stupid. This lady is not only beautiful, she's also highly intelligent. She took the best one. She took mine."

I smiled and shook my head, eyes downcast. Careful to be neither too forward nor too cold. I needed their trust.

When everyone who wanted an empanada had their half, I asked a question in English. Frankie moved next to me as though to stop me from circulating among the men. He translated my question into Spanish. I didn't hear any second translations going on from Spanish to an indigenous language, so I hoped they all understood Frankie.

I asked a question in English.

I asked, in English, whether Armando had any enemies.

The men glanced at each other, shifted their weight, stayed silent. Frankie said, "That kid is his own worst enemy. If he would learn how to work, he could get somewhere in the world!" He repeated to me how lazy Armando had been, especially this week, because he had been so tired from staying out late with his girlfriend.

I tried again to get a response from the group, this time leading with a soft lob of flirtation.

"You're all very handsome, very strong men."

Some clapped, others elbowed each other, wriggling off the tension.

A cascade of marriage proposals ensued.

"So, you are looking for a husband! The gringo husband left you? He's lazy, like a gringo man? I don't drink, I'm very loyal. I'll take care of you!"

"Yes, he'll take care of you like he takes care of digestion at night. The farts in our room, my sweet Savior, they make even the statue of the Blessed Mother cry! I'm the romantic one. Everything's roses, diamonds, and moonlight with me. Clean air all night long. Most gringas are so ugly. Really difficult to look at. But you. You are not one of these. Let me whisper you a lifetime of love poems written only for you!"

A third suitor strained up onto his tiptoes.

"We have twelve soft mattresses upstairs. Be my bride. We'll start making babies right now! We are going to complete a cycle! That begins with kisses. Continues with caresses . . ."

He hugged himself, cocked his head to the side with kissy lips, and rolled his shoulders in figure-eights.

Two other guys pulled him to the back of the group, grinning and chattering at him. In between breezy laughs, he said, in English, "Sorry, sorry, miss."

I think I blushed. Had I even brushed my teeth that morning? I suddenly felt very self-conscious. I wished I could've glanced at a pocket mirror.

"What I don't understand," I said, "is why with all these strong men, Mr. Tenorio still puts boys to work? Boys who are still finishing school?"

Frankie didn't bother translating that one. He answered me himself.

"Boys in El Pavo are born here, or very young when their parents come. They parents working here many years, save up money, rent a house from Señor Tenorio. That's what all of us do one day." He swept his arm to take in his assembled comrades. "We working, saving. One day we rent a house from Tenorio. In El Pavo."

I nodded. The American dream, writ small. To one day afford rent for a two-bedroom home on the frayed edge of town.

I tried some Spanish on the group. "El Señor Tenorio . . . les ayudan . . . a ustedes . . . mucho . . .?"

"Oh yes . . ."

"Yes, of course . . ."

"He is very good to us . . ."

"He helps us, he keeps us safe."

The assurances feathered over each other in downy layers. A few men pulled out driver's licenses.

"He secures documents for us."

"He keeps us safe."

"Safe from what?" I asked. Tenorio hadn't kept Armando safe.

The men dropped their eyes. Only Frankie looked at me, amazed by my question. He spoke the word for all of them: "Migra."

"Yes," I said. "That's good. He keeps you safe. Safe here. But what about all these places where you work? Where is the man you and Armando worked with? José Lara?" I asked Frankie, scanning the crowd.

One of the guys who had tackled Mr. Babies Now lifted his hand. "Presente."

I waved the supposed José over, showed him and Frankie the list of work sites recorded for their crew.

They squinted intently at the file. The two of them took turns lifting the papers, studying each one carefully. It seemed like they'd never seen this file before, which surprised me. Even the part of their lives that was documented had been obscured from their view.

I finished off my empanada half while they looked at the file. I also wanted to show the group the portrait of the mystery Somali girl, in case anyone knew who she was, but I'd left my phone in the car. It would have to wait. That was okay; there was still a lot I needed to figure out about these men who knew Armando.

"Twelve beds," I said to the group. "But more than twenty men?"

"No, no, no, I'm not like that, but he is."

"What, not me, he only says that because he's such a butterfly boy."

The shuffling and gentle shoves that followed seemed to expand and contract the group at the same time.

"We trade, miss," Mr. Clean Air called out. "One group working, another sleeping. Right now, one group leave soon."

They told me shifts with the mattresses ran from two PM to two AM and from two AM to two PM. Work shifts lasted ten hours. Crews could add men or boys from El Pavo, but those guys never had to work the full ten-hour shift. Two hours max on school days for the kids, eight hours max for the men who live in El Pavo.

"Tenorio is testing us, miss."

"Yeah, this is our probationary period."

"More like our purgatory period!"

I felt like I was gaining ground with the group. "Frankie says Armando was no good for working. Is that true? Is that why he . . . got deported?" I asked them.

A couple of guys cleared their throats. A few turned around to face away from me.

I suddenly remembered the interviewing lesson from Happy Face. No yes-or-nos.

"Okay, okay." I flicked my hands as though shaking them dry, to show I was starting over. "Who can tell me how Armando was as a worker?"

"Frankie just jealous, miss," came a voice from beside me.

José had stepped away from Frankie and the others to say these words in English. Frankie returned the file to me with a grunt, then walked away as though he couldn't be bothered with either of us.

"Go on" I said to José.

"I working with Nando," he explained. "Frankie say Nando is bad worker because he very jealous."

"Jealous of Armando? Because he has a girlfriend?"

"No, because he wants the job Armando has. The extra job, for extra money."

There was a knock on the back door. The men drew in their breath as one.

From across the room, Frankie rasped, "Arriba!" ducking his head as though something might drop on him. "Arriba, arriba!" He windmilled his arms toward the attic ladder, which still sat flush against the ground in the back corner of the building.

"Federal agents! Open up! We're going to kick this door in if you don't comply in three seconds!" The voice booming through the back door was male, unaccented. The speaker repeated his directions in textbook Spanish. Then he counted down. "Tres. Dos. Uno!"

Someone pulled me away from the flow of men rushing toward the ladder. It was José Lara. He led me by my wrist toward a set of stairs leading down to the basement.

He said something in Spanish that I couldn't understand. Behind us, the door was taking a royal beating. Each bang finished off with the sound of wood fibers splitting, but the door held.

José started down the basement stairs. I grabbed the top of the banister to keep from going any further.

"It's okay," I said. "I'm a citizen, they won't hurt me. You go, go." I tried to shake his grip.

"No, miss," he said, "there is no care if you citizen. Please. We go to little heat room."

"The furnace?" I said. "No, I'll be okay. You go."

If I hadn't stood there arguing with the guy, maybe neither of us would have ended up against the wall with semiautomatic rifles pointed at our chests, once the door broke open and agents poured in.

CHAPTER

27

THE ASSAULT RIFLE banished the illusion that I had a United States citizen's safety guarantee chip to cash in. My thoughts narrowed to basic body functions. Keep breathing. Don't pee all over yourself. Stop those knees from shaking.

"Did I hear you speaking English?" An agent with a stomach mound that pushed out from under his bulletproof ICE vest spoke to me with surprising softness, considering the deadly weapon he was pointing at me.

"We're together," I said, grabbing José's hand. I wanted to keep this new source of information from getting rounded up and carted off before I could really talk to him.

The warmth of José's palm was so innocent, so uncomplicated, I almost cried. He must have thought the impulsive gesture might keep him from being detained too, because he didn't pull away.

"Oh, Christ," the agent said. "Are you two for real?"

Neither of us spoke. I hadn't exactly made a false statement yet. By standing together and holding hands, we were, indeed, together at that moment. But I didn't have any more verbal tricks up my sleeve. And I was aware that any step further away from the truth would be a step further onto law enforcement's bad side, where I didn't want to be.

The officer marking us glanced over his shoulder and spoke to another Kevlar-vested gentleman half-heartedly pointing a rifle at a group in the corner. "Chelton, what do you make of this pair?"

The man called Chelton had his profile to us. Without turning his head, he answered "Jungle love."

The group in front of him stood so still they seemed to hold their breath. In the other corner, the ladder lolled out of the ceiling like a mute tongue.

Two other agents worked to zip-tie the wrists of each man in front of Chelton. Then they led them out the back door of the church, one by one, into a white van waiting in the alley.

Three had been moved out under their blanket of silence before one made a noise, a curse word, like a startled bird crying out, alone, in the night.

As though on cue, the back doors of the van clanked open, spilling a man onto his side, his hands still bound behind him. He rolled onto his knees, stood up, and ran.

The man guarding us yelled, "Here we go!" He moved toward the door, then half turned and shouted back at us as he left. "Stay put. I need some ID."

His feet pounded down the alley. "Stop!" he called in Spanish, "¡Alto, alto!"

José gripped my hand as though cracking walnuts. I attempted to squeeze back with the limited nerve function he'd left me. I looked into his face. His brow furrowed, his jaw set. I slid my eyes toward the stairs.

Chelton worked on tightening up his group. He had his back to us.

As one, José and I turned. Still holding hands, we tiptoed down.

I was in front. Fortune kept the carpeted stairs from creaking.

At the bottom of the stairs, I hesitated at the boiler room door. Quick as a fly zipping out from under a swatter, José went in and scuttled beneath pipes.

I needed to know what he knew. So I went in after him.

The furnace whooshed loud enough to cover whispers. I crouched down next to José, tried to force back a flood of panic. Only a matter of minutes before someone came for us.

"Frankie says . . . Frankie says . . ." I couldn't make my brain form words. I shook so much my teeth knocked together.

"¡Silencio!" José hissed. His eyes were bright, his expression one of complete alertness.

I put my head between my knees. Three deep breaths, I told myself. One . . .

When I raised my head again, my mind had thawed enough to access human speech, but my throat felt sandpaper dry.

"Frankie didn't like Armando." I said to José. "You said that's because Frankie is jealous. Why? Why is Frankie jealous?"

José squeezed his eyes shut as though I'd just aimed a blade of sunlight at his face.

"Why?" I whispered again.

"Tenorio gives Armando more work," José said. He spoke rapidly, trying to shut me up. "Extra important job. Pays a lot of money. Frankie don't get picked for this extra job because he's too horny. Tenorio says."

"What's the job?"

"I no supposed to telling. Secret."

No drugs, no prostitution, no violence.

It could have been any of those.

"If Tenorio says Frankie's too horny for the job, it has to be something with girls, right?"

José moved his head slightly. The small shake could have been "No," or it could have been the internal tremor of the unsaid.

"Very secret," he said again, his eyes on the door.

Everyone has a price. What did I have to trade?

I took out my car key, pressed it in José's hand. He eyed me in wonder.

I nodded once. "Take it. A swap. Un intercambio. Now tell me what you know."

"Armando driving up to the forest," he said. "Sometime bringing just groceries, sometime with a doctor." He slid my key into a pocket of his jeans.

"A doctor?"

"Very long drive. Very dark. It's difficult."

"You've done this before? You get this extra work sometimes too?"

"Yes, Armando and I taking turns."

"Armando drives, you ride, then you ride, Armando drives?"

"No. No riding. Just Armando drive the doctor, maybe sometime with Tenorio. Maybe sometime just Armando drive doctor only. Or groceries only. No Tenorio. Me, same thing. I only driving."

"When?"

"One night every month. When the moon have very little light. But also maybe just anytime."

"Where are you taking this doctor?"

"I don't know, we just follow this road Tenorio tell us to go on. Or the driver just by himself, bringing groceries up the same road. It's one time per month, usually, but sometimes it's all of a sudden, we just have to go, you know."

I felt I was so close to a key insight, I could sense the nearness of it like the tang of woodsmoke hanging over an evening chill.

I forgot we were hiding.

"What kind of doctor is he?" I said, in an ordinary voice.

José's eyes went to the door. He shrank back further under the pipes. Above us, feet shuffled, men's voices fell like hammers. But no one seemed to be coming for us. Yet.

"What kind of doctor?" I whispered.

"Is a lady. I don't know, but sometimes after, she smell like blood. Like blood, or like, you know, something human. Some human smell. Or sometimes a church smell."

"But you don't see where she goes or what she does? This doctor?"

With a chuff of finality, the furnace shut off.

Above us, footsteps thumped.

With the furnace noise gone, I could make out a man's voice upstairs.

"I'm exercising First Amendment rights!" It sounded like . . . no. Couldn't be.

"Keep talking," I whispered to the man next to me.

He shook his head.

I pointed to the pocket where he'd slipped my key, then paddled the air with my fingers in a "gimme" sign.

He pressed a hand against the outside of the pocket.

"I will yell for them right now if you don't keep talking!"

He gulped. Hugged his knees with his arms.

"Armando did not get deported. He got killed." I sent the words out like a jumper cable cranking out current, hoping to jolt José back to speech. "I have to find out what happened so I can keep it from happening again. In memory of Armando, tell me what you know!"

His breath became shallow. "If I take groceries, I no see any people. I drive to a gate, is always closed. Same for Armando. I leave everything in a big metal box. If I bring doctor, or doctor and Tenorio, I no see where doctor is going. Armando, same thing. I wait at gate. The doctor lady, and Tenorio too, walk up a little . . . how do you say . . . a little road only for people, no for cars."

"A trail. When was the last time Armando drove to this place?"

"Probably Sunday. We only drive at night. Maybe he's back very late Sunday."

"Does this place have a name?"

"They just call it Presidio, miss."

"He drove to San—?" I couldn't finish my question, because the kid actually slapped his hand over my mouth. He still had it pressed there when the door flew open. An agent I hadn't seen before pointed a rifle at me. The hand came off my mouth. I screamed.

"Put your hands up. Walk forward. Go stand against this wall!" The voice at the other end of the gun barked.

I crab-walked out from under the pipes. A chirping flock of pleas flew out my mouth.

"I'm a citizen, I'm a citizen, I speak English, I run a school, I'm a citizen."

"Save it for my sergeant!"

Behind the man ordering us around, I saw the Chelton guy from upstairs. His face seemed placid, empty of the violence that radiated from the man in front of us. Chelton held his weapon loosely at his side, pointed down.

He called over the shoulder of his fellow agent. "Ma'am, do you have ID?"

The man in front of me swung the gun back toward José. "I said against the wall!"

"No, no, he's okay," I said. "We're together."

"You're not wearing no wedding band," the angry one said.

I was making him nervous. I didn't fit his mental picture of how this raid would go down.

"Tell this man about our family," José said. "Our kids. Tell them, corazón!"

José was taking a big swing with this new story. If I played along to help him, I could get caught up with hearings, paperwork, more detention centers. I might even risk jail myself.

But I owed this man. He got caught by the feds because I wouldn't leave him alone.

I'd already slipped him my car key in the furnace room. What else could I do?

"You're right" I said, turning back to the agents. "This poor guy calls me sweetheart, but I've never seen . . . ah!" I widened my eyes. Clenched my jaw.

"Ouch! Oh, God! Aaahh . . ." I clutched my side, fell to my knees. "My appendix! Oh, I think it's burst, oh, God!"

"Your appendix is on your right side, bitch!" The fanatic one shouted in my ear.

I pressed my other side. "Oh, God, I'm dying, help me, help."

Footsteps pounding down the basement stairs froze us all for an instant.

Yori appeared, rushing toward the furnace room with a boom microphone, which he got stuck against the furnace room doorway. José ducked under him, scrambled up a smaller set of stairs I hadn't even noticed on the way down, and pushed himself out a window well.

"What the fuck!" said the angry ICE agent, trying to duck out after José. He got caught in the black cords Yori was dragging along with him, pulled his feet free, but then collided with the person behind Yori, a wide-eyed college kid of giant dimensions. The ICE agent stumbled backward, slipped on the cords, and fell on his ass. The college kid caught all of this on camera.

I hopped up. "Yori, it's me!"

"Boots," he said. "What the hell are you doing here?"

Chelton shot me a look of surprise. I doubled over again, clutching my right side.

"Not today, motherfucker," the angry one said, getting to his feet. He left to chase down José. Yori followed him, and the kid with the camera followed Yori.

Chelton, the remaining ICE agent, finally looked amped. "Stay where you are. Don't move!"

A car door closed.

Someone yelled, "Stop!" A thudding percussion followed the order, the sound of someone pounding on top of a car.

My engine made its usual chuffs before turning over. When I heard my car pull away, I was so relieved I hooted.

"All better," I said and straightened up. An anxious laugh escaped me.

Chelton seemed about to spit.

Yori came back in.

"Boots, are you all right?" Without waiting for an answer, he instructed the kid, "Get tight on her face, then on the agent, then we have to get a pano upstairs."

The agent and I obediently froze in place while the camera went from one to the other. After panning our faces, the young cameraman went upstairs. Yori gave me a tiny nod, his face unreadable, then turned around to follow.

The agent in front of me used his rifle as an expressive limb extension, spreading his arms open, which, thankfully, moved the rifle off to the side.

"So you know this guy?" he said. "You gonna show me some ID?"

CHAPTER

28

I LOOKED AT THE officer. "My license is in my wallet." He looked back. "Which is in my purse, which is in my car, which is . . . who knows where by now."

He grunted, motioned me upstairs ahead of him. Back on the first floor, Yori went from person to person in the remaining group of men that still huddled in the corner, holding the mic over them and introducing himself. "Yori Shimada, *North Coast Journal*. And this is my intern."

His intern aimed the camera at each face, asking people where they were from. Some answered "Zacatecas," others said, "Michoacán." A few of the men just turned their faces away from the camera.

"Don't be scared," the intern said in Spanish. "We're here to document this injustice."

The two agents who'd been zip-tying wrists stood beside the men, not touching them.

"You are interfering with federal agents," said Chelton.

Yori turned to him. "Either you let me stay, or I'm going to record this from the street. How will that paint you? Dodging press, pulling people out the back door, throwing them into a van hidden in the alley. Why not show the public you can do your duty with dignity for all involved? And what about her? You going to cart her off too?" The camera swung to me.

"I'm a citizen," I said right into the camera. "I run Daybreak Academy on Seaside Road. I've lived in Humboldt for over twenty years."

"Are you going to take her in?" Yori asked Chelton again. The camera swung back to him.

"We are going to remove all undocumented peoples."

"How's this for documentation?" Yori pulled out his phone with one hand, still holding the boom by the other. "Okay, wait—it takes a second to load."

He set the boom down, pushed at his phone a few times, stared at it, pushed at it some more. Finally, he raised the boom with one hand, held his phone out in the other.

"There's her picture. Not a very good shot—I think she's trying to look authoritative—but you can see it's her. You should read her bio. Always doing positive things for our community, a champion of the undocumented, on and on. I'm sure she's here to tell these guys about her school. She has English classes for adults there. Right?"

I nodded on cue.

"That school, look, it's the logo right there on her shirt. That school is beloved. She's beloved. I don't think you want to deal with a public firestorm for bringing her in."

My hero.

Chelton noticed the file I'd dropped when agents started breaking down the door. He picked it up and opened it.

"I brought that in," I said. "It's Braulio Tenorio's. A personnel file of his. Tenorio helps fund my school, and I . . . I was checking on one of his employees."

"Braten Staffing," Chelton said, reading the letterhead. "You got this from Tenorio?"

All I could do was nod.

"Ma'am, he should've told you to stay away today. Go on and get out of here."

Out on the sidewalk, I was at least five miles from my house, and farther from my school. I sat down on the back bumper of the *North Coast Journal* van to wait for Yori. I needed a ride.

Neighbors had come out to watch the commotion. One of them, mistaking me for a *Journal* employee, tried to start a conversation. "I'm so glad I called the *Journal* office. Somebody needs to be a witness to the inhumanity of this raid! We're treating undocumented people like illegal drugs. Toxic and disposable. What a tragedy!"

Another neighbor joined us. "This is a neighborhood of decent, law-abiding people. This church-slum needed to be cleaned out. I'm glad someone called ICE!" When the two of them got into it, I slipped around to the side of the van, pulled the sliding door open, and dropped onto the floor. The back seats had been removed. I found myself between various kinds of recording equipment. Eventually, I heard the ICE van drive away from the alley.

The intern and Yori came out and loaded their equipment. I scooted onto the floor between the front seats to make room.

"Guess you're coming with us?" Yori asked.

I shrugged. "Guess so. I let one of the guys from the stash house take my car."

Yori raised his eyebrows and grinned. "Some good, old-fashioned aiding and abetting. That's quality work! We have to drop this equipment back at the office, then we'll figure out what's next."

The youngster got in behind the wheel. Yori took shotgun. We followed the ICE van until it got on the freeway. Then we turned back toward the *Journal* office.

"Where do you think they're taking them?" I asked Yori.

"The agents wouldn't say. But my guess is San Fran. There's an ICE detention center there. Wish I knew for sure though. I hate how hush-hush immigration enforcement can be."

After the van was unloaded at the *North Coast Journal* offices, I wanted to rush to find the area José Lara had told me about. The area Armando drove to for his extra work. "They call it Presidio," Lara had said. The name of a well-known area in San Francisco.

But I had no wheels.

Yori was putting away the last of the filming equipment in a closet.

"Yori, let's go down to the city now. See if we can catch up to the ICE guys. Verify the facility where they'll hold those men. Follow up."

He shut the closet and turned to me. "Now you're a news hound? We have contacts who cover immigration down there. We'll check in with them later. No need to waste time driving all that way. It'll be at least four hours before they're close to the facility, if I'm right about where they're going."

I meant to shake my head and back away. Everything was all wrong. A young boy killed, Jaral out of reach. Me more confused and with less resources to help every hour. Now, no car.

I tripped over a trashcan behind me and ended in a half spin, half stumble, just to stay upright.

"Easy!" Yori said. "You're keyed up. I get it. That was a wild scene. Big drama, big guns. But seriously. Why are you so hot to go to San Fran? Maybe you should take it easy for a few hours. Looked like you felt kinda sick back there in the church."

"I'm fine. There's a kid who used to be a student of mine. He . . . got into some trouble. One of the guys living at the church just told me this kid was doing some kind of secret work at the Presidio. I need to get to the city and go to the Presidio and try to find out what the kid was involved with. To help . . . to help him."

I didn't want to bring up the murder with Yori, because he'd chide me again for getting involved, then pry for details. I didn't want to have to tell him Jaral was in jail for it. Jaral's arrest wasn't in the daily *Sentinel*, and I wouldn't be the one to feed it to the press. I wanted Jaral out, cleared, reputation intact.

Yori bent down to tie a shoelace while I was talking. He stopped mid-lace and looked up at me. "Boots. Seriously? The Presidio?"

"What?"

"You think the guy you talked to was saying this kid you know has secret work at a neighborhood next to the Golden Gate?"

"Why not?"

Yori pulled his rabbit ears tight and stood, leaning toward me. "You've got to come to my place."

"Um. No?"

"Yes. You're mixed up, shook up, hard up for transport. And probably hungry. Didn't we just work through lunch? I've got intel that will save you a bucket-load of time. Like, eight hours of driving time. Get some comfort food in you too. What do you think?"

The trip to Los Bagels had been like a very late breakfast. What about a very late lunch? I'd only had half an empanada at the stash house. Come to think of it, I was hungry.

CHAPTER

29

THE LAST TIME I'd been at Yori's six years ago, I came to end things. This time in, I noticed a few differences. Same giant ficus in one corner of the front room. Same gestalt of magazines, papers, and book stacks spilling from end tables onto furniture. But a small pair of women's tennies nestled cozy in the jumble of shoes by the door. And a new family of African drums occupied one side of the living room. Gorgeous, made of deep-toned woods that seemed to glow from within.

I didn't remember Yori owning any drums.

One djembe was common enough in the homes of West Coast lefties in those days. But five?

"Aren't those cool?" Yori looked up from chopping scallions at his kitchen island. He pointed his knife at the drums. "Nell used to tour with the Marley family."

The fiancée. Of course.

Yori went back to chopping. His strong wrists, the knife's quick cantilever, enchanted me.

He slid the scallions into two steaming bowls of miso broth and carried them to his table.

"For what ails you," he said. My mouth watered as we sat down.

"So you're into film now?" I held a spoonful of soup aloft to cool. "Don't you run a weekly paper?"

"We're launching a YouTube channel," he said. "Quick content hits covering under-reported issues on the North Coast."

"You talk like that in your own home? Are you ever not on the clock?"

He slurped a spoonful, shook his head. His hands were the color of hot sand.

"Here," he said, swiping a bag of yogurt-covered pretzels off the counter next to him. "Have some of these. Sorry I don't have much more right now. Nell's shopping at the co-op."

Probing after this Nell was a project for another day. I ate handfuls of pretzels between slurps. The white yogurt stuck to my fingers. My mouth was full of a salty-sweet mash when he asked how I ended up at the location of the raid. He said he knew I couldn't have just been recruiting for Daybreak School.

I swallowed, coughed into a paper napkin, and tried to think how to explain myself without spilling the awful truth that Jaral was a murder suspect.

"Wait a sec. You're supposed to be telling me something about the Presidio. What did you call it? Intel?"

"Quid pro quo, Clarice."

God. That should not have sounded sexy. But it did.

I swallowed some broth. Dried my lips with a paper napkin.

"When you called while I was being followed, you asked if I was trying to solve a murder."

"I didn't call." He popped a pretzel in his mouth. "You called me."

"Yeah, okay. So you were right. I'm helping the victim's family find out who killed this boy from El Pavo. He was a student of mine years ago."

"Isn't that a job for police? I thought the *Sentinel* crime blotter said they had someone in custody. No, wait. Let me guess. They've got the wrong guy? And now it's Boots Marez to the rescue! Whether it's grammar to be learned or murders to be solved, she's your mujer!"

"Don't judge. Anyone running around playing Michael Moore with an underpaid intern can't mock me for trying to help."

"You think I pay interns?"

I forced a laugh.

"I pay them, I pay them," he said, smiling back. "Not like some big boss types here in Humboldt. You hear about the Horizons Care Home raid? Your Tenorio called ICE on his own people. So he wouldn't have to pay them fairly."

"He's not my Tenorio. And what do you mean, he called ICE? That's ridiculous. At the very least, getting rid of employees that work through his staffing service would be bad for business."

The Horizons Care Home raid was the story Rosalva's neighbor, Happy Face Holland, showed me. All those women getting deported.

I tipped my soup bowl up, drank the rest of the seaweed-flecked broth.

"It's not ridiculous, Boots. For six days a week, each Horizons worker would be driven with her crew mates in windowless white vans to one of nine care homes holding this contract with Braten, Tenorio's company. They'd work twelve-hour shifts. After Tenorio took housing and transportation out of their pay, they had $36 a week for themselves. And you know they're trying to send money back to relatives. So they start to organize. For better pay. For eight-hour shifts with normal breaks. For decent living conditions. Then boom. They're locked up."

I already thought Tenorio might be a killer. So it was no stretch to think of him trading on human lives for profit.

"What about the men living at the church," I said. "They seemed loyal to Tenorio. At least the ones I talked to. Not the organizing kind. You don't think Tenorio called in that raid, too, do you?"

"Maybe those guys had to be out of the way for some other reason. Could be they knew too much about some piece of Tenorio's business. I mean, they had information you wanted, right?"

"I only heard scraps of what they know." I got up to put my bowl in the sink. "All the good Tenorio does, the boards he serves on, setting up a company to fund the school. It's all cover. I used to think he really cared about helping immigrants, people hardly anyone was helping. But he only cares about himself and his money. I see that now."

Yori stood up and moved next to me, took hold of my wrist. "What do you mean?"

I allowed myself a splash of a second to enjoy the energy jolt of his touch. But I couldn't get distracted by desire pooling around me. I drew my arm away.

"Wait. Why were you there, Yori? I was shocked by these guys with AKs coming in the door, but you just happened to be on hand to get it on camera?"

"Yeah, I'm good. But not that good. A neighbor called the *Journal.* Said someone should be there to record the injustice of incarcerating people who just want to work. But back to you. When you say Tenorio only cares about himself and his money, what makes you say that?"

There was a lot that made me say it, but topping the list was the fact that he had people living in his homes who worked for his scrape-by wages, who were so afraid of him they wouldn't even ask for help to get a cleaner to remove their dead son's blood.

"Yori, I can't get into it now. I just need to know what you meant about the Presidio. I have to get out there. As soon as I can. I gave you my quid. Time for your quo."

He ripped a piece of paper from a pad magnetized to his fridge, found a pen in a drawer, and started drawing what appeared to be a herd of amoebas nuzzling each other.

He muttered at me while he drew. "I can't believe I have to tell you this. You've lived here how long?"

"Since I went to college here at Humboldt State. You know that."

He sighed. Pushed the completed drawing toward me. "Okay, Boots. Since you didn't get this in college. One of the most well-known marijuana growing areas in Humboldt County is a hill known as The Hill. Real creative, I know."

"All right."

"When people radio or call each other about their locations on The Hill, they use these San Francisco neighborhoods so the feds think they're going out of town." He tapped the drawing. "Someone was trying to tell you the dead kid made runs here." He pointed to the top right blob labeled "Presidio."

"That's basically the north side of The Hill. But don't think you're getting anywhere near any of these areas. No outsiders allowed. Any roads off the highway are blocked by gates. Further up, they're guarded by guys with AKs. Some parts are too steep for roads, choked with vegetation. Or pot fields. You find one of those you're not supposed to find, you might not live to tell."

"Presidio doesn't mean San Fran?"

"Not for anyone up to something shady."

"You say there's no way in. But I have to find a way. Maybe I can pretend to be a lost hiker."

"Did you hear anything I said? First of all, even if you could get through the gates, it'd be a slow three hours' drive uphill on dicey dirt roads to reach The Hill. No one 'lost' would accidentally show up there. And worse, you come on a grow, at least you know what your problem is: you've exposed someone's illegal money farm and have to pray to the green god you can convince whoever you see that you're not a narc. You manage to get all the way over here, to the Presidio? You don't know what you'll find. That's not an area for grows. Not enough sunlight. It's a white zone, Boots. That's an area other federal agencies accession from public land for classified use. You won't know what the fuck you're walking into."

"That's a familiar feeling."

This was the part where I was supposed to feel hopeless. Outmatched. Out of my depth. Maybe a flicker of that showed on my face.

Yori reached forward to fold me into a California friend-zone hug. A lot of torso, with an invisible spacer holding us apart below the waist. He spoke into my hair. "What happens to the reputation of Daybreak if Tenorio's reputation tanks?"

Still interviewing me. I breathed in the scent of his sun-struck skin. "Yup," I said, my voice low. "That's a good question."

I leaned my head on his shoulder. It wasn't too much of a strain. He was only a few inches shorter than me.

Then he ran a hand up and down my back once. That hit a trip wire.

I kissed his neck once. Again.

I caressed the ridge of soft hair along the back of his neck.

He laughed. The sound was like warm cobbles moving along the bottom of a cool stream.

He pulled my arms to my sides and gently pushed me away from him.

"What's wrong with you?" he said. He was grinning.

I looked around the room behind him. I could push him into a chair, tie his hands behind his back with that phone cord stuck in the wall. Pop the fly on his jeans open one button at a time.

But even with his grin, this was an actual rejection I was in the middle of. How embarrassing.

"What's wrong with me? I should be asking what's wrong with you."

I moved to the door to get my shoes.

"Guess you're not the adrenaline junky I used to know and love," I said, with more bite in my voice than I intended. "You sound like a little old lady who's afraid to cross the street. Ooh, you can't get in there, nooo, don't go up there with the scary people."

On my way to the door, I'd seen a photo of Yori and the putative Nell on the fridge. What they were doing in the picture fired new currents of hope and urgency through me, blitzing out the moment's puny awkwardness.

I had my shoes back on and my hand on the knob when Yori called to me. "Where you going? I drove you here, remember?"

I pulled his door open and walked into a cold gust.

CHAPTER

30

If I could get into the area called the Presidio that night, maybe I could find out what Armando was mixed up with there, and get a read on how someone from this super secret "white zone" might've wanted to kill him.

I didn't know how arraignments worked, but I thought if I could find something that pointed to anyone besides Jaral for Armando's murder, they'd have to let him go tomorrow when he came before a judge. They'd release him, and I'd be there waiting with some clean clothes and a hug. We'd drive to Lumberjack Cookhouse for a fried oyster feast.

I'd sit across from him just beaming simple acceptance for once. No fussing about the future. Just talk about passing the dipping sauce. Because the chance to be near him, see he was okay, would be a gift of profound sufficiency.

Luckily, Yori's house was only a mile and a half away from Daybreak Academy. My school had a couple of things I needed as I was figuring out how to get to the Presidio.

I walked up through the Pacific chill, keyed in the door code on the security pad, and let myself in.

I could hear the night janitor moving around in the middle school wing. I slipped into the main office and over to my desk without turning the lights on. My cell phone had gone wherever my car had gone, but my office had a phone and computer I could use without Yori, or anyone else, hanging over me. Trying to talk me out of something.

After a few minutes of net surfing, I dialed Yori's number anyway.

"Can you loan me 20K?" I asked, as soon as he answered.

"You are batshit! What is this about now?" Then I heard him murmur, away from the phone, "It's okay, bunny. It's just Boots. Acting crazy."

I assumed "bunny" was Nell, who I assumed was the woman in the picture on their fridge that I'd seen holding hands with Yori while skydiving. The two of them belly-down, wind pulling the fabric of their suits straight up behind them, each clasping the forearm of the other with one hand while their free arms flexed in the ninety-degree bend for a proper jump. Whoever jumped with them must have grabbed the shot from a sports cam.

"What this is about is that I'm getting into the Presidio tonight. I have to. And I'm getting in there by an . . . unconventional route. All I need is twenty thousand to do it. I don't want to say why I have to go now, but trust me. It's an emergency. And you're the only person I could ask for something like this. You know I don't really have friends."

"Twenty thousand dollars is not 'friends' level, Boots. That's an amount you ask to get from a bank. Or a criminal. The only 20K I can get quick is in the *Journal*'s travel account. I'm not about to lose my job borrowing it for personal use. That's called stealing. It's embezzlement, Boots."

"Oh. Yeah. Good idea. I mean. Good point." I hung up.

The most promising find from my web search was still open on the screen in front of me. The "On the Dot Air Charters" site had a plain gray background with white font that said "Available 24 hours" across the top of the page. The site provided a phone number, a description of services and prices, and a promise they were "Humboldt's fastest and most confidential air service."

I could only hope that was true.

CHAPTER

31

THE LADY WHO answered the phone cut me off when I started to tell her my name.

"Ahht." She made a throaty noise, like someone correcting a puppy. "On the Dot is a zero-liability company, ma'am. Anonymity is key to our client experience." I asked if she could get me into the air while it was dark. She said, "That's the best time to fly."

My plan was for them to drop me off in a clear-cut I'd seen on Google Earth that looked to be just over a ridge from the area known as the Presidio. Since the Presidio had been Armando's destination for his secret night drives, I figured whatever was up there might be important enough to kill for. I hoped whatever I found would be enough to pull investigators off the trail of my son.

I could drive up there myself, but Yori made it sound like I'd have to bust through locked iron gates.

I could walk, but if I walked on the road I'd be a target for whoever guarded the land.

I could walk off-road, but I'd miss the arraignment. I'd have a miserable, nine-hour, uphill bushwhack ahead of me just to get over to the Presidio, and I'd have to wait for daylight to get started, so I didn't get lost. That was extra time I didn't have.

When I'd seen Jaral in the jail's visiting room, I'd dug myself a deep ditch of guilt by losing control and doing what I'd sworn I'd never do—reach out with my own hands to hurt a child. From now on, I needed to be there completely for Jaral, every second of every day. I'd show up at the arraignment, and I'd work even harder to free him until then.

The woman on the phone scheduled me for a three AM departure from the "back lot" of the tiny McKinleyville Airport, asked when I wanted my pickup for the return. I told her ten the next morning. I didn't have my car, but I could drive one of the school's minibuses to the airport. If I got picked up at ten the next day, that would put me back at the airport around ten-thirty, enough to make the twenty-minute drive from the airport back to town before Jaral's eleven AM arraignment.

A trip to and from the Headwaters Forest cost ten thousand dollars each way, including fuel, the pilot's time, all my gear, plus an expedited service fee for last-minute scheduling. I'd have to convert the money into something called bitcoin online, then use an encrypted browser to access the payment site.

"Unless you'd like to pay in Humboldt twenties."

"No, I . . ." Two hundred hundred-dollar bills? Where was I going to get that after five PM? Or at any time? "I'll have to transfer it."

I wish I could say my conscience told me twenty thousand was just too much to "borrow" from Daybreak Academy. But it was the automated banking system for the school's account that applied the brakes. After I ended the call, I found the Daybreak reserve account had a $15,000 per week transfer cap. I called back and said I'd just book the one-way departure tonight without the pickup tomorrow.

That left the question of how I'd get back before the arraignment unresolved. I suppose I thought desperation would give me godspeed. This area of the redwoods was the last place I could think to go for answers about why Armando was killed, the last place I thought I might find something to help get Jaral out. I had to get up there as soon as I could.

As I clicked through the steps to transfer the money online, the phrase “fireable offense” burst into mind. I shoved it down my mental basement stairs and slammed the door. I spun up the delusion that I’d find a way to pay the school back before anyone noticed the money was gone.

If I stopped to notice how it felt to hurt the school I’d poured my heart into, I would’ve shrank back from the heat of it, like watching layers of my own skin burn away. But that sensation had to be shoved down too.

All this beating back of reality gave me an adrenaline high, which was probably plain old fear at work, making the inside of my mouth taste like old coins.

I grabbed a backpack from the school’s lost and found box, then got a few things I thought I’d need from the maintenance closet and the computer classroom. I found Ty, the night janitor, cleaning whiteboards in a seventh-grade language arts room.

“Hey, boss,” he said, pulling headphones out of his ears. “I didn’t hear you drive up.”

“I forgot something. Just popping in, leaving soon. Have you already finished the elementary wing?”

“Yeah, it’s shiny new. I ran the buffing machine over there. I’m outta here soon too.”

I wished him a good night, then noisily opened and closed the front door as I went out. I made a loop around the outside of the school to the kindergarten room. I walked past their parked fleet of trikes, let myself in the outside door, and laid out some carpet squares for a makeshift bed. I was so tired I fell asleep immediately and didn’t hear Ty leave. When I jolted awake at 2:15 in the morning, I grabbed the bus keys in a half-asleep zombie daze and drove to the McKinleyville airport.

CHAPTER

32

I EXPECTED A BUSH plane to be waiting for me, like those you see in survival shows about life in the Yukon. What I got was a chopper smaller than Uncle Max's old Pinto.

At three AM, the airport asphalt is cool as the spring night air. Helicopter blades whirred above me. I sat cross-legged on the ground, shoving my hair up by the handful under a plastic helmet. The pilot paced in front of me, machine-gunning directives.

"Don't walk behind the bird. The rear rotors are invisible. They'll shred you like lettuce. We're five minutes from liftoff. Use the privy now, if you have to. No? Okay. When you jump, do not push off. Just fall forward. I will not hover. I will be going about forty miles an hour. Back here on the right, this pulls open your main canopy. This is your altimeter on your wrist. When it says five thousand feet, reach back and pull."

"Stop!" I shivered in the damp dark. All my insides seemed to be shrinking into themselves. I couldn't stop picturing a horror-show version of free fall where the wind pulled my flesh so hard it tore away in shreds. "T-tell me again. When do I pull?"

"Five thousand feet or a little before."

"Five thousand." It was just sounds. I couldn't get the number to mean anything. I tried to link up what the man was saying with the experience of my one tandem jump. But then, I'd had the animal comfort of my body pressed against someone else's. This time, I'd be completely exposed. So far up, and falling alone.

Right then, I never wanted to move from the actual ground.

"You okay, ma'am?"

"I just . . . I can't follow when you talk so fast."

He came over and squatted in front of me. Lifted one of my hands as though he might kiss the top of it. Took a sharpie from the pocket of his shirt, pulled off the cap with his teeth, and scrawled "5,000" on the top of my hand.

"Ma'am, you do not seem like someone with twenty-five jumps." It's how many the Internet said a person needed to be a licensed skydiver, so that's how many I told the woman from the air charter company that I had.

He stood, capped the pen, and pointed it at me. "You afraid of heights? I will not have you losing your shit in-flight."

I shrugged. "Just go on, okay?"

"Goddamn! The things I do for an honest buck." He shook his head, squared his stance, and continued. "On your left shoulder is your emergency pull. Let me see you pat it. Good. Yank it if the main canopy fails. Now switch this thing on. Yup, right on top. That's your automatic deployment switch. It opens the canopy at four thousand feet if you pass out on the way down. Does your helmet fit? Shoes on tight? When your canopy's open, toggle right to go right, left to go left. Face the wind. Pull in to descend. Flare out to land so you won't break your legs. All right. Last call, powder room. No? Ready? Let's board."

The rig had no doors. There were only two seats behind the cockpit or whatever you called it in a helicopter. I scrambled into one and fastened up.

The tiny chopper rose over McKinleyville into the marine layer that coats the north coast before sunrise. Tendrils of fog stirred around us, then broke apart. My hands felt cold. After a few seconds, we lifted above the fog into the star-spangled darkness of a new-moon night.

The pilot glanced back, gestured for me to take off my helmet, then pointed to his headset. I took off my helmet. A big pair of headphones like you'd wear with an '80s Walkman hung on a hook above me. I put them on. They connected through a spiral cord to a box welded to the ceiling of the cabin, and had a small mic in front on a wire arm.

The pilot pushed a button on the right side of his headset. "Where have you made your jumps? Your twenty-five." The pilot's voice had both velvet and wire brush in it. He sounded like a Yankee Phil Collins.

I pushed a button on the right ear of my headset. "This again? Here and there, man. None of your business."

"Uh-huh. Then I guess this will be review." He moved his head side to side as he spoke, scanning the sky ahead and the clouds below us.

"When you're in free fall, you want your body in an arch. Push your belly out. Bend your back up. You might flip around a little, at first. Hold your arms up at ninety degrees with your palms flat, like you're doing a little push-up. You'll fall into position. You want to be facing the ground. Once you're in position, glance at your altimeter. Keep your knees apart, bent slightly. Arch back, arms up, knees bent. Got it?"

I could feel it comin' in the air tonight. Oh, Lord.

"Roger that."

I moved the little foam-covered mic closer to my mouth. "You ever do return flights on credit?"

He chuckled. "Having regrets? Want to turn around?"

"No. Just asking."

"Maybe, if we have a guest with VIP status. Someone we know or someone who shows us some credentials."

"I don't even have a California driver's license, at the moment."

"They're sending you in completely dark? That's rough."

The guy must've assumed any civilian-looking person dropping into prime pot growing country was a federal agent or an informant. Though apparently, I didn't appear to be a Very Important one.

Without a return flight, I'd have to bushwhack my way down to the nearest road. Hitchhike back. I'd tried to prepare for this. But a children's academy is no place to find a machete. Looking through the maintenance closet for something to slash through the salal and greasewood undergrowth, I'd grabbed a pair of small pruning shears.

What would I have been sent in with, if I were a real federal agent?

With that question in mind, the pink backpack with flying ponies I'd brought from Daybreak's lost and found took on the qualities of classical Japanese painting. What was absent became more meaningful than what was present.

No weapons. No food. No communications equipment.

Along with the pruning shears, I carried only water, a raincoat, and a small, handheld video camera from our tech lab that still had some kid's recording of a banana slug dropping from a leaf to the ground on a glistening skein of slime.

No compass. Not even a flashlight.

After about thirty minutes of wakening to my stupidity, the voice of Genesis spoke in my ear. "Approaching drop zone, sixty seconds. Headphones off, helmet on. Take your position. Wait for a thumbs-up."

"Thumbs-up means looks good?"

"I can't tell how anything looks through this fog. Thumbs-up means drop your ass out if you want a prayer of landing near the coordinates you gave me."

"Why can't we drop below the fog before I jump?"

"Mortar rounds. I don't want anybody with antiaircraft getting eyes on this bird."

"Antiaircraft? How often does that happen?"

"Not as much as it did in the '90s." As though that settled anything. "Twenty seconds," he added.

I took the headset off, put the helmet back on. The cabin was so small, I couldn't stand all the way up. I grabbed a bar over the doorway on what would be called the passenger's side of a car. I had no idea what it was called in here.

Clouds rippled below us.

I moved one hand to a metal grip low in the doorway, released the bar over my head, and took a breath like I was about to go underwater. I sat down and dangled my legs over the edge. The flying pony pack bulged in front of me like a stage-prop belly, its straps looped over the straps of the chute kit on my back. I exhaled slowly. Used one hand to push the school backpack straps higher up my shoulders, against my neck, so they wouldn't cover the emergency pull.

The pilot glanced at his instruments, then held up a hand with four fingers. Three fingers. Two. One. Thumbs-up.

I leaned forward, one hand around the little handle in the doorway, the other squeezing the edge of the chopper. They wouldn't release.

I leaned further, slid off the edge, and dangled from that flimsy handle. The pilot frantically waved an arm to get me to let go. I felt the bird tilt toward me.

I must've let go then. I was falling through fog.

CHAPTER 33

HOW DO YOU mark time inside a cloud? Count Mississippis? Heartbeats?

Then I was through it, spinning. The dim earth wheeled in and out of view. Head up. Arch back. Hands are where? Up. Flat. Knees? Apart. Bent. Arch!

The ground snapped into place, below me. A ripple of forest surrounded a gray patch of clear-cut. I seemed to hang motionless as the clear-cut came at me.

A shoe must have fallen off when I went airborne. I felt the air pulling against my right sock. I reached back, which felt like pushing through syrup, to tug the sock on tighter. As my hand met my ankle, I flipped sideways, started spinning again.

Arms out. Palms flat. Knees apart. Legs bent. Arch. There you are again, Earth. There you are. Okay. Whether the sock stayed on or got ripped away was not my call. I had to stay in position.

My cheeks flapped around, turning my face into putty.

I glanced at my right wrist: 7,800 feet.

I looked back down again.

With nothing to do but fall, a spontaneous euphoria rushed through me. A pure feeling of release.

The flesh on my face stopped flapping around as I held the skin in place with an enormous grin.

Another altitude check: 6,500. Puzzlement replaced euphoria. Was I supposed to pull the chute at 5,500? At 5,000? Yes, that was the number in big black letters on my hand.

My brain gave back my hearing then. The tactile and visual senses had been so consuming, I hadn't heard the wind. Inside my helmet, it sounded like the roar of steam from a vast pressure valve about to blow. Instead of a constant, the sound was alive with rips, pulses, microgasps. None of the wind's netting held.

I felt like crying now but kept grinning, to keep my face still. Fifty-eight hundred. Fifty-six. Fifty-two. I had to answer the air. Cling to its rapid serrations.

I had to pull the handle. Where was it? There. At the small of my back, on the right side. A smooth piece of plastic, a little longer than a toy egg. I yanked it forward.

The chute rattled out. Then came an enormous smack, as air filled it. Five thousand ninety feet. I clutched the guylines. I was over the edge of the clear-cut, facing away from the middle of it, where I thought I'd land. I had a tiny breeze in my face. I hoped it would be enough to push me back into the center of the clear-cut.

I tugged the left guy to turn around, so I could see where I was going. I didn't release it soon enough and went into a lazy 360 spiral. I passed over the center of the clear-cut while an imperceptible hand pushed me gently on. I needed to drop fast or I'd miss the clearing and land in the forest canopy.

I grabbed all the lines I could fit in each hand. I pulled, sweating inside my suit. The lines barely gave. This seemed impossible. I wasn't dropping fast enough. I grit my teeth, pulled harder, at the limit of my strength.

There had to be some type of rigging that made these lines workable. Where was it?

I'd been so obsessed with looking down, I hadn't looked up until then. Only about a foot and a half above my head was a mat of loosely woven pieces of webbing that connected all of the guylines. In the middle of the mat hung a red cord with four inches of play, a plastic red toggle on the end of it. I reached up with both hands and yanked. The chute became a long, conical banner. I fell.

The suddenness of the drop scared me so much I pulled my hands even closer to my body in a moment's instinct, which made me hurtle down faster before I released the red toggle. The canopy billowed over me again. The ground slowed its oncoming menace.

I was still being pushed backward over the clear-cut. In forty yards I'd get pushed over the upslope edge of it.

I pulled the red toggle, gently this time, slowly applying more pressure until I was a few feet above the tallest stumps, twelve feet off the ground. Then I let the red line up to slow my drop. A gust lifted me about fifteen feet. I twisted my head to see behind me. Twenty yards of clear-cut left.

I pulled down on the toggle again. After a few seconds, I grazed the top of a stump with my toes. I tugged harder, dancing tiptoe to stay on the stump. The canopy's dying momentum pulled me off backward. I crashed into the scrub brush that had grown around the stump, landing in a tangle of manzanita thorns and mahogany branches.

I lay on my back, limbs enmeshed with woody stems. The pink kiddie pack settled under my chin. The earth greeted me with stunned silence.

I disentangled an arm, pushed the pack away from my throat. I waited. Tried to hear my way around before moving anything else.

No propeller blades. No mortar fire.

It took a lot of energy to breathe. My mind seemed whited-out. I kept at the job of breathing until I heard, from the woods behind my head, a lilting call here, a rustle of branches there. Eventually, the songs of far-off chorus frogs pleated the air. Crickets started chirping to each other in the clear-cut.

As the sounds of nocturnal life resumed, fragments of my mind managed to knit themselves back into something like rational thought. I had to get moving.

I thrashed my way out of the brush, landed face down on top of the pink pack. I pushed myself up to a kneel. I slipped the backpack off my front, shook the jump kit off my back.

The parachute lay in a rumple, the guylines tangled in the branches of the bush where I'd landed.

Shit. I'd thought I could repack the chute and sell the kit when I got back to town. Start repaying the school, or make a back mortgage payment, or hire a tutor to get Jaral on track to graduate in time. But it would take me at least an hour to untangle.

Screw it. One less thing to carry.

I pulled off the jumpsuit, wadded it into the mostly empty ponies pack. Although my lower back felt sore where I'd hit an especially knobby branch when I'd landed, the ripstop nylon had kept me from getting scratched up.

At least that part of my 10K bundle I might be able to use, if I needed a wind or waterproof layer. But I couldn't hike in the jumpsuit. There was no sneaking around in the swishy fabric.

The head of the ridge rose two hundred yards above me. Yori said the area called "Presidio" began on the other side. I shouldered the child's-sized pack and limped upslope, sock-foot, shoe-foot, into the forest.

CHAPTER

34

IN A REDWOOD forest at night, there are smells like my mother's Cote D'Azur Avon Body Splash mixed with rainwater sluiced off roofs and a used-up tin of tobacco. Smells like the feel on your tongue when a lady in a TV commercial rips a rinsed head of lettuce in half and droplets fly everywhere. Spice smells, root smells, cardamom and carrots. Underneath it all, a waft of some mulled elixir, heated and hidden beneath the damp.

It was one of the two things I loved about her. My mother. Her Avon scent, and then her Vasque Sundowner leather hiking boots. When she disappeared, I put the hikers on and wouldn't take them off except to shower. For seven entire weeks. At night, their weight kept me on my bed so I wouldn't wander too far away from her in a dream and miss the moment she came back in the door.

I was twelve years old, already her height—five foot five—with feet a full size bigger than hers. The stiff shoe leather pushed my toes into an anguished crimp.

When the flow of cops through our house started to recede after the first month, my father poured her perfume into the toilet. One of the cops had said, "We have to consider she just might not want to be found, sir." So the boots were all I had.

But after another three weeks, my dad, who had never said an angry word to me, hissed, "Take those goddamn things off. I never want to see them again."

I buried them in our backyard that day.

As painful as those old Vasques were, what I wouldn't have given for the pair of them that night, limping by thin new-moon light toward I had no idea what. I was used to the woods offering welcome. But in the dark, with the sudden memory of my mother drifting around me like shrouds of fog, the forest felt closed to me, heavy with menace.

When I got to the edge of the clear-cut, I heard a sound in the woods just beyond me. I was shaking. I shook harder when I saw wet eyes watching me, heard a snort. Then an explosion of leaves. It was gone.

A deer.

They say animals, humans included, have a sixth sense about when they're being watched.

My "someone's watching" sensor had gone haywire. After the deer took off, I felt the gaze of an entire forest needle my skin.

A nearby screech startled me, the same sound as my ringtone for Jaral, although my phone wasn't with me.

It was the call of a barn owl. Normally my favorite bird, for its unforgettable heart-shaped face.

But alone at night in the woods, hearing its screech just made me shudder.

Anger at my own helplessness grew in me.

At first, I thought the new sound, a low growl, came from my throat.

I stared into the branches of a maple tree behind me. My eyes had adjusted to the night, but I could only make out shapeless gradations of inky dark behind the leaves. It could have been a wolverine or fisher, the big weasels that lived in trees. But I didn't want to chance being followed by a mountain lion. I tried to appear larger by holding the backpack over my head. I ran at the tree, yelling and swinging the pack around.

A tawny cat about the size of an Afghan hound dropped to the ground. It loped casually away, not glancing back at me. It melted into the shadows after about ten yards.

I doubted that it meant to leave me alone. But I couldn't go through the forest clapping my hands, baying at shadows. Not if I meant to sneak up on whatever or whoever I could find at the Presidio.

Danger ahead, danger behind. Nothing to do but press on up the ridge.

My gratitude list: Two unbroken legs. One shoe.

I followed a deer path that cut a long angle up the ridge. Mud caked onto my shoeless sock, building something like a sticky sole onto the bottom of it.

The ridgeline was so heavily forested, I didn't know when I had actually come to the crest until I noticed I'd started walking downhill, instead of up.

The path led to the crenellated, exposed base of a fallen giant, then it followed along the length of the massive trunk. The grove on this side was older, more varied, than the even-aged stands I'd walked through. I saw split redwoods scarred black by lightning. Redwoods partially fallen against neighboring trees, still bearing leaves. Soldier-straight trees with bark that corkscrewed up to daring heights before even the lowest branches jutted out.

The major growers were said to love old growth, because the height of the canopy rendered their operations nearly invisible from the air. But the only thing moving on the ground in this grove, besides me, seemed to be an occasional spider, picking its way around the duff in a hurry.

I walked another hour. It was harder to find game paths on this side of the slope. I'd start, then lose, a faint trail. Most of the time I pushed or garden-clippered my way downhill through the undergrowth.

Some of the blackness started to fade to indigo in the eastern sky.

Mornings on the north coast start with something too muted to be called a sunrise. Rather than fire and rays, daytime just slowly seeps in.

I wasn't ready. I had no idea where I was. Was I even close? I had "lost hiker" as a cover, but I sure didn't mean to method-act it by getting lost. I'd wanted to get a look at this place, whatever it was, before daylight, so I could figure out how I might get into or through it. But now I might come onto it after the day had already begun, after the people there, whoever they were, started moving around. The odds of someone running into me or hearing me coming got stronger every minute the day came on.

A cry started up that seemed to rise from everywhere in the forest at once. As the first sound faded, a new cry came up. It repeated again and again. I'd heard this once before in the mountains of Colorado. The gravelly snarl at the start of each howl meant a large, wild feline. A mountain lion in heat, screaming for a mate. Maybe the same cat I'd chased off its perch in the maple.

The burst of yowls had the same pulse as the recordings some young couples play to soothe their newborns, a relentless in-utero heartbeat rhythm.

Rrow, rrow, rrow. Rrow rrow rrow rrow.

The volume was staggering. The misty air itself seemed filled with the fierce reach of this one voice. I crouched behind a mountain mulberry bush. I couldn't think. The muscles in my neck ached with tension. I gave my head a painful turn to the left, then to the right, trying to hear where the calls came from.

As best I could tell, the driving beat of caterwauls came from somewhere upslope. I waddled around in my crouch to face that direction.

My capacity for rational thought crept back out of the bramble of lizard ganglia at the base of my skull. This couldn't have been hunting behavior. There was nothing stealthy about these calls. This wasn't hunting, and I wasn't a target.

The predawn dimness continued to slowly brighten. I had to keep moving.

Against my every primate instinct, I stood. Turned my back on the yowling. Continued downslope on the deer path I'd been following.

Three more screams. Then nothing.

My uneven feet crunched dead evergreen needles. My denim pantlegs scuffed each other as I walked. The rest of the mountain held still.

A few minutes later, I came to a clearing with a low concrete building in the center. The structure had no windows. A small satellite dish perched on the roof.

I stood sidewise behind an ash trunk in a cluster of young hardwoods that had grown in front of some redwood giants at the edge of the clearing, watching the building as though it might move.

Across from where I stood, a gray flying squirrel made a graceful, diagonal glide down from one tree to the next. It slipped on the branch where it landed, scrambling for a grip to ride out the rebound sway. Jaral had always wanted to see a flying squirrel. Too bad I didn't have the camera going yet, to catch when it "flew." We could have laughed together over the comical landing.

Once again, the forest had rinsed anger from me, this time with the cold rain of my own mortality.

I glanced at the altimeter still buckled to my wrist. I'd gone up five hundred feet on the south-facing slope where I'd landed and descended another thousand feet on the other side. This put me squarely in the place code-named "Presidio."

The backpack zipper purred as I tugged the pull down slowly. I took out the shears, stuck them in my back pocket, removed the small camcorder, wedged the pack in the underbrush.

I walked around the building, twisted the handle on a beige metal door. It opened easily. I slipped inside.

The building was completely dark. I patted the wall next to me, flipped on a light switch. I stood in a long room with nubby institutional carpet. Standard office cubicles divided the space. Each cubicle held a desk with a headset for making calls attached to a computer with a tennis ball–sized webcam mounted on the monitor. The room appeared uninhabited. I heard faint voices. Female voices. Singing. My skin prickled.

Then I realized the sound came from outside the structure. I turned the light off, pushed the door open. I couldn't see anyone outside. The predawn light painted everything in its gray wash. I waited. The singing seemed like it was coming closer. I ran with my one-shoed gimp to the edge of the clearing and dove behind a fifteen-foot whorl of roots at the end of a downed redwood.

The sounds changed from faint notes to individual voices in a group passing through the clearing, all singing the same melody.

Female voices at dawn in a redwood forest. Had I expected something elfin? Otherworldly? Magical?

You can tell your dog to bite my leg,
Or tell your brother Cliff whose fist can tell my lip
He never really liked me anyway!

It was a country song from the early '90s. By the time the chorus started up, I was crawling forward on my elbows, palm-sized video camera strapped to one hand, recording, even though I still couldn't see anyone.

But don't tell my heart, my achy breaky heart,
I just don't think he'd understand.
And if you tell my heart, my achy breaky heart,
He might blow up and kill this man!

I hoped the mic was good enough to be picking up what I was hearing. The voices sounded young. I saw movement on the other side of the clearing, from the direction of the singing. A small trail I hadn't seen before led away into the woods. It sounded like this group of young women, or girls, had headed down this trail. I could still hear them.

The singing ended with soft conversation in a language I didn't recognize, punctuated by chuckles and grunts.

I walked around the clearing as quietly as I could, half crouching. When I came to the narrow trail, I walked in a pattern my mother taught me to stalk wildlife. Toe-heel, toe-heel. The trail led downslope away from the concrete building. It sounded like they'd stopped less than a hundred yards away from the hardwood stand where I'd first surveyed the area.

I crouched behind salmonberry bushes to listen. "We must speak just English," one of the voices said. "You don't know where they have microphones. Mr. and Mrs. will punish you if they hear."

"But I had one last night who wanted me to speak Somali," another voice said. "'Just a few words, please, please,' he said. I told him I'm in school to learn English and I can't talk my language, even in my room. But I wanted to tell him . . ." she finished off in the other language. I heard a few giggles in response.

The first voice spoke again, louder this time. "Do not toy with Mr. and Mrs.! They bring us here where we're safe. You'd be some Saudi's whore right now if they hadn't rescued you from Dadaab! Be grateful and complete your mission. Then you can go live on your own and speak how you want."

"Our mission!" said a third voice. "I don't even know what it's for. It started out like just having these video chats with Somali boys here in America, maybe showing them our hair or our bare arms, if they wanted to see. But that's all they see, and then what, we never talk to them again? Mr. and Mrs. just get their names, and I don't know what happens to them, after that. Some of them are really sweet. I don't want them to be getting hurt. And now American boys are finding us, and if they don't say gross things, which Mr. and Mrs. cut them off for, anyway, but if they don't start saying gross things, they start saying love, love, love to us, all achy breaky hearts!"

A little bit of laughter followed, then a pause.

"You know that music is in me like poison." This came from a new, brash young woman's voice, in the same accent as the others.

"It's only poison if you let it be," another young woman, or girl's, voice answered. "Try to clean it out of your head with some other song. Or a prayer."

A third voice said, "Mrs. Gwen says she plays this American music all night with the lights on to soften us up, so we'll answer her questions. But we don't have any answers! We want to know where Khadra is too!"

The first voice came back: "All night for three nights! I cannot survive a fourth." She said something else, but I only caught the words "little one."

All three voices, I realized, spoke with what I thought of as Kenyan accents to their English, with some r's rolled, others rounded off into breath as in British English.

Along with their voices, I heard what sounded like yard work. The plunk of a trowel wedged into the earth, the rip of weeds being dug up by the roots. The sha-shunk of a wheelbarrow pushed over the ground. And other female voices, talking quietly.

Finally, at the end of a long slide forward, I could see where the voices came from.

Inside a six-foot-high chain-link fence, about a dozen girls worked a square vegetable garden with raised beds.

The youngest looked like she might not even be thirteen. The oldest could've been around eighteen. Most of them had an openness in their faces that made them seem closer to fifteen or sixteen.

They all wore overalls and hijabs. All were pregnant.

I belly-crawled through the brush, to where I was only a few feet from the garden. I nudged the camera out from between some branches and kept recording.

CHAPTER 35

A TALL GIRL STARTED to thwack a weeding tool in a slow beat on the edge of a wheelbarrow. She sang something gentle that I couldn't understand, then quadrupled the beat and started chanting in English.

Don't tell my heart!
Don't tell my arm!
Don't tell my foot or my leg, heh!

Don't tell my bones!
Wherever Khadra's gone!
None of us can say a single thing, heh!

She kept drumming on the wheelbarrow until a girl who looked earlier in her pregnancy, more energetic than the others, stepped one foot across a row of lettuce and stomped a few dance steps straddling the row, before doubling over laughing into a head of leaves.

"That's the best country music," the dancer said, when she pushed herself back up. "Buraanbur, sung by our very own poet."

A few other girls clapped the beat that the drummer had stopped, but no one else got up to dance. I was too busy straining to see if any of them had a four-petaled birthmark blooming near her right eye to notice exactly when the clapping stopped and they all went back to work.

I counted eleven girls in the garden enclosure, with skin colors ranging from toasty cinnamon to deep cacao. Some tried to work fast, others seemed to struggle with their movements, as though fighting their way through resin.

"You can tell the rain," a different girl sang out. "Our Mister is a pain. I think we will never sleep again."

Big, confident laughs rang out from a couple of the girls. Those with heaviness in their limbs as though gravity itself exhausted them showed appreciation with breathy, small laughs.

A petite girl, working a hand rake around a mat of strawberries, yelled out, "Go tell your friend Nabil. Exactly how you feel. He won't be logging in again."

Another girl started in, softly: "You can tell your baby and her feet."

That quieted everyone for a second.

The bossy girl who'd warned everyone to speak only English broke the silence. "That one's stupid. Try another one."

A few girls threw in more made-up lyrics, but most had bent their faces back down to their work. They all seemed to be working faster, with a little more intensity.

Not one girl stopped to lay a hand on top of her belly or to comment on her baby kicking.

After a few minutes, the mom-to-be with the biggest baby bump sat back on her heels.

"Oh." She dropped her arms to her sides.

"Ohhh." She squeezed her eyes shut.

The other girls stopped what they were doing. The groaning girl's arms hung at her sides, hands in fists.

"No," she said, sensing the stillness around her with her eyes still closed. "No, no, it's fine, it's fine."

Nobody moved.

A grimace passed over her face, then she gulped a breath, opened her eyes.

"It's fine," she said again. She raised her eyebrows as though she'd asked a question to which she expected an answer, then dropped forward onto her hands. She continued weeding.

The girls went back to work, some trimming dead leaves off plants, others roving through rows to pick off caterpillars.

The area was completely fenced off with tall chain link, which must have kept out the deer and elk that live in the backcountry.

I lay on my stomach. My chin rested on top of one flattened hand. I felt the rise and fall of my chest against the ground. I watched the scene on the two-and-a-half-inch screen that popped out from the side of the camcorder, a red circle flashing in the corner of the view field to confirm I was still recording.

Usually, when I see pregnant women, I feel inferior. They are actually going to be birth mothers. I gave my kid advice, nagging, and cold breakfast cereal, but they gave minerals from their bones.

But these were not pregnant women. These were pregnant girls. What I felt watching them was completely maternal.

You tender dears. You fragile darlings.

The girl who had previously endured a contraction now pushed a wheelbarrow of chicken manure. The stubborn front wheel didn't move well in the damp ground between beds. She had to wrangle the thing right, then left, pull it back, shove it forward, for each few inches of progress.

In the middle of the row closest to me, she stopped, looked around. A shovel leaned against the fence a few yards from my face.

"Huh, nuh, la-la-la" she crooned, wordlessly repeating the melody they'd all sung. She walked toward the shovel. I watched her eyes scan the forest behind me in an unfocused sweep. A big Steller's jay screeched above me.

The girl's gaze swept over the brush, roving past my face. Then her head twitched. She snapped her focus back to me. We locked eyes.

"La-nah-laaaa—"

I put a finger to my lips. With my other hand, I slowly pushed the camcorder away.

Had she seen it? If so, my lost hiker cover story would never hold. There was no universe where innocent outdoor enthusiasts crawled through the bushes with fifteen-year-old documentary technology in one of the world's most notorious illegal marijuana-growing regions to simply record nature's marvels.

The girl walked toward me. Then she grabbed the shovel, turned back toward the rows. She started singing at the top of her lungs.

"Don't tell my heart! My achy breaky heart!" She spread fertilizer over a bed of tomato plants, singing the whole time. A few of the girls glanced up. The girl who had seen me worked her way backward through the tomato bed, which brought her closer to me again.

The smallest girl checked a watch on her wrist. Something I hadn't seen a teenager wear for at least ten years.

"Time to go make our calls! Then we will get breakfast," she said loudly, her voice strained. "Don't leave any tools in the dirt. Let's go!" She dropped her hand rake into a bucket that lay under a little tin awning tied to one section of fence. Then she left through a gate in the far end of the fence.

A few girls groaned. The girl in front of me said, "In a minute. I need to finish turning the beds. Go, go."

The other girls didn't seem particularly energetic about it, but each in her own time returned her tools to buckets under the awning and left, taking the path I'd just come up.

The last one to leave called over her shoulder at the girl dawdling near me, "Remember the gate, Amina."

"Sure," the girl in front of me said, swirling the back of her shovel around on the ground listlessly.

One came back because she had forgotten to put her kneeling pad away. Another returned because she had left a handful of weeds on the ground that she'd meant to drop on a compost pile just past the enclosure.

"The gate, remember the gate," each girl said, as she left, again.

The one named Amina spread what remained of her wheelbarrow's contents in a sloppy layer through a bed of corn.

For a few minutes, girls could be heard talking to each other as they moved down the path toward the clearing with the concrete building. When they'd gone, only the nattering of a Douglas squirrel and the patter of a nearby stream broke the silence.

The one called Amina, who'd stayed, parked her empty wheelbarrow in a corner near the gate. She placed the shovel in a rubber trash bin with other long-handled tools, then removed a hoe with a bright silver blade. She gripped the hoe high up on the handle with one hand, closed the gate latch behind her with the other.

Outside the enclosure, she moved around the perimeter of the fence toward me.

Even though I knew she'd already seen me, I tried to become still as stone. A mosquito strolled from my eyebrow to my temple. I surrendered blood without a flinch.

The girl stopped directly across the stream, about two feet from my head. She leaned forward with the blade of her tool pointing toward me.

"You that wild cat?"

The question unfroze me. I rolled on my side to look up at her.

"Am I dreaming you, wild cat person? Are you the one making so much screams? I don't sleep any for three nights. I am so tired, maybe dreaming. Maybe you're not here, but I see you. Say something."

I pushed up to a sitting position, unsure how to steer the conversation from "you that wild cat" to "who killed Armando Peregrino."

"You don't speak? You can't talk? Only scream?"

"I . . . I'm lost." My voice cracked.

Amina straightened up.

"So dumb. This is a dumb dream." She started to turn back around.

I cleared my throat.

"I'm looking for someone."

Amina faced me, eyes glazed.

"Where is she? Who can tell me where she is?" she murmured, as though in a trance.

This scared me more than the metal tool, now resting on her shoulder.

"Who can tell?" I said softly, trying to match Amina's tone. "Who can tell me where she is? Amina?"

Hearing her name, the girl shivered like she'd been hit by an electric current.

The hoe came down fast.

I shrank into a ball. The blade barely missed me, clanking off a cobble at the edge of the water. I scrambled to stand as she lifted the handle again.

"Don't say these words. Don't say 'Where is she, who can tell.' You don't say these words in this dream."

She shook the flat end of the blade at me. A dull fire lit her eyes.

"You help, or just disappear. Only reason for you to be in this dream. Help."

I patted one hand above my heart, raised the other above my face as a shield. "I'm not a dream. I'm real."

She considered this. I rushed on.

"I need to find a girl. You're Somali, right? She's a beautiful Somali girl, like you. She has a spot on her face that looks like four little leaves." I pressed four fingertips to the corner of my right eye. "Here."

The girl dropped her tool. She stepped back quickly, tripped over a small log, fell on her side.

She said something, but I couldn't hear what it was.

I slipped over stones in the stream to reach her.

"You okay? Amina? Are you okay?"

She propped herself up on one arm. She said something again, this time more clearly.

"Khadra."

I stood over her in an awkward straddle, my pantlegs dripping. I hauled her to a seated position by her overall straps. When I let go, she fell back, heavy with the weight of someone falling for two. The hypnotized expression had returned to her face.

The sight of a pregnant girl out of her mind disturbed me in a primal way. It seemed like the existence of everything hinged on whether I could bring this little mother back to her senses, up on her feet.

I repeated the name she'd uttered, hoping to call back her receding attention. "You said 'Khadra.' Why did you say that name?"

Then I tried this girl's own name. "Amina?" No reaction.

I crouched in front of her, draped her free arm over my shoulder, hooked my hands under her arms.

"Can you stand?" I strained to rise. She leaned into me for a moment, grunted, then grabbed my arms. She stood as I pulled her upright.

I felt such relief I thought I might collapse back down.

The girl stood in front of me, still gripping my arms. She looked exhausted.

"Are you hurt?" I asked. An aroma like damp wood shavings and incense wafted off her. The scent prickled with familiarity and foreignness.

"Where is Khadra?" she asked. "You find her? You help? Or, no, no, please no, you work for Mrs. Gwen."

"Who is Mrs. Gwen? Is that your doctor? Will she come when you deliver your baby?"

"Gwen is no doctor. The doctor is only here sometimes. Gwen lives here. But she's not here now. She is looking for Khadra. Where is Khadra? Why don't you find her?"

She shook my shoulders. Her voice rose.

"You have Khadra? Where is she? Where?"

"Who . . ." I started to ask again.

Suddenly the girl crossed her arms over her chest and tucked her chin down as though drawing into a shell. She rolled her eyes up to meet mine. This time, her voice came out small, reedy.

"You take me!" Her lips barely moved as she spoke. "You take me too! Please!"

Then her eyes raised to something just past my shoulder. I heard the crack of a branch behind me but didn't turn around in time.

CHAPTER

36

"DON'T MOVE, HONEY. I don't want to shoot you." A man's voice came from directly across the stream behind me.

"Do! Not! Move!" the voice repeated. "Come on! Why would you go for your back pocket? How do you think that looks to me?" I'd only made the tiniest twitch in that direction.

The voice gave a theatrical sigh. "Put your hands up, then, if you don't know what to do with them. Don't you watch cop shows?"

I lifted my hands.

"Good. What brings you here, sugar? Lost? You need food?" I heard him cross the stream. "I'll get you fixed up and on your way. You just tell me what you need."

A hand patted around my waist and along the rise of my butt.

"Ah, boy. What's this? A Leatherman tool?"

He flipped up my shirt, pulled the pruning shears out of my back pocket.

"Oh, so you're a trimmer, huh? That's odd. Harvest isn't 'til September. What's your name, sugar?"

Based on where his voice came from, he sounded like he had several inches on me.

"Yeah, I'm out here, um . . ."

Amina moved so that I blocked her from the man behind me. She caught my eye and mouthed a single word:

"Run."

"I hurt my foot." I held Amina's gaze while pitching the words over my shoulder. "Let me show you."

I lifted my shoeless foot, peeled off the muddy sock. "Right here." I pointed to my pale, pruney toes, wadded up the sock, lobbed it behind me. "Oops!"

I spun around as the man's gaze flicked up for an instant to follow the sock. He had a pistol lazily raised toward me.

Time slowed to the pace of droplets forming out of fog. Each moment had to bud. Then swell. Before falling into existence.

I grabbed the gun wrist and pulled down as a shot blew open a hole in the dirt.

The man tried to pull his arm away, but I hung on. He threw a punch at my head with his free hand. I ducked into a crouch and yanked down on the gun arm with all my strength. The man fell over the top of my back, shoving with his other arm and breaking my grip as he dropped.

"You bitch!" He sat up and switched the gun to his other hand. The arm I'd pulled hung lifeless. He struggled to push himself up.

I scrambled to my feet and saw Amina, wide-eyed, backing away into the trees.

"Where's Khadra?" she called to me, before disappearing.

I ran into the woods in the other direction. Four more shots rang out.

The rage spring-loaded in me since childhood had saved my life. I had enough violent energy at the ready to pull a man's arm from its socket. I needed to ride the adrenaline wave for one last push to reach a hideout I'd spotted twenty feet high.

A lightning scar opened into a dark cavern in a redwood trunk above me. Nearby, a big buckeye drooped close to the opening. I hauled myself into the buckeye and wriggled out on the branch. The branch bowed and bobbed under me. I heard brush moving near the clearing, but not the crash someone giving chase would make. I couldn't see the man or Amina.

The lightning scar was close enough that I wouldn't have to jump for it. I'd just have to get my feet under me, tip myself forward, and reach.

In the growing light of day, the ground seemed very far.

Someone crashed toward me through the undergrowth.

"Hey, stranger," the man's voice called. "Get out here! You dislocate my fucking arm, and now you think you're tough? Who's got the gun, sweetie?" Another shot.

"Hey, I know we had a bad start. Soon as I see you I'll stop shooting. If I gotta chase you, different story."

I heard him take a few more steps, then call again, his voice slightly more distant, as though he'd faced away from me.

"Amina! You better get inside. Where it's safe." The way he projected his voice, I could tell he didn't know where she was.

"Goddammit, I am not losing another one of you. Amina?" All was quiet as he waited for a response. "Get inside and call Mrs. Gwen from the landline! Tell her we've got company!"

He resumed moving toward me.

I crouched next to the trunk. None of my fingers would unpeel from the branches they held. The shiver of vegetation around the man showed his path. His angle would pass ten yards away. Then he cut right.

Dead on to me.

I threw myself at the hole in the redwood. One hand caught the edge, and the force of my drop nearly ripped my fingers off. I pedaled my feet against the trunk, flailing for a second handhold. I could only get traction on the spongy bark with my bare foot. I used my toes to pry off my remaining shoe and sock, then clambered up and over the lip of the lightning scar.

CHAPTER

37

ONCE INSIDE THE trunk, I still couldn't let go of the charred edge of the scar. The drop inside the tree fell away deeper than I'd imagined. Inky dark beyond my dangling feet.

Luckily, the lightning hadn't burned out the entire heart of the tree. I was in a hollow about three feet wide.

I switched my hands and twisted around so I could press my back against one side of the trunk, my feet against the other. I scooted to an angle where I could see out into the forest. Somehow I'd ended up about two stories high. I was panting so loud I worried the sound would give me away.

Below me, someone crashed through the brush. Coming closer. Then moving past. The trunk's opening, now on my right, limited my view to a patch of ground about twenty feet downslope from the base of my host tree. A muddy road cut through the trees. The man stumbled into view on the road, whipped around to scan the woods. One arm hung slack, the other raised partway as though the handgun at the end of it weighed almost too much to lift.

"You won't last a day out here," he called. "Just tell me who you work for. I'll get you a hot meal. We have beans, rice, cassava. Beats starving. You'll get a ride back to town. We can forget each other after that. If you don't come out, I will hunt you. I'll kill you."

He left the road and headed back upslope, scanning the ground. From my height, I could see how thick his wheat-colored hair was. Even wet from his tumble into the stream, it rode his head like a beret.

About ten feet from the tree where I perched, he stopped. With his gun barrel, he pushed up a broken salal branch to examine it.

If he came a few steps closer, he'd find the sock and shoe I dropped. And look up.

I wanted to slide out of sight and did nothing more than think about bending my knees, when one of my feet slipped off the sooty wall.

My back started to slide down the inside of the tree. I lunged for the lip of the lightning scar and kicked at darkness under my feet, dangling from a crumbling knob of bark.

If the gunman heard anything, would he start shooting into the tree? Or would he assume it was just the rustle of a squirrel?

My legs wouldn't stop flailing.

Could he see my fingertips? If I let go and fell, I might not be able to climb out. I couldn't tell how far down the hollow section went. I could end up becoming a decomposed part of the tree.

My legs finally got the message to be still. I hung, head tilted up, hoping to catch any sounds that told me what was happening outside the tree.

The skin on one of my ears felt like it had a bad sunburn.

Above me, a few thin spots in the clouds had brightened from gray to white.

There was the sound of needles in conference with a breeze. The sound of someone moving slowly uphill, closer to my tree. Then past it.

My fingers tingled. Tree fibers jabbed under my nails. I wanted to brace my feet on the inside of the trunk and vault myself over the lip of the scar, but I couldn't do that quietly or invisibly. I hung on in case my attacker was still near.

To tamp down panic, I ran through what I had just seen, before the man with the gun had shown up. These girls. Working together to obey someone but keeping secrets for themselves too. All of them pregnant. The strange way the one called "Amina" had spoken, like she was drugged or dazed.

What were they doing out here in the north woods? Were they forced to live here? Forced to work? Forced to work like . . .

With the thought of the word "slaves," I flashed on a memory that almost made me lose my grip on the tree. A description of a type of torture meted out during slavery in America, something I'd read, had been exactly how I'd seen Armando tied. Did that explain the horror of recognition I felt when I saw him? Or had it been something else?

I wished I could ask one of the girls here if they'd seen Armando. Living. If they knew him. But they were long gone down the trail now. My hands burned with the strain of holding on.

And just like that, Jaral's voice came to mind, a time he'd talked to me about my fear of heights. This was a year ago, maybe two. "My bio mom said facing a fear makes us tough."

"Sometimes facing a fear just makes us jelly-legged," I said.

He'd liked that, laughed, and did an imitation of me walking across a rope bridge like a wobbly drunk. We were in another north coast forest, had just crossed over a stream that wasn't even that far down, ten feet, maybe.

Then he sat down on a rock and lifted his acoustic air guitar.

"Are you strong enough to be my moooms . . ."

"Sheryl Crow? I don't think that's an '80s song."

"Would you be moms enough to be my moms?"

We hit the chorus together. "Lie to me, I promise I'll believe. Lie to me, but please don't leave."

I was not going to leave Jaral by dying in this tree. Time to kick my way up and out.

I shimmied my feet up the wall of the hollow until I was in a vertical crouch, feet up next to my hands. I pushed and clawed and heaved into a belly flop across the edge of the scar, half in the trunk, half out.

From a nearby tree a Douglas squirrel machine-gunned its scolding call.

No assassin to the right. None to the left. I had to escape before the man came back with a bigger weapon. Or with others to help him find me.

It'd be slow going climbing down the buckeye. I opted instead for an awkward flying squirrel leap at the top of a springy young hemlock. The tree obligingly bent forward with my momentum. A few feet from the ground, I let go and fell on my back. The tree righted with a diffident shiver.

I got up, wiped ash-covered palms on my pantlegs, fished my shoe and sock from a spiny huckleberry, put the shoe on one foot, the sock on the other and ran away from the road. I needed to stay out of sight, away from anywhere that man, or one of his people, could take a shot at me. The time on the wrist altimeter gave me two hours until my kid's arraignment. One hour fifty-nine minutes. Fifty-eight. Fifty-seven. It felt like I wore a detonator.

In a gully a quarter mile downslope, treetops changed from redwood and cedar to bay and laurel. There must be water down there. If what I'd seen on Yori's map was right, I could follow it down to the coast highway, hitchhike back to town.

As I ran toward the gully, I grasped at dashes of thought, scraps of sensation, to keep my mind off the stones and cones bruising my shoeless foot.

I'd come into the woods so hopeful. But I hadn't gotten anything I could make any sense of. I came in desperate and was leaving desperate. A spotted owl's two-note hoot trailed me for a while. It used to mean the forest was vulnerable. Something in need of saving still lived there. At this point, I had no idea what it meant. I couldn't read anything. All the world's signs had become a foreign tongue I couldn't decode. Tiny cracked eggs under a tree. Ferns reaching their soft fingers out, the wooden fan of buckeye branches. Mist and fog, heavy, seeming permanent, even as it began, imperceptibly, to clear. One orb of fog suspended, perfectly still as I ran beneath it. My heart pounded and my breath heaved.

The only reason I didn't turn salamander, curl in the dirt under a log to rest, was that Jaral would be brought before a stranger who would begin the process of adjudicating him. Was he a threat. Need he be caged. He would face a biased justice system, but he would not face it alone. I ran on.

The gully held a silver stream with game trails alongside it. I bullied through salal and willow, squished along mossy cobbles, not trying to be quiet. Just trying to be fast. Hot spots that would soon be blisters grew where my one shoe rubbed my Achilles. My other foot slammed the ground with nothing but a bunchy, damp sock for protection.

Yori was right to tell me I couldn't have walked up this roadless side of The Hill. It was so steep, I would've had to catch my breath every fifty yards, and who knows how long that would've taken. Every minute Jaral was in jail was a minute too long. Becoming a literal helicopter mom had been my only hope for getting answers as quickly as possible.

But coming down was a different matter. Gravity supported my goal of getting downhill.

Still, my rip and tumble descent felt endless. Finally, the slope got less steep. The light had increased to a milky daylight. I heard what, at first, I thought was a larger river. Then I realized it was traffic. The coast highway must be ahead.

I sprinted as best I could with my one-shoe gimp. Thirty-seven minutes until the arraignment. When I burst from the trees, I saw a ten-foot drop to the shoulder of the highway. I scrambled along the edge until I came to a slope of oatgrass and brome. I tried sidestepping down at an angle, but slipped and slid down, twisting as I fell, ripping up handfuls of weeds as I grasped their thin stalks. I slid to the shoulder, scraped my hands on the asphalt. I stood up too quickly and felt dizzy, shaking from the morning chill and the scare of the fall. A car pulled off the road ahead of me. I prayed to the hidden sun that it wasn't the man who had chased me.

A middle-aged woman with long ash-blond hair got out and walked toward me.

"Are you okay? Oh honey, you're filthy. What happened?"

"Who's that?" I asked her, lifting an arm that felt twenty pounds heavy to point at the driver's seat.

"My old man." she said. "You need help? Come here."

She moved to put an arm around me and guide me to the car. I hobbled, dew damp, dirty, and spent, toward her old man's ride.

CHAPTER

38

WHEN I OPENED the back door, a fat chestnut dog with a gray muzzle raised its head, thwapped its tail twice.

A logging truck whooshed by. I got in and draped myself over the animal to hide my face from all who passed.

"Real pet lover, huh? Dogs are the damn best." A short man with thick black hair spoke from the driver's seat.

The woman had opened her passenger door but hadn't gotten in. "Let me get a first aid kit out of the back," she said. "I think we have an old one there." The car dinged to remind us all she'd left her door open.

"Hi," I said to the driver, wiping my nose with the back of my hand. The cool morning air must've made my eyes water. "Can we just get going? I mean thank you, and please can we just drive?"

"Where you headed?" he said.

"Found it!" the woman's voice came from behind the car.

She opened the rear door and squatted down next to my legs. "Let's get a look at that foot."

"No!" I pulled my sock foot away from her. Her compassionate attention would shred up time I didn't have.

"Donna, c'mon," the man said to her, gently but firmly. "She says she needs to get going."

"Oh." The woman frowned, worried. "You want to bandage that foot up yourself?" She passed me a red first aid kit. I took it without raising myself up.

"Yeah, I need to get to the county justice center."

At this invocation of an impending brush with The System, the woman's affect changed. She straightened, nodded, and got in, shutting her door quickly. I shut mine, and the man eased the car back on the road when he saw an opening.

He glided into the fast lane and revved us up to a cruising speed of ninety-one. A radar detector on the dash stayed silent as we floated over the coast highway's curves, rises, and dips. Functioning shock absorbers are true marvels of engineering.

The man and woman stuck to the Humboldt code of politeness as we drove, never asking why I'd just burst out of the woods, dirt-smeared and haggard.

People around here cherish the right to refuse to explain themselves. And thank God for that.

The driver flipped through stations while I swung back over to my seat, still in a hunch. I peeled off my exposed sock, now encased in a cold layer of mud, and started swiping alcohol wipes at scrapes where twigs and cones had pierced the sock. I couldn't help making little panting noises at each antiseptic burn. The woman turned her head.

"You okay?"

"Almost done," I said, through gritted teeth.

I finished with the antiseptic wipes, bandaged two cuts on the bottom of my foot. The woman rummaged beneath her seat, then tossed what she found onto the floorboard beside me.

"Here. Least you'll have a matching pair. They're this guy's," she patted the driver. "But he won't miss 'em, right, Hank?"

"What was that?" he asked her.

"Your drugstore flip-flops."

"Huh." Then he glanced back at me in the rearview.

"That's gen-you-wine Hoopa sportswear you got there, ma'am. A true collector's item."

I smiled at the ridiculousness of all of this, and at the easy way they took it all in stride.

"I owe you both. Seriously."

"You got ten thousand dollars?"

"Whoa. What?" Hearing the exact amount I'd shorted my school sent a bolt of guilt through me.

"Hey, relax," he said. "Get it to me in the next life. Everyone knows Indians have nine lives, like cats, huh?" He elbowed the woman.

"I might be White, but I still got wisdom. I know you only got two lives. Your then and your now. And right now, you need to slow down."

The detector on the dash had settled into a fast beep. I poked my head up. Sure enough, the next corner we came around hid a highway patrol car with a radar gun.

The man slowed to a few miles above the seventy-five mph speed limit, and we went on by. The relief that came over me towed in all the exhaustion I'd held at bay. I finished taping gauze over the cuts on my feet and flopped back over top of the dog. He grunted and gave his own nose a lick. A few locks of the woman's hair draped over the top of her seat. They swayed when she turned her head to talk to her sweetie. Their small movements were so gentle, so reassuring. My eyelids felt heavy.

Memories came loose like pieces of a sandbank collapsing into water. Jaral in the visiting area, slumped in stripes, hands twitching in that horrible tweaker way. The words that cut me: *I wish I'd never gone to the white redwood . . . All my trouble starts there.* That meant he wished I'd never adopted him. Didn't it?

The next thing I knew, I picked my own drool-slicked cheek off the dog's back as I heard the woman's voice say, "We're almost there."

"Never got your names," I said.

They made no reply.

I wiped the dog fur from my face and sat all the way up. No use hiding as we drove through the edge of Eureka. I'd have to get out of the car soon, and if someone had followed us this far, the couple would have noticed. We were clear of whoever I'd run into on The Hill. I hoped that meant I'd have a good day of progress helping Jaral, now that I was back in town.

Hope is the thing with feathers you crush when you glance at the time on your wrist altimeter.

11:48 AM. I'd missed the arraignment.

"This goddamned kid!" I pounded my seat with both fists.

"Aw, it's your pup in there?" The woman turned around to face me. "Try not to be too hard on him. I'm sure he didn't ask to be arrested, did he?"

"But he wouldn't have been in trouble's way if he'd have just stayed in school that morning. Just gone to class like all the other kids."

"Yeah, they sure do get their own ideas. We know all about that." She gave the man's shoulder a quick squeeze. "What I can tell you is it's not that bad in there. His sister used to work at the jail. Used to be a lot worse."

The man nodded, glanced at me in the mirror. "Man, it would be so cold in the winter, water coming in the walls, mold from the rain that never dried. It's a lot nicer now. Your boy will do okay on the inside if he keeps his head down. As sad as it is, it could be worse. Just try and have a little faith in him. You're his mama. Maybe mama's all he's got."

"I don't know if he wants my faith or my help or any mama at all right now. He said something so . . . something I can't get over. I need him to take it back. I just can't get past it. And you know the sad thing? I used to wish I knew where he was twenty-four/seven. And now I do."

Twitch. Jitter. *Snap. Snap. Puullll.* Jaral's hands on that shirt hem.

If I had a little more faith in Jaral, if I got over the shock of seeing him in those jail stripes, if I tried really listening to him, would it make any difference?

I wanted to talk to him again. But the next visiting hours for inmates with last names beginning with "M" weren't for another two days. Then I thought of something.

"Hey, do you think we could make it by noon? Just drop me at the side door that goes to the jail. Not the big doors for court." There was still a time window today that I could hurl myself through if I was lucky.

The car bucked over a couple of speed bumps. The radar detector kept quiet. We passed Adel's Restaurant, then the Catholic school playground around the corner from the justice center.

"Can I get you some gas money? I don't have any now. But can I get it to you? Soon?"

"We've had times like that too," said the woman. "Don't worry about it."

"Here." I took off the wrist altimeter and dangled it between them. "Take it. As a thank you. Both of you, really . . . I feel like we're connected."

"I don't think so, lady," the man said.

At 11:56, I cracked the door open while the car was still moving to park along the curb.

The man braked. The woman said, "Go, go. We don't want to be near this place anyway. Just go."

I stepped out of the car, closed the door with a quick wave and turned away. My mud-caked sock and shoe drove off with them, next to the wrist altimeter I'd laid across the floor mat. I limped down concrete steps, then yanked open the door to the CJC.

CHAPTER

39

CROSSING OVER THE justice center's tiled waves in grimy jeans and an old pair of flip flops, I felt mortified and defiant.

When I got to the front of the line at the check-in counter, a deputy on the phone registered my wild hair with a quick glance blank as a square of linoleum. He turned away from me to hang up the phone. Then he passed the clipboard sign-in sheet under the window.

I clacked the clipboard down in front of me and began to fill in the next empty row.

Name: Lucia Marez.

I used my middle name this time, in case I was banned under my own name after getting cast out of the visiting area the day before.

Time in: 11:57 AM.

Reason for visit:

I stopped at that column. Because I noticed an entry right above mine with a line through it. Under "Reason for Visit," the crossed-out entry read: Jaral Marez.

"Who is this?" I tapped the crossed-out visitor's name: Gwen Cates.

Lino-face glanced at the clipboard. "I can't discuss other visitors."

"Why was she here?" I said to no one.

A portly White man called out from one of the blue plastic chairs. "Maybe a public defender. What's the last name?"

"Cates."

"Naw, never mind. There's one public defender, an assistant, eight deputies. None of them's got that name."

"Gwen Cates?"

"Uh-uh."

"Ma'am, you going to fill that out? Check-in's supposed to be at a quarter til. I'm doing you a favor, here." The man behind the glass motioned to the clipboard in my hand. I finished writing out my information, duplicating the "Reason for Visit" the person on the line above me had written. She'd tried to see Jaral Marez just fifteen minutes ago.

I handed the clipboard back.

"Wrong day, ma'am," the jailer said to me.

Talking my way in on the wrong day was my whole and only plan. But I did wonder what an arm could do, angled up under the glass.

I tightened my throat with pretend feminine helplessness. "I didn't know I'm sorry but I really need to see him it won't take me very long can I please just see him I'll come on the right day next time I didn't know please officer?"

He sighed. "Give me your ID."

"It was stolen. But I'm his mother. Aren't I on some special list?"

The man waiting in a chair harrumphed at that.

"Ma'am, you'll have to come back when you have your ID. I cannot admit you without it." He crossed his arms over his chest, a light in his eyes.

Cry? Yell? Whine? Cajole? "Well . . ." I drummed my fingers on the metal counter while I tried to decide which gamble paid.

"Wait." He pulled the sign-in clipboard back toward him. "Let me check something."

He clacked the computer keys in a short burst, then turned back to me.

"Doesn't matter that you don't have your ID. Or that you're here on the wrong day." He pointed to where I'd written Jaral's name. "He's been moved to third floor. That's twenty-three-hour lockdown. No visits."

"What? Why didn't I hear about this?"

I extended the fingers of both hands into the metal tray. No more Betty Boop for this guy.

"Let me see my son!"

The deputy's hair, I noticed, must have been recently dyed. His scalp had muddy smears along the part. Not very committed to his role in our drama, he straightened a set of papers off to the side. "Try again in a week. He'll be evaluated then."

"Why? Why was he moved? What do you mean, no visits? Are you talking about solitary? Are you saying my son is in solitary confinement? What the hell is going on?"

"It happens, ma'am. Lots of reasons. For discipline, maybe. Or if there's a credible threat to the inmate's safety, we move 'em." He handed me a card with the sheriff's department logo on it.

"Call this number half an hour before your next visiting period. Use this inmate number." He wrote a number on the back. "The automated system will tell you if this inmate will be available that particular date."

I hadn't moved, but the corrections officer said, "Help you?" over my shoulder to a woman who had rushed in, out of breath. She pushed her way up to ask him, "Am I here in time for visiting hours?"

"Yes, ma'am. Just by a nose."

I stormed out through the interior hallways, barreling toward Criminal Investigation.

CHAPTER

40

I BANGED OPEN THE door to Alvarez's office. She jumped up from her desk, hand on her weapon.

"Tell me why he's in solitary!" I said. "Twenty-three-hour lockdown? That's prisoner abuse."

"Back off, Boots," Alvarez said in a low voice, not moving her hand off her gun. "I've been looking for you. You're America's Most Wanted School Administrator. Believe me, I want to hear all you've got to say. But just take it easy. Sit down." She extended her free hand toward the chair in front of her desk.

"Most wanted?" I thought of the school bus I'd run off with. And the ten grand.

"Sit down, and we'll talk. As for Jaral, we moved him into AdSeg for his own safety. Believe it or not, we're trying to protect him in there."

"It's my job to protect him! No one else's! I am his mother!" In two steps I was around her desk and looming over her. Just as quick, her hand whipped something out of her belt and I was flat on my back, stunned.

She fucking tased me, I thought, staring at the ceiling. I had to get control of myself before I made things much worse.

The cop's face appeared over me. "Think of that like the nice girl's bullet."

I grunted and sat up, trying to clear the haze of surprise and unwelcome electrons from my head.

"Talk about protecting that boy," she said, back behind her desk. "He made his first court appearance today and you weren't even there. Some other lady came for him though. Blond, real short hair. She came over and said something to him while he was being led away. You want to hear his reaction?" She tilted her head at the chair in front of her. "Sit down, I'll tell you about it."

Seasick with exhaustion and fear, I pulled myself up into the chair and sat forward, gripping the edges as though I were on a tossing ship.

Alvarez looked satisfied. "First, you're going to tell me where you were last night. Let me guess. Mud wrestling?"

"Funny," I said. "Not a word 'til you tell me why he's in solitary."

"Ah, yes," Alvarez melted her gaze into a show of nostalgia. "Solitary confinement. Those were the days. When we used to call something what it was." She shrugged. "Now we call it AdSeg. Administrative Segregation. Same diff though."

I stood up. "How can you be so casual about it? This is my boy's life we're talking about."

Alvarez shook her head. "Ya, ya." A phrase used for fussy infants. I stayed standing, shot daggers with my eyes.

"He requested AdSeg for his own safety. In a manner of speaking. Woman comes up to him, leans in. Says something real low, then walks away. He starts jerking his arms and legs like he thinks he can pull himself out of the cuffs. Guard can't keep a grip on him, so he has to throw him to the ground. The kid's screaming, 'Get her away from me, keep her away, judge, you can't put me in there, I have to be away from everybody, judge, they'll get to me in there, they'll get to me. Please!'"

My legs turned to jelly. I sat back down, hard. "Who will get to him?"

"They will, Boots. Same 'they' all the nutjobs hide from. CIA? FBI? Aliens? Who knows. Anyway, judge orders a psych eval. Wouldn't you know it, those only happen once a week! So? Your kid gets his wish. Goes straight into AdSeg. It's no big deal." She shrugged. "Standard ops for everyone who's pre-eval to be held there."

"This is a nightmare."

"You look pale, Boots. And what's with your clothes? You sleep outside last night or something?"

She opened her desk drawer and pulled out a small bag of pretzels. "Here, eat these. I do not have the time for you to be passing out here in my office. And don't chew with your mouth closed, cause it's your turn to talk. So talk." She pushed the pretzels toward me.

I snatched them up like she might pull them back, ripped the bag open, and ate them one by one. Trying to think. Jaral was no head case. But I had no idea what this woman could have said to him to make him panic like that.

I tossed the empty bag back on her desk. "There's one more thing I need." My voice came out raspy. I coughed as the last crumbs tickled my throat. "I need whatever the jail cameras recorded from the time I visited Jaral. That was . . ." Dear God, was it only yesterday?

"I know when it was," Alvarez said, looking smug. "But why do you want to relive that joyous milestone in your life as a parent?"

Because I can't see him today. Because maybe if I replay the last time I saw him, I'll catch something I missed. Because right now that visit, and his terrified phone call, are the only times I've heard anything in his own words since all this started. That makes every word precious.

I put my palms on her desk and leaned forward. "Maybe this will get your attention. A bunch of pregnant African girls. A White overlord. Where was I last night? What I saw? It's a chance for you to be a real hero. Make your mark in this department! Get the respect you deserve! And save twenty-two lives. Eleven girls and their babies."

Alvarez twisted her mouth, considering me. "Oof," she said finally. "You need a psych eval too?"

I pounded on her desk. "This was on The Hill! What, you think you already know everything going on up there? I give you something you never heard of, it must be imaginary? I was there! On The Hill, in a part called the Presidio. You get me that footage and I tell you everything."

"Presidio?" Her eyebrows raised. "Hold on." She punched a few numbers on her desk phone and picked up the receiver. "Thiel, where did you say that new white zone is? The one we heard about a couple months ago?" She waited for his reply. "Oh, Lord. I hate those things so much. Pain in my protecting-and-serving behind. All right. Meet me in the conference room and see if you can pull up the CCTV archive files. The Marez mom is here. Says she was in that white zone and saw something we want to hear about. Yeah, I know. But she won't spill unless we get the justice center security footage from when she visited her son. Yesterday afternoon. All right. Thank you."

She hung up. "You met my partner? Thiel? He's getting the footage cued up in the conference room down the hall. I want you to give whatever you've got to give before we hit play. Write it all down on one of these." She opened a drawer next to her and pulled out a statement form. She slid it toward me, then pulled it back. "If I find out you're bullshitting, I can turn a false statement into a big problem for you and your kid."

I stood up. "I'll write it all out when I see you've got the video. Where's that conference room?"

She pointed down the hall. "You might as well start now. It'll take a couple of minutes for him to get it ready. Our archive system is very touchy."

"I'll meet you down there," I said and left her office headed the opposite way she'd pointed.

CHAPTER

41

I FOLLOWED SIGNS TOWARD another hallway for the women's room. After using the facilities, I went back into the hall and slurped from a fountain so cold, my teeth ached. Then I sat down in a chair next to a fake plant. I needed to think before submitting an official statement, to find an angle in what I'd discovered that pointed away from Jaral.

But exhaustion fragmented my thoughts. I couldn't focus. The ornamental plant beside me gave off the faint outgassing of newly manufactured plastic. The fake plant's odor triggered an awareness of my own aroma: crushed redwood needles, the living earth, microbes in mud. Wet skin, bark. All smells I loved, but they didn't serve me well in the tiled world.

I got up to return to the ladies, thinking I'd at least wipe some mud off my pants and feet. But when I pushed the door open, I heard my name spoken inside. I stood behind the half wall just inside the door to listen.

A voice with a soft southern accent was having a one-sided conversation over near the sinks. Probably on her phone. Her voice picked at a memory I couldn't quite access, but after a night of no sleep, every sensation rang with the tin-on-tin clatter of déjà vu.

"You say she's tall? Like, freakishly tall? Long dark hair? Yeah, I've seen her." A rush of sink water covered what she said next. I peeked around the wall. Luckily, she had her back to me, pulling paper towels out of a dispenser. She had blond hair one clipper setting away from a buzz cut. Trim, fit. In a smooth beige bomber-style jacket. She seemed familiar.

"I'll go myself," she said. I ducked back behind the wall. "Berribou Street? I know where that is. I'll get her."

I lived on Berribou Street.

A calmer soul might have tried waiting outside the bathroom behind the plant or around the corner to then follow this woman down the hall and try to find out who she was, what she was up to.

But a calm soul I was not. Hearing the words "I'll get her," I fled. I ran as best I could, toes clenched to keep the flip-flops tight to my feet. When I turned the corner to the Criminal Investigation hallway, I slowed to a brisk walk, tied my hair in a knot behind my head, and slumped forward to take a bit off my height. That was as close as I could get to a disguise.

When I reached the conference room door, I glanced back. Didn't see her. Maybe she'd gone the other way.

I went into the room, closed the door behind me.

The meeting room had an oval-shaped redwood table in the center, a pulled-down projector screen at one end. Thiel and Alvarez were already there when I walked in. Thiel glanced up from a podium near the screen, gave me a quick top-to-toe, then kept typing into a laptop on the podium.

"They said it was on the T-drive," Alvarez told him.

"A lot of shit's on the T-drive. That don't mean I can find it."

Alvarez pointed to a chair next to her. I turned away from her toward a bank of windows facing the hallway. I twisted the blinds closed over each window, then went to the opposite windows overlooking the street.

There was the short-haired woman in the bomber. She climbed into a mud-spattered white pickup truck parked alongside the CJC. When she pulled away, I caught the last two letters on her plate, S and Y.

When I turned toward the table, I was too keyed up to sit, but a sudden dizziness meant I couldn't stand either. I put my hands on the tops of my legs and bent over, like I'd just run a hundred-yard dash. My heart raced.

Alvarez sat ramrod straight, hands stacked on top of the table. She eyed me with a vice principal's glare.

"You all right?"

"Not even close. Did you dispatch anyone to my house? In the last few minutes?"

"Why?"

"I heard someone talking about me in the bathroom."

As soon as I said it, I remembered where I'd heard that woman's voice. Seen her. I think. She'd been at my school. Hadn't she? I didn't see the woman's face just now, but I thought it could be the person who'd interrupted my class. Right before Jaral called in a panic.

"Paranoia makes you sound more crazy," Alvarez said, blunt as a snub-nosed gun.

I didn't feel crazy, but I did feel slow. Like my brain was boiled molasses. "You should send someone out there. To my house. Just to make sure? There might be a prowler, a stalker. She had really short hair. Like that woman you said scared Jaral in court."

"So you got a look at her? This person you overheard talking about you?"

"From the back." Not wanting to play into the picture of paranoia, I didn't add that I thought I'd seen her before.

Bent double before the short cop, I was no longer the warrior who had beaten off an attack by an armed gunman. Thirty-seven hours since I'd slept in a bed. Nineteen since I'd eaten, minus tiny pretzels. The showdown in Alvarez's office over not being able to see Jaral had lit the last crumbs of gunpowder in my soul. Nothing left of me but a mewling mammal desperate for a scrap of safety. And rest. I hated it and welcomed it at the same time, fierceness being such an iron weight to carry all the time.

I sat down at last. "Please. I heard a stranger say my name, the name of the street where I live, and then 'I'll get her.'"

"Okay," said Alvarez. She slid some papers and a pen toward me.

"Okay?" I felt the first tingle of relief. "Okay you'll send someone over to watch my home?"

"I'll see what I can do. Meantime, Thiel's retrieving that recording of you and Jaral in the visiting area. So you can start writing." She pointed at a stack of the same statement forms she'd had in her office, handed me a pen, and left.

Thiel kept typing, scrolling, muttering under his breath. His attempts seemed real enough. Not wanting there to be any reason not to start the video when they found the spot I needed, I grabbed the pen and gave a selective account of what I saw on The Hill.

I included the pregnant girls working in the garden, left out their odd singing as they walked through the woods. I included the aggressiveness, the killer intensity, of the man I ran from, the man who probably wanted to kill me now and who maybe could've killed before. I left out how I'd gotten into his territory in the first place—the clandestine chopper flight paid for by money skimmed from my school.

I included the girls talking about a "Mrs. Gwen," and added that a "Gwen Cates" was listed in today's jail visitor log as a visitor for Jaral.

Had I ever gotten the name of the short-haired woman who had visited my school a few days ago? Was I sure it was the same person I glimpsed today?

These questions distracted me from my written account. I shook my head to refocus. I ended the statement with José Lara telling me this part of The Hill was an area Armando drove to at least one night per month. I wrote that if he'd crossed someone up there, or discovered something he wasn't supposed to see, it could've gotten him killed.

I was about to sign what I'd written, when I thought to add one more thing. I hadn't been able to reach Braulio Tenorio since he'd shown up at Daybreak, but Armando's neighbor saw him parked outside Armando's house the morning he was killed. I couldn't remember if I'd already told Alvarez this, but I thought it was worth repeating. Tenorio could have been involved in Armando's death. I just couldn't guess how. Or why.

Alvarez returned and read the statement forms. When she'd finished looking through what I'd written, her face was blank.

"You don't think these girls you saw are there for the trimming sheds?"

"Harvest isn't usually 'til the fall, right? And they're not Mexican, or Central American, or Laotian. Not the usual trimmigrant stock."

"Hmm," she said.

"These girls need help," I said. "They're scared. Drugged, maybe."

"This man who was with them. Why did he chase you off?"

"I think I surprised him. He thought he was tucked away in this secret hideout. And he said that name, Gwen, too. Can you run a check on that name from the visitor log? See what you find out about who she is?"

"Boots." Her tone pretend-gentle, as though shaming a little kid for forgetting a basic rule of conduct. "I do not work for you."

"Obviously."

She rolled her eyes, then pointed to the statement. "You have any photos of any of this business with girls on The Hill?"

I thought of the camcorder mulching the base of a rhododendron.

"My phone wasn't with me. I had a camera, but I left it behind. When a man with a gun came after me."

"How about descriptions?" Alvarez asked.

"Well, I think the girls are Somali."

She sat back for a moment and looked at me, eyebrows raised.

"I mean, they spoke some English. But they talked about speaking to Somali boys on video chats."

"Head coverings?" Thiel asked, over his shoulder.

I nodded. "Yes."

"And you have a line on identifying people from northeast Africa?" Alvarez asked.

"Call it an educated guess. From my days with the library's ESL program."

"How did you know the girls were all pregnant?"

"They were all showing."

She shifted in her seat.

"What about the man? Give us a description."

My memories of the hand-to-hand combat were dominated by close-ups—ankles, fist, gun—I told her what I remembered. Tall White man, light brown hair. Strong. Maybe mid-forties.

"But no name?" Thiel prompted. I shook my head.

"No identification. No idea who he works for or why he has these females with him. Nothing concrete tying him to the victim." Alvarez ticked off the deficiencies in my statement, one finger at a time. "In other words, nothing we can use."

She picked up the top page of my statement and ripped it up. She started in on the next page.

"These girls need help!" I chewed my top lip to stop a twitch. "They're drugged! Sleep deprived or hypnotized!" I rose to my feet. "He's keeping these girls against their wills! And what if Armando knew all about it? Knew too much? That could be enough for this guy to want to get rid of him."

Alvarez finished her page by page destruction of my account, then stood up beside me with arms back, chest thrust out, like she meant to get in my face. But she only menaced the hollow of my throat.

"Let's say our vic *was* connected to this place. That still doesn't mean anybody but Jaral Marez killed the kid."

I wanted to stomp the earth into a quake with my two feet. "Aren't you worried about these girls?"

"I don't even know if these girls exist." Alvarez sat back down, facing the flat screen. She glanced over at me. "I just like hearing another version of what the hell is going on in my county. You were in a white zone, Boots. A place we've got no jurisdiction. A place we know only by rumor. More mythical than Sasquatch."

"Which white zone?" Thiel asked.

"FVSC," Alvarez said. "Supposed to be run by that intel ops couple who ran Abu Ghraib interrogations."

Alvarez gave me a hard look, as though waiting for a reaction. I had the feeling I was supposed to be catching on to something. Something almost clicking.

Alvarez finally turned back to Thiel. "There's this one weird thing I remember about them. In some documentary I watched. They weren't the poor army grunts who took the fall for all that craziness up there. No, they're the ones who told those army kids what to do. To get detainees ready for whatever the interrogators had in store. Which was never on camera, I guarantee. But one thing I remember is how an army kid said the contractors asked them to keep people up all night with music. To soften them up for questioning. And the army girl says how they tried heavy metal, but it wasn't upsetting enough. I mean, the guys started to like it, started singing it back to the guards in the morning at top volume. What they found really made those Iraqi prisoners nuts? Country music. They played country all night to turn them dazed and desperate."

I sat back down and spoke to the table top. "These girls were singing country. I just didn't write it in that statement you fucking tore up, because I thought it was irrelevant. And now you won't believe me, but they did act sleep deprived. I heard them singing 'Achy Breaky Heart' while they walked to their garden."

Thiel and Alvarez looked at each other like a couple of middle schoolers who'd just seen someone biff a skateboard trick and land on a cow pie.

"You're a trip, Boots," Alvarez said. "I'm going to miss our time together when Jaral pleads out. Let's watch the young man now, shall we?"

She nodded toward the screen. A graphite gray image of my son entering the visiting room of the jail was paused just at the moment he saw me waiting for him. It was too grainy to see the details of his face, but I thought I remembered him having a cocky expression.

But now, in blurry black and white, what appeared as wide eyes and a clenched jaw cabled terror.

CHAPTER 42

THIEL STARTED THE video. Jaral walked over to my table, sat down, and immediately began fiddling with the edge of his standard-issue shirt.

"There's no audio," I said to Thiel. I wanted to hear Jaral. Dissect his words, one by one.

"These only record visual."

Ugh. All this effort, and I wouldn't even hear his voice.

I watched a Jaral the shade of a bold pencil mark say, "You high, Moms? Talking about pots and pans . . ."

Even without sound, he spoke plain as day in my head.

"What are we looking for?" Alvarez asked, watching my face.

My lips moved as I watched his lips move, but I didn't say anything.

"He's tweaking," Alvarez said, quietly.

This was a mistake. I had remembered the worst of his words exactly as he'd said them. *You want to help? Are you even trying?* And that horrible dismissal of our years as mother and son: *I wish I'd never gone to the white redwood.* This gave me nothing new. Worse, I'd served up a chance for Alvarez to add drug charges against Jaral. Even if I had all the faith in the world in this kid, I couldn't help making things worse for him.

When he'd skipped school Monday, I hadn't taken his phone like a normal, competent mom. Which meant the cops got it for evidence.

Now I was basically narcing him out to the lead detective investigating him for murder. Jaral was right. He would've been better off if he'd never gone with me to the white redwood that day six years ago. He would've been better off if I'd never adopted him.

We reached the end of the twitchy hands segment. The part where I grabbed Jaral came next.

"Nice parenting," Alvarez said.

"Fuck off." Oops. Said that one out loud.

When me-of-the-past was shown the door by a uniformed corrections officer, Thiel dragged the progress bar for the video back to the start. In walked Jaral. Neck crack. Sit.

"What are you doing?" I asked Thiel.

"I'm watching," he said, his face three inches from the screen. "Same as you."

Alvarez stood next to Thiel, both of them staring at the movements of Jaral's hands.

"Hold up," Alvarez said to her partner. "You seeing what I'm seeing?"

Thiel nodded, almost imperceptibly.

"Need my pen," he said, still mesmerized by the silent film in front of him. He pulled a small notebook from his pants pocket without looking down.

Was he going to take notes for the drug charges?

Alvarez handed him a pen from her shirt pocket like a nurse passing over a scalpel. I'd never seen Thiel give his superior a directive. She kept her feathers smoothed.

He pressed the notebook against the wall beside the screen and wrote:

H M

He added an "E," crossed out the "M."

"You teach your son Morse code?" Alvarez asked me.

"What?"

Thiel kept writing. I wanted to see the notepad, but he moved it down to his palm.

"Morse code," Alvarez repeated. "Your kid doesn't seem the Boy Scout type. Where'd he learn it?"

In an instant, I realized what Thiel and Alvarez must have noticed when they replayed the video.

When I'd been living that scene, sitting across the table from Jaral, his fidgets with the edge of his shirt drove me nuts. I couldn't concentrate. But it hadn't been aimless jitters or drug-induced jerky movements. Jaral was making a pattern. A code.

"The Civil War," I said. "And Vietnam."

Thiel paused the video.

"How's that?" said Alvarez, bringing me back to the room where we assembled, trying to puzzle out this boy.

"The Civil War and the Vietnam War. We watched some TV show about codes in wartime. He had two favorite examples. One was about how a Confederate general's daughter raised and lowered her window shades to pass battle plans to a handsome Union officer billeted in town."

"I bet the other one," Thiel said, notebook at his side, "was how that American POW in Hanoi blinked in Morse during the video his captors made."

I nodded. Thiel's voice got animated.

"Every soldier knows that story," he said to Alvarez, in answer to the question on her face. "The Viet Cong made this American hostage say out loud, on camera, that he was fine, that he was being treated very well. But the one word the VC didn't want spoken, this captive soldier said with his eyes. Literally."

"Jaral thought those stories were so cool," I said. "He taught himself the Morse alphabet. I only learned a few letters, and that was years ago." I felt my throat tighten.

Alvarez turned to her partner. "What word was that soldier blinking?"

"T-O-R-T-U-R-E. One letter at a time, he spelled, 'Torture.'"

Thiel moved closer to Alvarez, showed her the notepad. "Should she see this?" he asked her.

"So we all see that he wasn't tweaking, right? We've got that down?" I said. I still couldn't see what Thiel had on his notepad.

"This is the pattern Marez repeated," Thiel said to Alvarez, pointing to what he'd written. "This series of dots and dashes. The long pulls on his shirt hem were the dashes."

"And the short tugs were dots," Alvarez said. She nodded at me. Thiel handed me the notepad.

Ink marks for Jaral's dots and dashes took up the top few lines. Below them, Thiel had printed the decoded message, with the one mistaken letter crossed out:

H ~~M~~ E L P G O W R N O W

"What's WR?" Alvarez asked, speaking the question that wailed from the page like a siren.

"What help does he want from you, Ms. Marez?" Thiel added. "Are you in on all this? Or is he doing your time?"

My hands were cold. The building had the summer AC blasting. My guts felt cold. My eyeballs felt like shimmering marbles in my head.

The only patches of heat on my body were the bruised pad of my right foot and a searing pulse at the top of my bullet-burned ear.

The girl who found me in the woods kept saying "help" too. She wanted help finding someone named Khadra. Is that who Jaral drove off with? Did Jaral want me to help her?

For whatever help he'd meant, Jaral wanted me to go somewhere, now. But I couldn't interpret WR any more than Thiel and Alvarez could.

"One of the girls from the Presidio is missing," I said.

Alvarez leaned over the chair next to me.

"What do you mean, missing?" Thiel asked. "How would you know that?"

Alvarez was very close to my face now, watching my mouth move as I spoke.

"I know who she is. I mean, I know her face. I saw a book of sketches. There were all these drawings of the same girl in it. A Somali girl with a birthmark next to one eye."

"Where'd you see these drawings?" said Thiel. "Somebody told you the girl in them is missing?"

"Braulio Tenorio drew them. I found them in his notebook. Doesn't matter how I got it. How I know she's missing? I asked one of the girls at the compound up on The Hill about her. I described her birthmark. It's unique, four dots like a cloverleaf. And she said I had to find her. No one knew where she was."

Alvarez went to the pad of paper by the screen. She wrote something down and handed it to Thiel. "Take care of this for me."

He powered off the projector, closed the laptop. Then left without a word.

"So that's big, right?" I said to Alvarez. "Say this girl is Tenorio's obsession. Now he's hiding her somewhere. Maybe he abducted her or is trafficking her. Armando finds out, tries to help her. Gets killed for it. But before he does, he lets Jaral know where she is. Now Jaral wants me to help her."

Alvarez smirked. "That how you think this goes? I'm floored by your brilliant deductions and release your son immediately? Maybe throw in a dozen roses to make up for how mean I was? You think Tenorio could have killed Armando for taking a girl he wanted for himself. Nice idea, but no. The evidence shows Armando didn't swing that way. He had traces of semen in his stomach when he was killed."

My hair stood up on the back of my neck, as though I'd sensed a ring of unseen predators closing in. "That doesn't prove anything about who killed Armando. And yeah, I do want you to release my son immediately. At first I thought, why is she gunning for Jaral? Why is he the only focus? Then

I read about you on the Cop Watch blog. You've been passed over for a promotion twice. Your kids need more cushion in their college fund. And you need a place for your aging father. Old man getting to be a handful, huh? Time to shuffle him off to the old folks home? Jaral has to be guilty because you already arrested him. You need him to be guilty for your numbers! But to not even consider other leads? You're letting the real killer off. If it's just to set yourself up to sit pretty, you're an embarrassment to the badge."

Alvarez slow clapped. "Judge Marez, everybody!"

She sat down across from me. "Now, just to be clear, I don't owe you any explanations. But I'm about to share a little more of my perspective. Call it my professional opinion. Because it appears you're the type to run your mouth when you're backed in a corner."

She got up and started pacing.

"Yes, the victim could've had ties to a mystery guy in the woods who's the killing kind. Sure, he could've been menaced by his landlord, Tenorio. But were either of them close enough to this boy for sexual contact? Not in recent days, they weren't. Not according to the DNA we just got back this morning."

She stopped pacing and pulled out the chair next to me. She rested one knee on it and leaned forward.

"Did either the mystery man or Tenorio text the victim, saying, 'Whatever you do, do not tell your mom'? No, they did not. I'd call that text the language of threat. And as you might remember, that text came from the suspect we have in custody. Jaral Marez. Looks now like he's a young man desperate not to be outed. DNA confirms the physical evidence collected from the victim's stomach was Jaral's. And yes, in case you're wondering, DNA can remain intact in the stomach for hours, even days. Those building blocks of life are tough. So I know Jaral was intimate with the victim. Shortly afterward, he killed Armando Peregrino out of desperation, wanting to keep the relationship secret. When he got caught, he pretended to flip out in front of the judge, to keep himself out of gen pop.

It's common knowledge what happens to young men with his tendencies on the inside."

I let out an indignant yelp. "You said he was reacting to what some woman said to him in court when he got . . . emotional. That's what you said set him off. What if she figures into this somehow? What if she knows something about the murder?"

"I said he got wild after she spoke to him. We get random do-gooders at those public proceedings, trying to connect with the inmates. Probably just someone saying she'd pray for him. Letting him know they run a Bible study on the inside every Tuesday. What he was reacting to was getting led away without any offer of bail, getting led away to sit in jail another fourteen days while he waits for a hearing he knows will go bad. Because he's guilty."

For a heavy second, I toyed with believing her. I hadn't heard about this physical evidence before. It was plain I didn't know much about what was going on in Jaral's life. Maybe his lost childhood was a ticking time bomb inside him. And this, the explosion, at last.

For one leaden breath, I let go of the last frayed hope I'd held on to and felt a jarring relief. No more for me to do. No more fight against the unknown, against the system's bias. They had who they were supposed to have. I only had to accept it.

I rationalized this attempt at letting go with the thought that Jaral had already given up on me.

He wished I'd never adopted him.

He wished he'd never gone to . . .

Wait. Where he said all his trouble started. That's where he wished he'd never gone.

I assumed he meant he wished he'd never gone there with me six years ago when I adopted him. But what if he meant he wished he hadn't gone there recently?

My expression must have changed. Alvarez removed her leg from the chair and cocked her head at me.

"Did you remember something? Got an idea how to crack this coded message?"

It wasn't an idea. I knew. I knew right then where Jaral wanted me to go. He'd said he wished he'd never gone there. He didn't say he wished I'd never taken him there. He must've gone there himself. That could be where he went when he skipped a whole day of school and came back saying he was trying to help a friend.

But he didn't say it out loud because he didn't want anyone but me to know. I wasn't sure how I was supposed to help when I got there, but I knew where he was asking me to go.

I stood to leave. Alvarez's voice stopped me at the door.

"Won't get far without your car."

I turned to her. My car? Right. I'd let my fake husband drive off in it to get away from an immigration raid.

"Your vehicle was at the bus station. Funny how important pieces of your life keep showing up there."

"So that's where it ended up." I could only hope the man who'd helped me had slipped out from under the immigration radar this time.

"Ended up? You saying your vehicle was stolen?"

"I lent it to someone."

"I see. 'Someone' left it sitting overnight in a short-term parking spot, keys tucked under the bumper. It was set for towing. Would've been a couple hundred dollars to get it out of impound. Lucky for you, we wanted it for evidence. And that lot's just out back."

"Evidence?"

"Yeah, we held on to it. That's one reason I wanted to reach you last night. It's all good now though. Our team is done going over it. Let me make a call and I'll get you reunited with your ride."

Alvarez left but didn't go far. I heard her out in the hall on her phone.

"It's ready? Okay. Let whoever's in the kiosk know I'm bringing the owner. They can release it to her."

It didn't occur to me this was too easy. There was something in it for her, me having my car. All I could think about was that I had to drive out to where Jaral asked me to go.

To show him I'd heard.

CHAPTER

43

When I slid in my car, it had the faint smell of men's cologne. I put the key in without turning on the ignition, turned the wheel a quarter turn, tapped the brake three times, put the radio dial on 107.9, and tried opening the hidden panel under my steering wheel where I'd left my phone. It didn't budge. I repeated the steps, turned my interior light on and off at the end, then tried again.

Bingo.

But the phone was dead. I fished the car charger and my wallet out of the hidden compartment before closing it. The part that went into the adapter on the lighter clicked in fine, but the phone was a fussy mate with the smaller metal end of the charger, only lighting up when it was pressed to one side and pinned at an angle. I dropped in into the cupholder and tried wrapping the cord around the drive stick. The light flickered off, then back on again. I looked in the door, cupholder, glovebox, for any loose change I could use to get a coffee and some food. I knew there was nothing but air and maxed-out credit cards in my wallet.

After scraping together $3.16 in pocket change, I drove out of the lot, waving to the attendant who pushed the button to raise the exit arm with a scowl and nod. An old Honda in a back corner could have been Jaral's, pulled in from outside

Armando's house. It was the right tan color. But I didn't have time to check.

I was in a hurry to get to where Jaral had sent me. The car had a full tank, courtesy of José Lara or whoever had left it for me. Gente decente, as my mother used to say. But I needed fuel for myself before setting off. I couldn't risk falling asleep at the wheel. Or fainting from hunger.

The line at Los Bagels was miraculously short. I walked out with a day-old Everything and a cup of Signature Costa Rican, and almost missed my own face staring out from the *North Coast Journal* bin out front.

"Local Educator's Son Arrested on Murder Charges" read the headline. The byline was Yori's. Next to my standard headshot was Jaral's senior picture from the yearbook. In the photo company's bowtie and jacket, he smiled into a future second star to the right of camera, straight on 'til morning.

I juggled the coffee and crinkly bagel bag into one hand and pulled open the door of the bin with the other, propping it open with my elbow so I could yank out a copy.

Standing on the sidewalk, I read the first part of the article. It told about Jaral's arrest at the bus stop, and reviewed the facts of Armando's murder that had been released publicly, which weren't much. Just that he'd been killed at his home on Tuesday morning, and that he was a student at Eureka High. And it talked about me, the head of school for Daybreak Academy.

Maybe the last time I'd see my name with that title.

"That you?" someone said, walking by.

"Not any more," I said, as though the betrayal by Yori had remade me. That's how it felt.

When I'd gone to his house, an electrified cord of sexual history still bound us. Now that connection was dead. He'd used our conversations for a one-time scoop, guessing I had personal reasons for going to extremes. He must've found a way to verify Jaral was arrested.

I left the paper on the table and got back into my car. The phone had enough juice to turn on when I pressed the power button, but then it shut itself off again. I tried finessing the charger to get the charging light to light up again, then drove off sucking Signature Costa Rican like it was lifeblood, ambrosia, and communion wine blended together, which it was.

Eight missed calls from Daybreak. Probably Mrs. Murray running up a scale of progressive alarm. Where are you? Where's the minibus? What the devil did you need ten thousand dollars for?

I wanted to call her and beg her not to tell anyone about the missing money, to just give me a few days to get it back into the account somehow. And to ask her about the woman who'd visited our school, get her name.

But then I noticed a white, mud-splattered truck a few cars ahead. I angled over a lane and got a glimpse of the plate. Same last two letters as the one I'd seen leaving the justice center: S and Y. I changed lanes and sped up to try and see the driver. It was the woman who was coming for me.

I dropped a few cars back, hoping she wouldn't see me back there. We went through the same intersections, heading north.

A thought dawned on me with sickening dread. Were we going to the same place? She'd found out about my home address. But she hadn't found me there. If I truly was the one she wanted to find, could she have found out about Uncle Honey's place? I knew Whitepages.com showed known relatives and people you'd lived with at previous addresses. It only stood to reason that she'd try to find me at other Humboldt addresses associated with those names. And there would have been only one. Uncle Honey's yurt.

He'd died in Alameda County, but my Uncle Max told me to keep the forest property in Humboldt in his name as long as I could. Max said there was no reason for public records to know every last detail of where I might be at any time.

But if I was right, the woman had been able to figure it out anyway—that if I wasn't at home in Eureka, I might be up in the north county at the yurt.

If she was heading there too, I wanted to get there first. That's where Jaral wanted me to go. Where he'd said all his trouble started. The white redwood. I had to get up there before this person, and hoped it was plain enough when I got there what help I was supposed to give.

CHAPTER 44

THE TRUCK AHEAD of me went through a tricky freeway entrance, and I followed a few seconds behind. We both merged onto northbound 101 and sped up.

I was racing a hemi-engined truck to the yurt. I could not win in an economy-class car of the previous decade.

But if I took the backroads, she wouldn't see me coming. If none of the backroads were washed out, and if she got a little lost on the way, I had a chance of getting there first. I hoped she was relying on GPS. That would guarantee a few wrong turns up in the woods.

The white truck accelerated as it passed the Moonstone Beach exit. I veered onto the exit ramp, then skidded to a halt at the stop sign that marked the end of the ramp. A baby blue VW bus toodled toward the beach on the gravel crossroad.

I glanced at my phone. One battery bar but no service. I was back in the county dead zone.

I gunned my car away from the beach where, just yesterday, I'd tried to get Marta to spill some hidden knowledge. I'd been heading the wrong direction then. Not listening to Jaral. I wouldn't make that mistake again.

If Jaral really meant for me to go to the white redwood—if his trouble started up there, and he needed me to end it—if, my God, if he and Armando helped this missing pregnant girl escape, hid her up there at the yurt—then maybe she was up there now, alone, waiting for the boys to come back. If that's what happened, she'd be starving, needing help, and may have been up there for days.

Gravel sprayed in a rattle against the car body as it fanned up under my tires.

I bounced over hillsides, across swales. The forest closed in, then opened onto straw-colored meadows, before pressing up to the road in a throng of leaning trunks. The gravel thinned, then disappeared, leaving a rutted old dirt road. Unable to avoid every pothole, I steered toward those that looked shallower, less rock-toothed. My little car shook in protest. The front tires hit the walls of holes I'd misjudged with an accusatory bang.

After fifteen miles of continuous punishment to my car frame, the road turned under a highway. It became smoother, sandier, behind Prairie Creek Redwoods State Park. Where it skirted the park's southwest edge, the road became a grassy two-track that ran another two miles. It ended in a copse of maple and bay about a quarter mile from the back of my family property.

When I got out, I found a thick sycamore to pee behind, as though anyone were watching. A nuthatch hopped down the side of the trunk, probing for bugs under flakes of bark with its tiny spear of a beak.

Back at the car, I pulled out my phone to double check that no Miracle of the Satellites had occurred to suddenly grant me reception. Nope. I dropped the phone back into its secret compartment, looked around in my car for anything that could be used as a weapon. Newer cars had heavy jacks and silver lug wrenches in their trunks. In my trunk I had jumper cables plus a dollar-store set of beach toys.

I considered the cables briefly. I could swing the metal clamps at someone's head, if I had to. But they seemed clumsy and small.

I raised the hood on the car, then lifted the thin piece of metal for propping the hood. It may have been held in place by a snug plastic clasp once. Now nothing but a hinge brittled by rust attached it to the car. It depressed me how quickly the metal snapped off when I yanked it against the direction of the hinge. Piece of crap car.

But at least I had a weapon now, lightweight and jagged-edged. I dropped the hood back into place. Last week I was struggling to clean up my email inbox. Now I'm looking for something to beat a head with. When they say parenting changes you, I don't think this is exactly what they mean.

Getting nostalgic for desk work gave me a chance to laugh off a little of the cold fear I brought with me.

I didn't know what I was going to find up here. Maybe the driver of the truck had gotten here first. If she was the counterpart of the man at the Presidio, she had at least three reasons to kill me. I'd talked to a captive at her clandestine camp. I was the mother of someone who might've taken a girl out of there. I had to confront the woman if she was trying to take that girl back.

I set off, switching at the grass with my primitive defense tool, a shaft no thicker than a riding crop.

After a few minutes, I could see the back of the yurt. A Steller's Jay cranked out an alarm, then hopped up to a higher branch in silence.

At the edge of the clearing where the yurt stood, right under the white redwood, the ferns had all been dug up. Thinking maybe a mountain lion had put a cache there, my skin went cold. It was an odd, hot, sunny day in the north county, the kind that were getting less odd every year. But my skin felt glazed with rainwater. I shivered.

If the boys brought the girl named Khadra here on Monday, that was four days ago. What if she had wandered out to find food and a mountain lion got her?

I ran in a crouch to the spot with the disturbed earth. This part of the clearing faced one of the yurt's windows. I glanced up, cringing, expecting to see a stranger's face watching me. But the weatherproof flap was fastened tight over the window. If anyone was inside, I couldn't tell. There were no cars near the yurt, but that didn't mean anything. The main driveway was a three-hundred-yard bend. Anyone arriving from that direction could have parked out of sight and walked up.

A few roots poked out through the disturbed soil. I thought they might be rhododendron tubers. I brushed dirt away from them, then pulled my hand back as though I'd been stung. I fell back in the duff, wiped my hand on the leg of my jeans.

Human fingers and rhizomes have some resemblance, but only one of them might display a gold class ring.

I lifted the finger. Up from the dirt came a human hand, an arm, then I couldn't pull any more. The arm, it seemed, was still attached to a shoulder a few inches underground.

I dropped my makeshift spear, clawed the dirt over the area where the face should be. I uncovered portions of skin that became features, features that became a face, a face that had bloody bruises on the forehead, a smashed nose with blood crusted below it. A death-swollen face. Still, a face I knew. Braulio Tenorio.

I sat back on my heels, mouth-breathing to avoid the odor escaping through turned earth.

"Where's my shovel?" I mumbled, my only benediction over the corpse. I didn't see it propped against the shed where I thought I'd left it. Overhead, puffs of wind stirred the redwood canopy.

As I turned my attention back to the body, I caught a glimpse of the shovel blade winging toward my temple. I ducked.

The blade glanced the top of my skull hard enough to whip my head to the side. I rolled toward a pair of denim-covered legs that appeared below the arc of the swinging shovel. The flat of the blade found the small of my back. I threw my arms around the legs, pulled upward.

The person who fell on her butt with my bent arm cinched around her ankles was a tall Black teenager, eyes the color of embers, in a face framed by a black hijab. A round belly strained against the faded overalls she wore.

I recognized the four-leaf clover birthmark next to her right eye.

"Khadra," I said. Her eyes widened.

I lunged for the shovel she'd dropped. I grabbed the top of the blade. She gripped the free end, pulled herself to her feet. She was my height, slight-boned except for the belly. I yanked the shovel to dislodge her, but she came with it. The surprise of looking another female in the face at eye-level stopped me for a second, which was all the time she needed to bite my hand hard enough to rake open the skin on my knuckles.

I let go and grabbed my hood prop off the ground. The girl raised the shovel again so quickly it toppled her a little off-balance. I ducked to one side, whipped the jagged edge of my broken metal rod toward her throat.

She backpedaled to get her footing, shovel still raised, then froze when she saw the sharp piece of metal aimed at her.

"Don't test me." I said. The angry part of me I'd smothered under motherly feelings churned to life. "Set the shovel down."

The girl's arms quivered. "No."

A spot on her neck beat in time with her pulse. I inched my weapon forward until the ragged end kissed her thrumming skin.

"I can help you," I said. "But you have to tell me if Gwen Cates is here yet."

The girl's eyes widened at the mention of that name. She took a few steps back from my improvised spear, dropped the shovel, and ran.

CHAPTER

45

SHE SKIRTED THE undergrowth, circling around toward the front of the yurt, her eyes on the woods, searching for a break, a deer path, some means of escape she could dive into. When she came around to the driveway, she saw something that made her change direction. She tripped, crashed to one knee, toppled forward. The heel of her hands plowed the duff in front of her as she fell onto her forearms.

I couldn't see what scared her. I ran to the edge of the clearing and crouched in the brush, watching.

Khadra raised her head, looking down the driveway, and uttered one word that came out like a growl: "Mrs."

"Khadra, here you are! Girlie, I have been hunting around something fierce for you." This was a voice from the forest, from somewhere down the curve in my driveway. The same voice I'd heard bouncing off the bathroom tiles at CJC.

I shrank back to melt into the undergrowth and stay hidden. Two things happened at the same time that made this impossible.

Khadra sighted over her right shoulder to hold me in a look that could burn salt from the sea.

The short-haired woman I'd seen at the CJC—and earlier, at my school—appeared in the driveway. She followed Khadra's gaze and locked eyes with me.

This must be "Mrs. Gwen," who the girls were so afraid of. Who I knew was trying to get to me.

The woman dropped low. She raised something like a wooden pistol with a plastic rat's tail coming out the back. She cranked the rat's tail down, then fired.

To my right, a wild rose exploded, petals flying into the air. An arrow pinned a rose leaf to a buckeye tree behind me.

It took me a second to realize I was crawling off to the left. My limbic system had executed a goalie's gamble. By luck, left had been the direction to go.

I heard the snick of the "tail" being cocked again.

For cover, I ran straight at Khadra. I thought if this woman wanted the girl dead, she would've tried to kill her already. Since she hadn't, she must've wanted Khadra alive. In that case, if I got near Khadra, I wouldn't be shot at. Arrows sprayed gravel around me as I ran.

When I got close to Khadra, she sprang aside and shoved me to the ground.

I had the wind knocked out of me. Before I could get air again, the girl yanked my arms back at an excruciating angle. She rested a heavy lug-sole between my shoulder blades, without putting her full weight into it.

"There you go," the woman said. "Step all the way onto her. Pull those arms back."

"Don't come any closer, Mrs. Gwen!" Khadra yelled. "Stay away, or I let this lady loose to kill you." This was the first full sentence I'd heard pass her lips. She had the same accent as the girls I'd seen working the wilderness garden. Her voice had a surprising depth coming from such a slim, dimpled face.

Gwen had stopped within ten feet of where I lay. Her grayed army surplus boots with dirt-smudged yellow laces were right in my ground-level sight line. I couldn't see where she had her weapon pointed.

"Khadra!" I wheezed, my mouth clogged with leaves. "I can help you. I can get you away from Gwen." I coughed against dead leaf bits moving toward the back of my throat.

"Now, Ms. Marez, that's just silly," Gwen said. "This little miss knows I'll take care of her. She's ready to come back with me, aren't you, girlie?"

"You go away from here. Then this lady takes me to Los Angeles," Khadra said.

"Is that what you think, you little tramp? You got a man in L.A. says he'll marry you. You think he'll save you? Well, he's dead now, girlie. All you've got is me."

"Let me go!" I tried to rock side to side under Khadra's shoe. "We'll fight her together!"

"Dead? He's dead? My Hanad? Dead?" The teenager's fingers tightened so hard around my wrists I thought she might cut off blood flow.

"Yup. He's a goner. I sent Mr. Cates to SoCal to take care of it. And this idiot you've got trapped here? She's just an airy-fairy do-gooder. I don't know what you think she's going to kill me with. Good intentions?" She squatted down to look me in the eye, her bow armed with an arrow aimed at my head.

"Or maybe . . ." She murmured low, like someone about to put an animal down. "She burns me with the light of her self-righteousness?"

"What is this? Telling me my Hanad is dead?" Khadra's voice had a wildness to it now, high and desperate. "How do you know who he is? Why should I believe you?"

Gwen straightened and spoke in a frightening monotone. Her southern sound was gone, replaced with a flatness that was almost mechanical.

"You honestly think we didn't keep copies of all your recordings? All your conversations? All your work for us? Sure, we take your notes, about which young boys are the most in need of male role models. The boys wracked with guilt for lusting after all the parts of you they can't see. And the boys embarrassed they feel nothing when they see you."

"Our notes are your gold," Khadra said, her voice shaking. "That's what you always told us."

"Of course they are, girlie!" Gwen's voice became animated again, her southern accent back in play. "You let those boys pour shame all over themselves. They're primed for contact with a strong male figure who can build them up for manhood. Our undercover agents provide that. They reach out to these boys online, convince them they are still worthy of respect, still capable of honorable acts. They show how the highest path to honor lies in jihad. Gently, gently, they encourage these skinny little birds to stretch their wings into the free air of violence. Or at least the idea of violence. For God. For honor. Then we catch them. We lock them up before they can do any real harm. Which means you've saved hundreds, maybe thousands, of people with that pretty face. You had a big part to play. But then you got stupid."

"There was nothing about my Hanad in the notes I gave you." Khadra's voice came out raspy. Her foot on my back pressed down and up, then down again more heavily, as though she were trying to keep her balance. I took shallow breaths and tensed to move if Khadra let up again.

"That's what was so stupid!" Gwen said, eerily gleeful. "We know about 'your Hanad' because we watched your entire archive as soon as you went missing from our compound. The recordings of every chat you've had over the past twelve weeks, not just the ones you chose to report up. That's how we saw your treachery. Your treason. You had entire conversations with this guy that you reported nothing about. That's right! We heard 'em all!"

Gwen kicked at the ground for emphasis. I squeezed my eyes shut and tucked my head in against the flying dirt. Gwen laughed, on some kind of sadistic roll.

"We learned from your recordings that you are a little ungrateful bitch who spits on the nation that pulled you from that filthy refugee camp in Kenya. Why would you betray us to run away with the first pathetic boy who said he'd marry you, just to live broke and on the run? Call that freedom? Girlie, you have no idea what *that* word means."

"I left so my baby would know its mother!" Khadra interrupted.

"Oh, you did it for your baaay-beee? You think that baby would be better off in a stink-ass HUD high-rise, bawling into the night with all the other poor babies bawling through the paper-thin walls? Or would he—yes, that's right, it's a boy, we've known for a few months now—would he be better with a nice American family desperate to give a child three squares a day, a college education, a standard set of middle-class advantages? Doesn't that sound better than the food bank and lines at social services? Hell, he could be shot in the street, he grows up wrong."

I twisted my head up at a painful angle so I could see Gwen's face. She had her weapon aimed at Khadra's belly.

"Turn around. Go in that structure." She jerked her head toward the yurt.

Khadra released me and jumped back. I'd gotten my neck and shoulders off the ground when Gwen sprang forward and kicked me in the forehead.

"I've got to make sure you stay put," Gwen said through a ringing in my ears, "while I deal with this girlie."

I rolled over to see the silver tip of an arrow like the blind face of a hard, metal grub aimed at my eyeball. I tried to push the wooden not-toy from my face, and she kicked my head again.

She twitched the archery gun up again to aim at my forehead. "Got any rope here? You must have hung bear bags before. I see some nice strong branches."

I raised both hands up, surrendering where I lay.

"Die!"

The shout came from behind us. It was Khadra with the shovel. She connected with Gwen's skull in a blow that only served to piss off Gwen. She shot an arrow in Khadra's thigh. Khadra swung the shovel at her head. Gwen dropped her crossbow, caught the shovel handle right above the blade. Khadra yanked her end of the handle. With Gwen pitched forward, I scrambled up and kicked her in the back. She sprawled to the ground.

Not until then did Khadra notice the shaft of an arrow sticking out of her thigh. It had burrowed through denim into her flesh, at least four inches of shaft lost in her leg. The girl, still holding the shovel in one hand, marveled at this foreign object stuck in her. She raised her arms wide, as if to say "tada." Her jaw was slack, eyes wide.

Gwen rose to a crouch. She made a quick motion to pull something up from near her ankle. I lunged for the crossbow as Gwen sprang toward me with a knife.

Just as my hand connected with the bow's small stock, the whole clearing filled with an explosive sound.

Gwen stumbled, then fell. I pulled her wooden weapon up out of reach.

When she hit the ground, Gwen curled into a fetal position. She snaked a hand out to cover the bicep of her knife arm. Blood seeped out between her fingers.

Salal rustled in the woods. Thiel ran at us, his gun drawn on Khadra.

"Set the shovel down, honey. I'm not going to hurt you." Thiel's words were meant to reassure, but his voice was sharp.

I held the crossbow awkwardly in front of me, thinking I should keep Cates from getting back up, when I heard "Drop it."

Alvarez emerged from the woods behind the shed, her gun pointed at me.

CHAPTER

46

So long as I still had the crossbow, I might have a say in how things played out. I didn't want to give that up.

Khadra dropped the shovel. She wrapped a fist around the arrow shaft sticking out of her leg.

"No!" Thiel yelled. "Don't pull it out! We have to get you to a doctor!"

With one hand still on the arrow, she lay her other hand over the rise of her belly. Behind her, the white redwood stirred in a breeze. Khadra's mouth hung open in astonishment. She looked up at us, then back down at the arrow protruding from her leg.

"Don't," Thiel commanded.

She tightened her hand around the arrow and started to pull.

I dropped the crossbow and sprinted to Khadra. Thiel charged in from the other direction.

Khadra cried out and yanked the arrow free. A dark red patch soaked her pantleg with terrifying speed.

Thiel dropped to one knee next to her. He holstered his gun. He mashed her bleeding thigh between two hands.

"It hit the artery," he barked. "Get me jackets. Female products. Bedsheets. Anything!"

I turned and ran past the still supine Gwen to the yurt. I heard Alvarez bark at her: "Hands where I can see them."

"I'm FBI, motherfucker," Gwen fired back.

"Unlikely," Alvarez said. "Now toss that knife away."

Inside the yurt, I grabbed paper towels, table napkins, a pile of sheets from a tub next to the bed.

Outside the canvas walls, I heard Alvarez talking to Gwen.

"You're ex-military. You do security dirty work for one of those bloodsucking contractors. I know who you are. I know what you did in Iraq."

"That was different."

"Did something come loose out there at the hard site? I hear you used to drive golf balls off the roof of the building in the evenings after your interrogations. Now, that's living."

"All I do is help the country stay vigilant."

"Ever vigilant!" Alvarez raised her head as I ran past with my arms full. Gwen lay face down, wrists zip-tied behind her back. Alvarez bent over the prone woman's legs, patting her down.

I ran back to Khadra, unaccountably worried that the sun was in her eyes. At the angle where she stood, with her arms at her sides, still clutching the bloody shaft she'd just pulled from her flesh, she could barely open her eyes against the glare. The shadows of the white redwood and its parent tree fell away from us, back into the forest.

Thiel tugged the sheet out of my arms, spilling the rest of what I'd brought onto the ground in front us. He started winding the sheet around Khadra's leg. I ran to the shed to get the metal shaft I'd brought with me.

"Can you use this for a tourniquet?" I asked Thiel, running it back over to him.

He took it without a word, twisted some more of the sheet around it, cranking in clockwise circles.

"No tampons or pads in there?" he said, tilting his head toward the yurt.

"Just some blankets," I said. It wasn't like the place was stocked for long-term habitation. Or trauma wound care. "Should we take her in where she can lay down?"

As though in reply, Khadra slumped to the ground, flopping on her back, the arrow beside her in the duff.

I knelt, tried to cradle her head on my knees. Her face was still in the sun, so I rotated the angle I was kneeling to shield her face. Her eyes opened all the way then.

She turned toward where Gwen lay. She drew a few deep breaths, as though gathering herself. Then she yelled over to her, "You made us into lions. Hunting the weak, the sick! Most boys want nothing to do with us. But my Hanad, he knew we could have a family. We could have a life together. I got away from you for that reason. I had to rescue myself to start my new family."

Thiel stood beside us, shouting codes into his radio. Instructions crackled back through the speaker. The tourniquet he'd set above Khadra's wound bunched the fabric of her pantleg. The skin underneath was probably twisted painfully, but the flow of blood from the hole in her leg seemed to have slowed from a gush to a steady trickle. Her blood soaked the ground all around us. I could feel it dampening my knees.

"I rescued you!" Gwen yelled back at Khadra. "Don't you remember? I saved your life. You and the other girls. Alone and pregnant in the Dadaab camps, abandoned by your own families, no one to protect you. All of you were nothing but outcasts. The throwaway tier of the world's throwaway people!"

Khadra howled, a sound like the cougar I'd heard throwing a flaming ring of sound around her territory.

"What is it?" Thiel said, shoving his radio back in its holster. "Are you having contractions? Any pain here?" He squatted down to pat the underside of her belly.

"The pain comes from hearing that woman speak. I had to get away from her. I left so she wouldn't take my baby from me. But now, as I speak, I feel weak. I think I die. You take this baby. Not Mrs. Gwen. Not her."

Her voice had become a hoarse whisper. Her eyes rolled.

CHAPTER

47

"BREATHE," THIEL SAID. "Just breathe. You're going to be okay. How many months along are you?"

"Eight," Khadra rasped. "Maybe nine. Take this baby out of me."

"No," Thiel said. "Don't say that. We're going to get you the help you need."

Her gaze came back into focus. She took in my upside-down face, bending over her. I nodded encouragement. "Stay awake!"

She blinked. I massaged her arms below her shoulders, thinking to pull more blood from her extremities back toward her heart.

"Untie me, you fuck!" Gwen screeched. "I'll have you court-martialed! When you hear in November that a plot to bomb the living nativity in Nashville was stopped by the FBI, you'll have the work of these girls to thank. When you hear a teen in Minneapolis was going to knife random shoppers at a mall but got stopped at the entrance, that's the work of these girls. They're like magnets. They pull boys to them who are isolated, scared, primed for violence. They pull them forward so we can see them. Then our agents chip away to discover which of those boys has a terrorist inside him. Then they get 'em. And we have a new domestic counterterror op ready to spin up. You let these girls do their work, they'll be melting the hearts of corn-fed White kids in anti-immigrant hate groups too."

Her rant had filled her own sails. She shouted like a corner preacher foretelling Armageddon. "You're costing the national security effort millions of dollars. You don't know what you've gotten yourself into. People will die if you—"

BAM. Alvarez shot in the air, right next to Gwen Cates's ear.

"Overconfident much?" Alvarez asked, as though checking whether Gwen took cream in her coffee.

The sound of the gunshot made me wince, but it put Gwen back in a fetal curl, wracked with waves of full body shudders.

"Got a little PTSD?" Alvarez said to her. "You probably don't like this sound." Alvarez fired again, right next to Gwen's ear. Gwen added gut-level heaves to her shudders.

"I got a couple more of these ready to go. I'm kinda bored, thinking I might shoot them off. But you know what? Why don't you tell me a story instead?"

"I'm not telling you shit."

BAM. Gwen curled up tighter, her hands spasming open and closed behind her back.

"Let's start with these pregnant girls. Why don't you let the girls keep their babies? Khadra here tells us she ran away from you so she could keep her child. Why wouldn't you have let her keep him?"

"D . . . dju . . . do you have any idea how expensive babies are?" Gwen asked, through chattering teeth. She sounded like a child just out of the pool after swim lessons. "Well, n-no, you w-wouldn't," she said, looking at me.

She turned her gaze back to Alvarez. "We d-don't have the b-budget. The s-state takes them off our hands. Adoption. Our girls have a chance to become adults with their heads h-high. Find a nice Somali h-husband."

Khadra closed her eyes, murmuring. I thought she was speaking her own language, but when I bent close, she said, "This baby is the only family I have left. You have to take him out of me. He has to live."

"Khadra!" I commanded. "Open your eyes!" I thought if I assumed a godly tone, I'd have godly power to match.

"Take him. Out of me." Her eyes remained shut.

"Look at this tree behind me!" I said. "Look!"

She fluttered her eyes back open.

"Back there." I twisted my head toward the white redwood. "See how beautiful that tree is? Different from all the others. But without green needles, it can't make its own food. Its roots are attached to the big parent tree next to it, so it gets food through its roots. We'll help your baby. But you have to stay with me. Stay awake. You're still feeding your baby through the blood inside you. Like that bigger tree feeds the one attached to it. Please . . ."

Khadra gave a rasping sigh and closed her eyes again. I thought I'd lost her. Her blood spread on the ground beside me. Then she spoke again, her eyes still closed.

"Do not sell him. Promise me."

"Why would you say that?"

"You came here to sell me."

"Is that what you thought that man came here to do?" I whispered to her. "That man who's in the ground now?"

"Not sell me," she said, seeming to grow short of breath. "Own me. Men who wish to own women have a way they look at you. I stopped him before he could take me."

"I didn't come to sell you or force you to go anywhere."

"Then why . . ." She took rapid, tiny sips of air. "Why are you here?"

"I don't know." I really couldn't remember right then, so encompassing was the sensation of being carried along in the ebb tide of her dying. "My son told me to go here. Because . . . because you needed help." I was beyond sorry I hadn't figured that out sooner.

"You hear that?" Alvarez said, to the still-shivering Gwen. "That's a real American hero."

At first, I thought she meant Jaral. But she was talking about Khadra.

"A young girl, fighting to keep her child. We never would have known about these girls you have, these captives you keep for your twisted intel op, if Armando hadn't stolen her from under your nose. But now we have a rescue underway. Because of her."

"What rescue?" Gwen scoffed. "I'm the one who rescued them."

"Our SWAT team is closing—"

Before Alvarez could finish, Khadra pushed herself up with a burst of energy.

"Stole me?" Khadra said, with a scratchy sound that I realized, only after she started talking again, had been a laugh. "I snuck into that boy's car. Hid in the back. When he started driving away, I just appeared there in his back seat, like I was born under the blanket where I hid myself. I forced him to drive me away from there."

She leaned back against my legs, her eyelids drooping again.

"What do you mean, forced him?" I asked, to keep her talking.

"That boy wanted to drive me right back to her." She pointed at Gwen. With her accent, "her" sound like a jab of breath in Gwen's direction, "heh."

"I told him no. He said Mrs. Gwen would hurt him if she found out he took me away from her. But I told him I'd cut his throat if he didn't. I had a knife, yes. I said, 'Take me to Los Angeles.' And I told him don't bring me to police, because they'll bring me back to Mrs. Gwen. Don't sell me, because then Mrs. Gwen will find me quick. I told him if Mrs. Gwen finds me, then I will tell her he kidnapped me.

"He was very, very scared. He said he'd get his friend to drive me. He told me he can't drive his car very far. His boss checks his miles every week.

"So the boy drives me only to his home, where I stay hidden in his car over night. The next morning, his friend takes me here, like a kidnapping, not to L.A. Wait here, he says. He returns that night with some vitamins and a few pieces of fruit. Imagine, I am waiting here since that time, one day, two days, three days. Neither of those boys come back for me."

"Something happened," I said. "Those boys, they . . ." It seemed an unnecessary interruption to how hard she seemed to be concentrating on breathing, to say that one boy was in jail and one was dead. "They wanted to come back, but they couldn't."

"Take this baby out of me," she said again. "If you rescue the other girls, put them somewhere far away from *her*." Khadra's eyes fluttered shut once again.

Thiel held her wrist, pressed two fingers to her neck. I could see him mouthing numbers for seconds. When he got to ten, he set her wrist down so gently you would have thought she was his own sleeping daughter.

"Take my duty knife." He pulled a folded knife from the front of his belt. "Sterilize it quickly. Run it under some hot water or put it through a flame."

"What . . .?" I stared at the handle he held out to me.

"Now!" he said. "We're going to save this baby."

"He once cut an unborn fawn out of its dying mother," Alvarez said, in answer to the questions my eyes must have asked. I drew out the knife.

Gwen had gone quiet. Whether it was from the solemnity of death, the suspense of what was unfolding, or the satisfaction of a kill, I was glad for her silence.

I laid Khadra's head gently on the ground and ran past Cates and Alvarez into the yurt.

What happened next came in a strobing series of images, sensations.

The blue flame that sprang from the long-nosed lighter I kept next to the stove.

The flame's reflection on the blade's smooth tip, on the thirteen peaked teeth toward its base.

Sun flashing off the blade outside, a splash of quicksilver that slashed my vision.

The girl's overalls and underwear peeled down so the top of her pubic hair sprang out like some hidden, insistent truth.

Latex gloves over Thiel's hands. Thiel measuring three fingers up from the bony core of her pubis.

The crackling voice on the radio spattering directives.

The knife's first contact, the hold-resist-give of the initial puncturing of flesh. Then the blade's buttery movement through skin, muscle, blood as Thiel drew the tip lengthwise across her belly.

The cut was a slightly concave arc about six inches long. With rubber-gloved fingers, he pried apart a layer of skin, fat, muscle to reveal another layer of muscle.

He pressed one hand down, then in, to push the solid form on the other side of that last flesh barrier away from the blade.

Next to a slack area at the edge of his fingers, the knife made a new opening. There.

Thiel tossed his knife aside and jammed his hand in up to its knuckles, trying to work his fingers around the slippery head.

Then he had two hands in. With a pull that stretched apart the layers of the incision with an impossible giving way, he lifted a boy into the sunlight, and to my complete surprise, handed him into my arms.

Thiel retrieved scissors and a clamp from a first aid kit behind him. He cut the cord about five inches from the baby boy's body, tied it off, clamped it. Then he began removing the placenta.

"He's not breathing on his own, tonta!" I'd forgotten Alvarez was there. She was still standing with her gun on Gwen, who lay on the ground, uncurled, with her face away from us.

I set the boy in the shade of the white redwood's parent tree. Alvarez was right.

I rubbed the limp little limbs. I swiped a finger through the tiny mouth, like swabbing out a little mud-lined hole in the earth. "Come on, baby. Come on, baby," I called. I lifted the chin up with a pinky. When I tried to seal my lips around the little thing's nose and mouth, I thought of playing the flute. What was the proper embouchure for launching life?

Alvarez yelled something at me, but I didn't look over. The skin felt damp beneath my lips, warm from the furnace of the birth canal. Up close, the creature smelled like pine pitch and rain.

I pushed air into his mouth and nose slowly, just until I felt the chest rise under my hand. I'd heard about CPR providers bursting infants' lungs with over-enthusiastic puffs of air. Then I removed my mouth, with a sense of regret, to turn my ear to the little mouth and listen. I wanted to keep depositing breath in those lungs until the end of time, with no pause for death to creep in.

I heard my own breath leave his lungs, then nothing.

"Compressions, compressions!" I finally registered what Alvarez was trying to get across. "Compressions first, before rescue breaths!"

I felt for the sternum, placed two fingers there, just below the level of his pebbly nipples. One, two, three, four, five, I made infant pushes no firmer than those I'd use to depress the keys on a laptop keyboard. I watched the still face as I did so, smooth except for a suite of wrinkles at the top of the forehead, as though he awaited an answer to a question he'd just asked. "Press down more," shouted Alvarez. "Try to get down an inch and a half." I pressed in hard, like a jab, worried I was hurting him. Six, seven, eight, nine. Then heaven cracked open with two beams of startling light. The child opened his eyes.

CHAPTER

48

THE FLIGHT FOR Life helicopter, twice the size of the fake medivac rig I'd ridden in, sounded like an enormous projector overheating. As it touched down in the clearing, I scooped up the newborn, turning us both away from the blast of air and debris. The baby started to wail, which I only knew from the shape of his open mouth and the feel of his ribs opening like bellows.

Two beach-blond male medics leapt sidewise to disembark. One took the baby from me, the other bent over Khadra. "I need help getting her into the chopper!" the second medic called to Alvarez. "We have oxygen in there, blood if she needs it. I can stabilize her, but I need to get her up there right away."

The girl's belly had been sewn up with surgical thread. Thiel must have been working on that while I resuscitated the baby.

"Marez! Watch this suspect. Make sure she doesn't go anywhere." Alvarez waved a hand at Gwen, now cross-legged, arms cuffed behind her.

Still stunned from my brush with birth, I walked over to the woman, holding my shaking arms in an empty cradle. My eyes fixed on Gwen, but I was aware, in the periphery, of shouting, a stretcher being run out, that ongoing chord of propellers ripping the air. Tree limbs swirled around the edge of the clearing.

When I knelt in front of Gwen, I realized her eye color was fake. Up close, her dull sapphire contact lenses gave the feeling of looking into dark sunglasses. No detectable window to the soul.

"You called my school," I said. "Then you showed up there. You thought I was hiding this girl in the air ducts?"

"I called the school to get you a fat contract for polishing up our girls' English. Get them ready for our next op. They got so skilled at getting the attention of teens and young men whose families immigrated from Somalia. We were going to have them try sweeping White supremacist boys off their feet next. Think about it. We know those groups just need a few stirs to cook up a bombing plot or some other kettle of bullshit. But wouldn't they want to warn their little sweethearts, first? Like a Romeo and Juliet thing. Warring houses, doomed young love. Then we'd have more intel to feed the feds and keep everybody safe. You could have been part of something great. And when I showed up at your school? Yeah, I wasted some time there. Thought your kid might trust you to hide my girl. But no."

"He trusts . . . I mean . . ." I caught myself before tumbling into the insecurity trap she'd laid. "What did you say to Jaral in court? You were the one who set him off at his arraignment. That right?"

She shrugged. "A little advice never hurt."

"What about holding these girls against their will? How's separating new mothers from their babies part of something great?"

"These unmarried, pregnant refugee girls would've given birth in the dust of a shithole camp in Kenya, alone. By the time we got this group, they were showing enough to be outcasts, too far along to terminate. They had no one. Anyone willing to protect them was likely a pimp waiting to sell them in Saudi. You think a pimp wants babies around? So yeah. Technically, these girls make sacrifices. The exact same sacrifices they would've had to make in their old lives. The difference is, now these sacrifices have meaning."

Until then, I'd always thought Braulio Tenorio was the most manipulative person I'd ever met. But here was a person so calculating that she'd split up new mothers from their children and call it a favor. So twisted that she'd gone over the edge torturing others for information. She may have left behind her days as a state-sponsored perp, but the experience of it was in there, churning up her mechanistic view of other people.

I was trying to process all of this when the helicopter lifted off behind me. I glanced over as Alvarez and Thiel scuttled out away from its rotors.

I wanted to ask them if Khadra would live. If the medics had brought blankets to wrap the baby. But those questions piled up behind a realization that had been rising in me like the headwall of a flash flood.

"It was you," I said, turning back to Gwen. My voice came out gravelly, unfamiliar, possessed. "You killed Armando." I rose from my crouch in front of her. Thiel and Alvarez came alongside me. I spoke louder.

"You killed him for taking this girl. Khadra."

I watched Alvarez for a reaction. She drew in a breath and waited.

"Not for taking her," Gwen said. "I made him hurt for that, for sure. But I killed him for not telling me where she was. He wouldn't say, and he wouldn't say, and he wouldn't say. That dumbass kid."

"You're admitting it?" I asked Gwen. "You're saying you actually took that teenager's life. You erased his whole future because he wouldn't give up a person's location. Why did you need to find Khadra so badly? She's just an asset, a thing, a tool for you, not a young woman."

Almost on its own, my foot jerked back for a goal-kick at her ribs, but my arms sprouted cops. The two held me back.

"I've heard about you, Cates," Alvarez said. "I didn't remember your name at first, but I remember your story. You're sick." Her tone was so matter of fact, it shocked me out of my fight impulse. I stopped lunging against her grip, but she didn't let go. "In your last few months in Iraq, you started killing interrogation subjects. Five, wasn't it? Or six? If they didn't collapse under your pressure, you just ended them. Anyone who stood up to you had no right to live. Armando refused to tell you where the girl was, so he had no right to live either. When you came back from Iraq, you brought it with you. The idea that anyone who doesn't obey needs to die."

"Playing shrink now?" Gwen said to Alvarez. "Well, you got me about four-point-eight percent right. Nice work, Freud. And you." She swung her dead fish-eye gaze to me.

"You have so many ideals. Are you willing to sacrifice for them? Willing to kill?"

"I don't like yes or no questions," I said.

"Take her to the squad car, Thiel," Alvarez said. He dropped his grip on me, put two hands under Gwen Cates's armpits, stood her up.

"We have other business," Alvarez said, steering me toward the yurt.

CHAPTER

49

"ANY PLASTIC BAGS around here?" Alvarez asked. "I need to take this knife in. It won't fit in a baggy. Has to be a one-gallon storage bag." Cates's blade lay in the duff like a piece of surface archaeology from a bygone era.

"Why aren't you surprised she confessed?" I asked Alvarez. She followed me into the yurt.

"Not much surprises me," Alvarez said. "People confess for lots of reasons. Sometimes they do it to justify their own sense of grandiosity. Look how dramatic and powerful I am, that type of thing. Sometimes they do it to make more trouble. And sometimes people experiment with a powerful drug called truth."

"But aren't you surprised she's the killer? Or did you already have something that pointed to her? Even while you kept Jaral locked up?"

I handed her a freezer bag, my heart pounding.

"What happened to your hand?" She nodded at the raw skin over my knuckles where Khadra bit me.

"Just a scrape from some branches," I said. "Don't act like you didn't hear me. Didn't you think Jaral was the killer? Isn't that why you arrested him?"

"When I arrested Jaral Marez, we had enough evidence to hold him. A judge thought so too."

"But you had doubts. Yet you kept him in jail anyway."

"Like it or not, we also kept him safe. If Cates found him after she found Armando, well, you don't want to think about that."

I would not go walking into that inferno of speculation. "I'm just trying to figure out why you thought you had to hold him."

"I didn't have a clear picture."

"What's that mean?"

"The vic had taser burns on his back. That means anyone could have subdued him. Didn't have to be a male."

"What else?"

"No murder weapon at the scene. The kitchen knife with blood on it was smooth-edged. The coroner said a partially serrated blade killed Armando. The kitchen knife was staged by the killer so we'd think we had the weapon."

She held up the empty freezer bag. "Cates's knife is the right type. That's why it's going in here. Forensics will tear it apart to find flakes of dried blood. Stuck in a joint, maybe. Under a screw. Between the casing and the metal."

"So you had an idea someone else had gone in Armando's house? Someone besides the family or Jaral?"

"Or you," Alvarez reminded me. She patted a quick rhythm on the countertop. I couldn't tell whether it was a gesture of nerves or irritation.

"We found short hair at the scene. Blond. Possibly female."

I gasped. She shrugged. "Everyone sheds."

What is the sound of one hand refraining from pounding a sergeant detective's face?

I groaned, backed away.

"Think of it this way," said Alvarez. "If your son hadn't been picked up, you never would have gotten involved in all this and led us right to this very spot where we could get to Gwen. Off her goddamned white zone and trespassing on private property."

"What do you mean, led you?"

"We'd been waiting on a warrant for this place, but in the meantime Thiel put a tracker on your vehicle. Earlier today, when you came storming in. Then you did us the favor of coming right here, where I figured you had some type of secret stashed."

I shook my head. That's why it'd been cake to get my car back.

"You said you'd heard about Cates. She was at Abu Ghraib?"

"You have any trouble imagining her there?" Alvarez said

"When you had her on the ground, in cuffs, I finally remembered why there was something familiar about the way Armando's wrists and ankles were tied behind him, linked to that rope pulling his head back."

I'd come across it twice before. Once in a written account of torture examples from the history of U.S. slavery that I'd read in college. The other encounter had been more recent.

"I saw that same thing in photos from Abu Ghraib. The second set that came out a few years after the first scandal. They didn't get as much press, but I remember one showed men bent up and tied like that. A row of them. Lying naked on their sides. Bags over their heads."

"Women's underwear," Alvarez said.

"What?"

"Not bags. They had women's underwear over their heads. To mock their beliefs about women's modesty being sacred. I remember those pictures too."

A human moment of recognition passed between us. Fellow onlookers.

Alvarez walked out to where Gwen's knife lay on the ground. I followed.

She pulled on a set of latex gloves. Bending to retrieve the knife, Alvarez spoke as though talking to herself.

"Be good to have someone else place Cates at the scene too. Loose cannon like her could recant any time."

Holding the handle with her fingertips, Alvarez dropped the knife in the bag. She pressed the edges together to zip it closed, going over the seal repeatedly as though to keep what was inside from leaping out.

"What happened to the fawn?" I said suddenly.

"The what?"

"The fawn Thiel delivered. Did it live?"

"Oh no, he never did that. I read it in a poem somewhere. But he definitely saved some lives when he was in the army. Nothing he'll ever talk about. Just what I hear from his service buddies. Now come on." She snapped her fingers. "Think. I'll get your kid released from CJC. But we want this confession of Cates's to become a conviction. Not anything she can take back. Who could have seen Cates at the Peregrinos' house? We tried the neighbors. They're not talking to us. Who else can we ask?"

"Try Ernie the Alley Man."

"Ernesto Galvan? We already questioned him."

"You asked him about Jaral. He told me that. Now you can ask him about the real killer."

She started walking back toward the driveway, a route that would take her past the shed.

I scrambled to stand in front of her, blocking her path.

"When can I pick up Jaral?" I wanted to get that locked in while I was on Alvarez's good side.

"After I tell the DA to file a 'decline to prosecute' notice. By the time they actually file it, then notify the jail it's been filed, that can take up to twenty-four hours."

Evening shadows stretched across the clearing where we stood.

"It's Thursday," I said. "Are you saying it can take twenty-four weekday hours, starting Friday? Meaning he might not be out until Monday?"

"Could be," Alvarez said, distracted by a noise behind me.

Thiel drove the squad car up the driveway at an angle that gave him a clear view of the side of the shed. Cates glared from the back. He stopped the car in the center of the clearing, got out, then moved straight to the disturbed earth.

"Whoa," said Thiel. "What's this?"

"A white redwood," I said. "They're very rare."

Alvarez started toward him.

"What is it, Thiel?"

We walked up next to where he stood, examining the discolored, bloated face of a recently buried corpse that now bore my fingerprints.

"Dang," Alvarez said to me. "Just when we were starting to get along."

"That's not mine," I said. "I'm holding it for someone."

Tough crowd.

Alvarez recognized Braulio Tenorio and gave me an on-the-spot interrogation. I had to sew together a parachute as I fell.

"The girl, Khadra," I said to her. "She said she snuck into Armando's car when he drove up there, to escape where she was being held in the Presidio, right? He must've been doing a delivery run alone. He went up there around the same time every month, always at night. Khadra planned her getaway knowing when to expect him. By the next day, Cates figured out Khadra had left with Armando. She thought he stole her. So Cates went after him. When she didn't find the girl at Armando's house, who would she try next? The man who sent Armando up to the Presidio in the first place. Armando's boss. Tenorio. Cates must have thought Armando passed the girl to Tenorio."

"Tenorio was one of your close associates," Alvarez said. "But why'd he come up to your property? That didn't go so well for him."

"Up here? On my property?" I needed to think.

Thiel went back to his vehicle to call in his discovery.

"I told Tenorio about this place."

"When? Where were you when you told him? What were the circumstances?"

"We were arguing at my school." Mistake. I didn't need her red-flagging the fact that I'd recently argued with the deceased. Her face remained still.

"I told him that I had a yurt up here behind Prairie Creek. He knew Jaral had been at Armando's house the morning Nando was killed, so he must have thought Jaral took the girl."

"Why would he have known the whereabouts of your son the morning of the murder? We didn't release his name when we arrested him."

"Rosalva Peregrino would have told him. The people of El Pavo see Tenorio as a Godfather type. A protector. Someone with control over their lives, yes, but also someone who can help them."

"I believe it. He owns almost every house in the entire neighborhood. But why would Tenorio be looking for this girl? If she's the one you said he was obsessed with, I'm going to need that sketchbook you told us about as evidence."

I had to be careful here. If Khadra lived, I wanted her to be free to start a new life without a murder charge. If I helped prove Tenorio was obsessed with her, that could be just a few legal dance steps away from the damning truth, which is that his rabid possessiveness gave her a motive to kill him.

I wanted Khadra's boy to grow up cared for by his mama. Inside me, the child's eyes were still opening. Dense beads, dark planets, black holes pearled with the dew of new life, asking everything of me.

"I don't have the drawings," I said. "I saw them once when I was in Tenorio's office. But I don't think Tenorio would have been frantic to find the girl because he was obsessed with her. I think he was trying to keep a client. Or save his own skin. This couple from the white zone would have been ready to kill him themselves if they thought he'd taken her. The only reason Armando had to be driving up to that compound the Cates pair ran is that it was a job Tenorio arranged for him. So Tenorio himself had to prove he wasn't involved in the girl's escape, by bringing her back to them."

If this Cates couple contacted Tenorio in a fury to find the girl, it would also explain why Tenorio was hanging around outside Armando's house the morning of the murder. He wanted to see whether Khadra was there.

If, while watching Armando's house, he saw Gwen Cates's car turn into the alley, he would've driven off—fast. Not wanting Cates to think he knew where the girl was or that he had a role in hiding her. He didn't.

That's how he could've been outside Armando's house that morning but have driven away right before the murder.

"Tenorio hasn't been dead more than a day," Alvarez said. "Your son was in custody at that time, so he's clear. But you could have come up here earlier."

"Cates could have been up here earlier too," I said.

"You're saying Cates offed this guy yesterday?"

"I don't know what happened here yesterday," I said. But my guess was that Tenorio came looking for Khadra. Khadra knew, the way a woman can know, that he was coming for her with a hunger that would devour. She wasn't going to leave with him.

"Your whereabouts yesterday," Alvarez said. "You got anyone can verify them?"

"There was a girl at the Presidio named Amina. If she's one of the ones the SWAT team got to in time, she'll tell you I was there."

"Wagon's on its way," Thiel called over from the squad car. "We can get the crossbow and some photos, but the evidence tech's coming up to help, too."

Alvarez nodded. I tried to pick back up with our sense-making.

"My son's the reason Khadra's been up here safe, not serving as anyone's traffic. Armando's texts to him must have been about not wanting to tell their parents about this runaway. To protect her."

"Smart kids," she said. "They knew if any law enforcement got to her first, they'd just return her to her legal guardian. Which appeared to be Mr. and Mrs. Cates."

"What's going to happen to Khadra? Her baby?"

"We'll interview the girl when she's out of ICU. If she makes it. There are foster placements specially set up for young mothers. That's likely where the girls from the Presidio will go, into foster homes willing to accept pregnant teens. It all depends on what social services and the Office of Refugee Resettlement decide."

"Will they find good places for them? Will the girls be safe?"

"Your concern is touching, Marez. But we have a conversation of our own to finish up, me and you."

She asked me why the burial was partly exposed. I told her about seeing something sticking up from the dirt, uncovering Tenorio. I left out the part about Khadra's confession.

"You left Eureka to come here because . . ." Alvarez prompted.

"I was coming to help the girl. Make sure she was safe. See what she needed."

"If you weren't party to transporting the girl here, how did you know to find her here?"

"From Jaral's message. 'Help. Go WR now.' WR was the white redwood."

She glanced up at the tree. "And there it is."

She squared her stance in front of me and cocked a pointed finger my way.

"Just because you helped us bust some weird underage labor thing, we are not through. Let me recommend you keep yourself available to me in the coming days. We'll need to talk more about your on-site human composting. Got it?"

"You release my boy," I said, "and I'll stay in a rusty old lamp for three thousand years, if you ask."

I had no work and no friends left in Humboldt. But there was an event coming up at the high school I'd been waiting six years to see. No chance I'd leave town before that.

CHAPTER

50

I SPUN THE RED tassel around on my finger. The student aide in the high school had handed it over, along with a mortar board and gown sealed in plastic, with nothing more than a quick glance at my face when I gave her Jaral's name.

It just so happened that regalia pickup day at Eureka High was Monday morning. Jaral wouldn't get released until Monday afternoon. But hey. What were moms for?

After picking up Jaral's graduation wear, I stopped in at Daybreak Academy. Mrs. Murray had said she'd give me a week's grace period before "discovering" the missing money in the school account and reporting it to the parent board, on the condition that I resign immediately.

When I came in the office, she walked out past me without a word. "Thank you," I said to her back. She pretended not to hear. I left my letter of resignation on her desk. Classes were in session and the hallways were quiet. I picked up a framed photo on my desk—a selfie of Jaral and me in front of the yurt on a s'mores night, our laughing faces smudged with dabs of chocolate. It was the only thing I took with me.

I stepped out in the foyer and said a quiet goodbye to both hallways full of classrooms, thinking the job and a 10K refinance loan I'd turn right back around to the school were a price I'd pay again a thousand times to have Jaral safe.

With the money I'd repay just as soon as I got the loan, Mrs. Murray would only have an account irregularity to report to the board, not missing funds. What they chose to do with that info would be a problem for another day. Or maybe no problem at all. Since I was out of the picture now anyway it was possible the board would just drop it to avoid bad press for the school. A future question that would only be resolved in the future. Today, I had a very important mom-taxi run to complete.

* * *

When I walked into the waiting area at the jail, I had the tassel with me as a memory aid. I had a few things I wanted to remember to tell Jaral right away when I saw him. I wanted to enjoy showering a person with nothing but care and truth.

The truth that I loved him.

That we were going to go eat that huge plate of oysters at the Lumberjack Cookhouse.

That I was sorry I hadn't listened to him sooner.

That I'd brought his car home from the evidence lot this morning.

And that I'd talked to the high school to get his make-up work for the week he'd missed. He could cross the stage and get his diploma along with his friends.

Inside the jail, there was a door to the left of the check-in desk, a different door than I'd gone in for visiting hours. I was taken through it into a smaller waiting room that faced the back of the desk. I handed an officer the bag with clean clothes I brought for Jaral.

No sign of the corrections officer who'd thrown me out last time.

This waiting room held the recently released who wanted to wait inside for their ride, and family members of the soon-to-be-released. Opposite the desk was yet another door, through which I watched three newly released individuals be escorted.

Each one was told, "Wait here for the retrieval of your personal effects." Each one waited for his name to be called by an officer working the part of the desk that faced into the room.

I was so surprised to recognize the couple standing at the check-out desk, the tassel I'd been twirling flew off the end of my finger and landed on a plastic chair with a nylon splat. I picked it up and walked over to Lita, one of my adult students, standing with her husband.

I heard he'd been locked up on domestic violence charges. Looked like he wouldn't be getting prosecuted. Lita wore a T-shirt that said, "Always with us, never forgotten," with a rainbow background and a picture of Armando's sweet, smiling face.

"Maestra!" she said. "We worrying! You sick? Something happen?" Her "something" sounded like "son-thing."

I threw an arm around her shoulders. She shrank away from me with a warning glance that said, "Don't ask."

Her husband flashed me a charming smile. He was bright eyed, clean shaven, with an undeniable magnetism. If he'd gotten convicted, he probably would've been deported. The fact they were back together meant Lita and her kids still had his income to support them. Knowing this, I didn't need to ask the why-are-you-letting-him-come-home question that her eyes begged me to withhold.

Anyway, I had another question.

"Where did you get this shirt?"

"The church, maestra."

"Which church?"

"River of Hope, maestra. They having memorial service for Nando yesterday."

"But the rainbow . . ." I said. "¿Esta iglesia acepta personas . . . gay?"

She turned her back to me.

The back of the shirt said, "River of Hope/Rio de Esperanza—Todos son bienvenidos." Another rainbow poured like a waterfall from a pink heart at the center of a cross.

"I thought the Peregrinos got the idea from their church that gay people belonged to the devil."

"Maybe Rosalva think that, maestra, but the church, no. Really, they have no been to that church in three, four years. I there every Sunday, don't see them."

I'd mistaken Rosalva's pathological homophobia as the bias of her social crowd, when it had really been personal zealotry.

Lita and her husband's departure left me and three other men in the room. They sat close to the desk, crossing and uncrossing their legs, leaning forward, leaning back.

I went to the desk to ask how much longer it might be. Jaral had called me about forty-five minutes ago to say he'd be ready soon. When I started to ask what the timeline was, the door behind me swung open. There stood Jaral.

"Wait here for the retrieval of your personal effects," said the officer behind him, before closing the door again.

Jaral gave me a bear hug that ended too soon.

"What up, Moms."

All the things I'd meant to say were sunk under a wave of emotion.

I planted a smooch on his cheek so loud it echoed off the linoleum. One of the guys in the chairs chuckled, a friendly sound.

Jaral wiped at the messy spot on his face with a half smile. He had the warmth in his eyes of someone who knows they're safe with you. Being seen that way, after all I'd done, was like standing under a crystalline cascade of mountain water.

We sat down side by side. I placed the tassel in his palm. He fist-pumped with it. Then he whispered, "Is Khadra safe?"

"Maybe," I murmured.

The two officers behind the desk chatted, stapled, filed, typed. The other men in the room wanted no part of anyone else's business. But Jaral's question required a complicated answer. I moved to the last row of seats. Jaral followed.

"She's barely holding on," I told him. "I went up there to try and help her, but one of the people she ran away from hurt her. I think it was the same lady who scared you in court. But that vicious lady's in custody now. And the girl's finally safe. She just . . . she lost a lot of blood."

He hung his head for a moment. Then he gave me the look of a man who had aged five years in a week.

"We talking about a blond lady? Short hair and spooky eyes?"

I nodded.

"She just leaned right up to me as I'm standing up from my bench in the courtroom. Says, 'Where's the girl? Tell me right now or you get all types of trouble in there.' Nando warned me about her. He worried she'd find a way to get to him and his family. And I think she's the one that did . . . that did what . . . that did what happened to Nando."

He swallowed, turned away. Then kept going. "Nando told me she was shady as hell—heck, sorry—so I thought if I'm on the inside, mixed in with everybody else, I'm a sitting duck. Whoever she's got in there working for her could get to me, easy. So I went off. Made a show crazy enough to get thrown in AdSeg."

"Were you . . ." I could barely speak through the searing guilt of not having saved him from six nights in jail. "Did they really leave you alone in there?" I meant: was he really okay?

"Yeah. I did a lot of push-ups. Got chilly in there when I wasn't moving. But that was the worst of it. I'm okay, Moms. What about you? You limping?"

"It's nothing. I just hate that I wasn't there when you had to face the judge. I tried. I really tried to get there."

He patted my hand like someone visiting a pitiable relative in an old folks' home. One more way to show I wasn't needed. But at this point, it was fine. He was all right.

"Don't take it too hard, Moms. Hey, you figured out what I was trying to tell you. That's amazing. Then you tried to help. And now that lady's put away. I hope for good."

"She actually confessed," I said. "So, yeah, let's hope she's away for good."

He asked if I knew about the other girls she had trapped. Nando told him she had some kind of harem doing online video chats with boys all over the country.

"The whole place got busted," I said. "They never caught the head guy, the husband of this lady who confessed, but the girls will be placed with foster families. I guess there are families specially set up to receive pregnant teens. And those will be secret placements, so wherever he is, this guy called Mr. Cates, he won't be able to get to them. But can you believe this? Khadra's baby . . . he was actually born right there, by the yurt."

I told Jaral about the emergency C-section, giving the newborn CPR, then handing him to the paramedics.

"I think the baby's in good shape," I told him. "He seemed strong. Not just alive, but kicking, squalling."

"Moms, didn't you think about what could have gone wrong? I mean, helping start a new life off in the world. Sounds brave."

One of the three men who were waiting was called up to the desk to sign for his items. The other two shifted in their seats.

I wanted to answer Jaral, but my throat felt clogged with a mesh of roots.

"It wasn't bravery," I said. "It was focus. More intense than any I've ever felt. It shifted everything away except the action right in front of me. It was new to me. Like I learned something about existence itself. Witnessing a birth, being so focused."

"Learning goes on our whole lives. I know I've heard you say that."

"You know, I also did some learning about you these last few days."

"Uh-oh."

"It's nothing bad, I just have to ask. Why didn't you tell me about . . ." I lowered my voice further. "About you and Armando? I'm open and affirming, right? What was there to hide?"

He flicked his eyes around the room, then spoke to his hands as he cracked the knuckles on each finger, one by one.

"It's like this. I need a corner of my life just for me. If you knew? You'd start matching me up, asking a buttload of questions, do I like him, do I like her, what about this friend, that friend. I just needed a part of my life that wasn't . . . that wasn't . . . that you couldn't take over."

"Well, that's an honest answer. I'm not sure how to react. I do have one more question though."

The next man got called up. There was only one left to be processed ahead of Jaral.

"I understand why you needed to raid the emergency cash," I said to him. "You needed to buy a bus ticket for the girl. I'm guessing you went in one door of the high school Tuesday morning, then out another, not too long after. You got the idea to grab that cash from home while I wasn't there, pick up Armando, and drive together to the yurt. You thought the two of you would get Khadra, bring her down to town, and buy her that ticket to get to LA."

He nodded.

"And I'm guessing you brought her to the yurt in the first place on Monday because you needed space and time to keep her away from the people she was running from while you figured out how to get her down to SoCal."

"That's right."

"And then you wanted to turn right around Monday night and get those vitamins to her, because you realized you were partly responsible for Khadra's well being at that point. But what I don't understand is why you shoplifted those vitamins on Monday. They weren't that expensive. Why not ask me to borrow a twenty?"

"You would've asked me what the money was for," he said. "I would've had to lie to you, which would be bad, or tell you, which would be worse. You'd get all freaked out, not listen, insist you knew what to do. Probably end up calling social services. Then the girl would be right back where she came from, never get a chance to keep her baby."

"You did all that to keep a baby and his mom together," I said. I wanted to say that if he ever felt torn open in a way that would never heal, because he was apart from his mother, I would just listen. I would not insist I knew what to do. Being apart from my son for just a week had nearly undone me.

I tried saying it in code. I smoothed down his shirt sleeves. Patted the back of his hair.

He gave a half smile, then said, out of the blue, "You ever think about how much your mom must have missed you? After she left?"

"Where'd that come from?" I shrank back a little, feeling sliced open, but wanting to know his mind.

"Well, I missed everyone when I was on the inside. You, my bio mom, my friends. Ernie the Alley Man. Even the man in the moon. And Nando. Man, that guy . . ." He got choked up, cleared his throat a few times. It was obvious he didn't want to let it all go here in the CJC.

"It's normal to miss people," I said.

"Yeah, and it got me thinking about what it's like to be connected to someone but apart from them. I was actually surprised I missed you, since I'm pretty much grown, and you know, you get crazy sometimes."

"Moms gotta mom," I said.

"That's the thing. With all that time to think, I realized my bio mom has a part of her, like her spirit or something, that's still looking after me. Like you are. Still trying to help. You ever feel like your mom tried to work things out for you from a distance, in some weird way?"

The third man got called up to sign for his things.

"The first two years after my mom left, I was so angry at her, it ate me up inside. Did you know that the year she left, I was the age you were when I adopted you?"

He shook his head.

"After those two years, I was either going to spontaneously combust from outrage or make a change. I was fourteen by then, thought I was pretty much grown, so I vowed not to think about her and moved in with my California family. She caused me and my dad so much pain, I wasn't willing to think about whether being apart from us was painful for her. When I imagine what it'd be like to play out those thoughts, I picture myself swimming far out in the cold ocean, way past where I could see the shore."

"Maybe go in a floatplane," Jaral said. "Who says you have to swim out alone?"

Who, indeed.

The newly freed man gathered his things and left. The officer at the back of the desk called out, "You must be Jaryl Mare-is."

Jaral jumped up, Guns N' Roses at the ready. "Oh, won't you pleeeease take me ho-ome."

The officer froze for a half second, placed a tray on the counter tagged with a number, then slid a form in front of Jaral with the same number on top. "If everything listed on this form is present in this tray, sign here."

The tray held everything Jaral had at the time of his booking. Among his keys, wallet, and wallet contents—driver's license, coffee punch card, wrapped condom, student ID, and a bus ticket to Los Angeles—lay a small sand dollar about three inches across. The bleached out, desiccated test. Perfect, intact, beautiful.

He signed the form and started to reassemble his wallet.

I tapped the bus ticket. "You never got to take this to Khadra."

"Maybe I can use it myself," he said. "I still want to visit my bio mom. After graduation."

Did I dig in with questions to scrape details out of him, then shove a pile of "shoulds" right at him? Yeah, some. But just in my head.

Now that Jaral had brought up my own mother, at a time when I was already so raw, a surprising thought occurred to me. There might come a time when we'd both be out looking for our mothers. After sealing that particular chamber of my heart up, I'd never thought it might be possible to see her again. But I had no reason to think it would be impossible either.

The idea made me feel slightly disembodied, as though I couldn't even recognize my own hands as mine. I'd have to put away those musings for another day.

Today, I wanted to focus on supporting this older, wiser young adult.

"I'll take you to the transit center, son. See if they can exchange the ticket for a different date."

"Some other time," he said. "Right now, I need to relax with my Moms and a huge plate of oysters."

He picked up the sand dollar, flashed the five-petaled pattern at me.

"My lucky charm," he said.

Then he wrapped his red tassel around the sea treasure and pocketed them both.

As soon as we broke out of the waiting area's double doors, Jaral sang, "Love somebody, love someone." Background vocals for a Sting song about freedom. I started up the tambourine beat with the keys in my hand and followed behind Jaral. We spun and danced over the tile waves, up the stairs out to street level, into an evening rich with the promise of rain.

ACKNOWLEDGMENTS

The uncertainties of manuscript drafting all get offset by the excitement of seeing a book exist where readers can find it. For this I thank Toni Kirkpatrick, acquiring editor, trailblazing autora in her own right, and Lisa Abellera, agent extraordinaire, a monarch in the kingdom of strategy. Thanks to Jennifer Hooks and Lunaea Weatherstone for smart and discerning edits. Thanks especially to the Crooked Lane Books production and marketing team: Mikaela Bender, Mia Bertrand, Dulce Botello, Megan Matti, Rebecca Nelson, Thaisheemarie Fantauzzi Perez, and Heather VenHuizen.

For unreserved frankness about life in Humboldt County, and for your work to feed, caffeinate, educate, empower, and protect communities there, thank you Barbara Brinson Curiel, Karyn Lee-Thomas, Andy Nieto, Teodolinda Salas-Meza, Maria de Jesus Torres, Michael Twombley, and Stanley Wickham. Writing by María Corral Rocha, Emily Brady, the *North Coast Journal* staff and the Women's Refugee Commission was very helpful.

Big thanks to Juan Morales, Juliana Aragón Fatula, Iver Arnegard, Barbara Brinson Curiel, Cory Marciel, John Gallagher, Cory Hanyok and Blas Falconer for reading early drafts, to Rigoberto González, Elizabeth Honor Wilder, Toni Lopopolo and Jacob Krueger Studio mentor Christian

Lybrook for crucial edits and insights, to Barbara Nickless and Catherine Dilts for miles of companionship and mentoring, to Sisters in Crime, Susan J. Tweit, Guthrie Miller, Chris Goff, and Santa Fe Art Institute for opportunities and support to grow the book, and to all the volunteers, staff, and presenters who power the Association of Writers and Writing Programs, BoucherCon, Creatures, Crimes & Creativity, International Thriller Writers, Left Coast Crime, Pikes Peak Writers, Rocky Mountain Chapter of Mystery Writers of America, and Sleuthfest.

Thank you Francisco Aragón, Frankie Y. Bailey, Rachel Howzell Hall, Naomi Hirahara, Ausma Zehanat Khan, Cynthia Kuhn, Gigi Pandian, and Linda Rodriguez for your support, your generosity in leadership, mentorship, and service, and for changing the face of publishing.

To my Melendez, Gallagher, Chinnavaso, Espinoza and Little families, love always. Thank you for your examples of vitality and creativity.

Mil gracias to you, reader, most of all.